A LOBSTER AND A LADY

A LOBSTER AND A LADY

Jeanne Whitmee

Chivers Press • Thorndike Press
Bath, England   Thorndike, Maine USA

This Large Print edition is published by Chivers Press, England, and by Thorndike Press, USA.

Published in 2000 in the U.K. by arrangement with the author.

Published in 2000 in the U.S. by arrangement with Dorian Literary Agency.

U.K. Hardcover   ISBN 0–7540–4253–7 (Chivers Large Print)
U.K. Softcover   ISBN 0–7540–4254–5 (Camden Large Print)
U.S. Softcover   ISBN 0–7862–2810–5 (General Series Edition)

The text of this Large Print edition is unabridged.
Other aspects of the book may vary from the original edition.

Set in 16 pt. New Times Roman.

Printed in Great Britain on acid-free paper.

British Library Cataloguing in Publication Data available

Library of Congress Cataloging-in-Publication Data

Whitmee, Jeanne.
     * A lobster and a lady / Jeanne Whitmee.
         p.   cm.
    ISBN 0–7862–2810–5 (lg. print : sc : alk. paper)
    1. Music-halls (Variety-theaters, cabarets, etc.)—Fiction.
    2. London (England)—Fiction.   3. Foster families—Fiction.
    4. Women singers—Fiction.   5. Birthmothers—Fiction.
    6. Young women—Fiction.   7. Large type books. I. Title.
PR6073.H65 L63   2000
823'.914—dc21   00–042624

A boat afloat, a cloudless sky,
A nook that's green and shady,
A cooling drink, a pigeon pie,
A lobster and a lady.

ANON

CHAPTER ONE

'Are you going to sing that song downstairs, Kate?'

Kate paused in her humming and turned from the mirror where she had been putting the final touches to her hair. Polly's amber-green eyes were staring at her with a mixture of pride and envy from where she sat on the bed.

'I'm not singing to that rabble!' Kate shrugged her slim shoulders and tossed the glossy blonde curls. 'Those days are over!'

Kate was a music hall artiste. She was on one of her rare visits home to the Eight Bells where her sister, Florrie and brother-in-law, Sid, worked long hours serving the constant flow of customers from the docks.

'I sing for them sometimes,' Polly said eagerly. 'They give me pennies!'

Kate wrinkled the beautiful tip-tilted nose in distaste. 'You watch it my girl or you'll find that's not all they'll give you!' And with a swish of her skirts she swept out of the room.

Polly drew her knees up to her chin and clasped her arms round them. Ever since her fifteenth birthday almost a year ago she had been filled with strange yearnings and dreams. Until now life at the Eight Bells had been pleasant. There was never a dull moment,

1

especially when a ship had just docked and the big, smoky tap-room downstairs was full of sailors with plenty of money to spend. It was true Florrie would keep her hard at work, scurrying back and forth from the kitchen and washing up at the sink for hours on end, but all this was made up for on the occasions when Sid would lift her onto one of the trestles at the end of the long room and she would sing one of the pert songs Kate had taught her. Amid cheers and laughter, her audience would toss pennies onto the table and although she was not allowed to keep all the pennies herself, the fact that they meant appreciation never failed to bring a glow to Polly's heart.

Only one thing puzzled her: other girls of her age were allowed to wear long dresses and put up their hair but Florrie wouldn't let her do this. She still wore the long red-gold hair hanging loose to her waist and the childish pinafores grew uncomfortably tight across her rapidly developing bosom. Polly looked longingly at Kate's dresses hanging on a piece of string that Sid had stretched across one corner of the room for her. Rich jewel colours, beautiful soft velvets and rustling taffetas. She sighed. Kate was doing well, she was so lucky. Polly never tired of the stories Kate told of all the admirers waiting at the stage door to take her to supper and give her expensive presents. One day she meant to have a life like Kate's and earn her living on the halls; after all,

2

hadn't Kate herself started here at the 'Bells' singing for the customers just as she did. One night a gentleman with a cigar had asked to see her and offered her a job on his music hall circuit and since then she'd never looked back. It had been hard work but Kate was strong and full of vigour. She had delighted audiences all over London with her rich throaty voice and her pretty, bold face and figure and now she had left the circuit days behind to work at the bigger theatres.

Polly slid off the bed and took down one of the dresses, holding it against her. A thrill of excitement went through her as she saw that since Kate's last visit they had become about the same size. The dress would surely fit her! With trembling fingers she pulled off her own frock and slipped Kate's—a shining creation in green taffeta, over her head. It was difficult to manage the fastenings but she didn't need the whalebone stays that Kate wore underneath. At last she managed to fasten the last hook and stood to survey herself in the spotted mirror.

Two spots of bright colour burned in her cheeks. She was pretty! She scooped the bright hair on top of her head and secured it with some of Kate's pins, then she stood back to admire the result. Why, she was as pretty as Kate dressed like this—prettier! The low cut of the dress revealed the creaminess of her skin and the soft curve of the young breasts.

Polly shivered with excitement as an idea suddenly presented itself. Kate had gone out— she'd never know. Tonight she would sing for the customers dressed like this! Her hand flew to her mouth as the shock of the idea took her breath away. What would Florrie say? Dare she really do it?

Polly had never known her real mother or father. In fact she knew nothing of her origins at all. Florrie had told her once long ago that Sid had found her one night wrapped in a shawl and left in the doorway of the Eight Bells. Ever since then she had lived with the Harris family, looking on Sid and Florrie as her mother and father and Kate as an elder sister. They were kind enough to her in their rough way but there were often times when Polly would dream of her real mother, longing for the warm love and understanding that mothers were reputed to have.

The stairs were boxed in by walls on either side and at the bottom a door led straight into the stone flagged kitchen. Polly cautiously opened the door a crack and looked in—it was empty. It was nine o'clock and the tap-room was full of the noisy crew of the 'Aphrodite' which had docked at high water and now floated high on her moorings, relieved of her cargo. Florrie had called up the stairs to her several times to come down and help but she had waited, watching for her chance. She would give them the song before Florrie had

4

time to stop her—work afterwards when she had changed out of Kate's splendid dress.

Stealthily, she crept towards the door of the tap-room. She was in luck, Florrie was nowhere to be seen. Slipping past Sid's broad back, bent low over the beer engine she bobbed under the counter flap and in a second she had stepped up onto the trestle at the end of the room, lifting her skirts daintily.

A hush fell over the room as all eyes were upon her. She began to sing one of the saucy songs that Kate had taught her, her voice a little more strident than usual with nerves but as soon as the sailors' raucous voices joined in the first chorus her confidence grew. She began to shake her shoulders and swing her slim hips as she had seen Kate do giving an occasional saucy wink, her eyes shining with excitement. Among the sea of faces Sid's stood out, his mouth agape with amazement. She could see Florrie too, her mouth a grim line of annoyance—but she didn't care. For the moment the world was hers; the coarse, upturned faces gazing at her were her public and for now she existed for them alone.

When the song was finished there was a roar of approval and the clatter of pennies was deafening, some landing at her feet, some ringing on the stone floor. To Polly it sounded like the sweetest music and she would dearly have loved to comply with the shouts of 'More'—'Give us another song, Pol'. But one

5

look at Florrie's menacing face told her she'd better not! Bowing graciously she stepped off the table and immediately found herself surrounded by men all reaching out eagerly to touch her. Suddenly Sid's huge brawny shoulders shrugged through the throng and his large hand descended on Polly's arm.

'That's all!' he shouted. 'She's got her work to do now—let her be.' And she found herself propelled at speed through the tap-room and out into the kitchen. The door shut behind her with a slam and she'd barely had time to catch her breath when Florrie's hand struck her a ringing blow across the cheek.

'You little slut! What do you think you're playing at?'

Polly stared at her, one hand to her stinging cheek and the tears springing to her eyes. 'I never meant no harm.'

Florrie rolled up her sleeves, her face crimson. 'Asking for it!—That's what you were doin'—asking for it! Get upstairs and get out of that dress. This settles it,' she added half to herself. 'It's what I've always been afraid of!' She opened the stairs door and as Polly passed through cuffed her ear. 'I'll settle your hash, my girl. I'll not have you bringing the place a bad name!'

Upstairs Polly stood looking at her tear-stained reflection in the mirror. What had she done that was so terrible? And what had Florrie meant when she'd said she was 'asking for it'? Asking for what? She was only doing what Kate had done and everyone treated Kate like a lady now. Kate was somebody now and all through singing—so how could it be wrong?

Florrie's shrill voice brought her quickly to her feet. No time to indulge in self-pity. By the sound of her Florrie was still angry and if she didn't make haste she'd feel the weight of her hand again! Hurriedly she took off the green dress and hung it up, her hands lingering over the rich material, then into her own childish frock and down the stairs to the kitchen again.

'Shall I collect the dirty glasses?'

Florrie swung round. 'Don't you dare to go in there again! You'd best stay out here tonight, there's plenty to get on with. You can go out to the tip with the rubbish for a start, then there's the washing up to do.'

Polly hated taking the rubbish out to the yard at the back after dark. At night the rats played there—big as cats and twice as bold. The yard was bathed in moonlight that cast eerie shadows and Polly hurried over her task, tipping up the buckets as fast as she could. Suddenly there was a movement behind her, she jumped, startled and the next moment found herself caught in two burly arms. She let out a squeak of alarm but a large hand closed over her mouth.

'Ssh—don't make a noise—it's me. You was winkin' at me in there, don't you remember? I

7

bin waitin' for you.'

Polly felt hot breath on her cheek as the sailor bent and pulled her roughly to him.

'Please—let go of me—I wasn't winking at you—I don't know you!' Her heart pounded madly as she tried in vain to push the huge man away. He laughed hoarsely.

'Don't know me, eh? Well, you soon will!' His rough face grated against hers as he tried to kiss her, one arm like an iron band around her waist while the other tore at the neck of her frock. All the breath went out of Polly's body as she felt his rough hand on her flesh; the yard spun crazily round her and she made a last desperate effort. Taking a deep breath she let out a thin scream, but the noise that was coming from the tap-room would surely drown it. Then a miracle happened.

'Let the girl go and be off with you!' The deep, authoritative voice cut through the roaring sound in Polly's head and to her great surprise the sailor let her go—so abruptly that she staggered back against the wall, lost her balance and sat down with a bump on the cobblestones.

'Be about your business, fellow!' Again the voice spoke boldly and although the sailor swore under his breath he shuffled off meekly enough. Peering through the shadows, Polly saw a tall figure in a wide brimmed hat bending to look at her.

'Are you all right?' The voice was softer and

kinder now. She nodded, swallowing back the threatening tears and accepted the hand he offered her. He pulled her to her feet and looked at her with humorous brown eyes. 'Why, it's the little song-thrush—though robin would suit you better!'

Polly shook her head shyly and he laughed delightedly. 'Oh, come now, you weren't so shy in there,' he nodded towards the tap-room. 'I'll warrant that big fellow thought you were his for the taking!' He bent closer. 'But you're trembling—you're only a child. Come, let me take you inside. I was about to ask the landlord if he could let me have a room for a few days. Does he have rooms to let?'

Polly nodded. 'Sometimes.' She looked at the stranger's clothes. He wouldn't fancy the doss-house next door where Sid let the sailors sleep off their night's drinking in the straw, she knew that. But occasionally Florrie let the spare room at the 'Bells' to a ship's officer or someone of that class. 'I'll ask if you like,' she offered, then paused to look up speculatively at the stranger. 'You—you won't tell, will you? About that sailor.'

He laughed gently. 'Of course I won't—if you'll promise me one thing—' She looked up at him enquiringly, her head on one side, reminding him again of a robin. 'Just that you'll sit for me—' He saw her uncomprehending look and explained: 'My name is Edwin Tarrant. I'm an artist and I've

9

come to Wapping to do some sketches of the docks and the people here. I'd like to paint you.'

Polly stared at him. 'Me? Oh, yes, sir. I'd like that!'

He smiled. 'And I'd better know your name, hadn't I?'

'Polly, sir.'

'No, I like Robin better—I shall call you Robin.' He laughed again and took her hand. 'Come, we'll see about that room.'

The next day Kate left to move into her new rooms. She had indicated that she wouldn't be coming back to the Eight Bells so frequently now that she had gone up in the world and when she had left Polly felt strangely lonely. With all Kate's things gone the little room seemed bare and empty. Only the tantalising waft of her perfume remained, reminding Polly of the sweet new life she led now, so far out of Polly's reach.

In the meantime Edwin Tarrant was enjoying his sketching holiday. He loved the sights and smells of the docks; the clamour and bustle and the colourful people he met and talked with at the 'Bells'. Florrie's good plain cooking suited him well and when he had asked Sid if he could paint Polly the big man had agreed proudly. Florrie had vague misgivings about it but at last she was persuaded and Polly found to her delight that she was to be allowed to sit for Edwin in the

afternoons when business was slack. It was at
this time that Florrie had her 'forty winks' but
she made sure Sid had his orders before she
went upstairs.

'Don't you leave him alone with her,' she
warned. 'I don't trust his sort further than I
can spit! An artist *and* one of the gentry—what
a mixture! Black sheep of the family, I
shouldn't wonder!'

Being painted wasn't as exciting as Polly had
thought it would be. For one thing she found it
difficult to keep still for so long and for
another, Edwin, who by now she adored,
seemed to see her as an urchin rather than the
beautiful woman she visualised herself.

One afternoon her annoyance got the better
of her. The last straw had come when,
reaching into the fireplace Edwin had smeared
her cheek with soot to give her—as he put it
'The right gutter-child look'.

His words touched her on the raw and she
sprang up from the stool on which she sat. 'I'm
not out of the gutter—and I'm not a child
either!'

Edwin looked up at her, his brown eyes
amused. 'Really? What are you then?'

'A woman!' Polly stamped her foot on the
stone flags. 'One day I'll show you! I'll show
them all!' Tears sprang to her eyes as he threw
back his head and laughed his rich throaty
laugh. She flew at him furiously but he caught
her wrists and held her away.

11

'A woman, is it? More like a little she-cat! A little dockyard she-cat!'

She thrust her chin out defiantly but the tears ran down her cheeks and her lower lip trembled. Suddenly the merriment left his eyes and he said softly:

'I'm sorry, Robin. I didn't mean to hurt you.' He let go of her wrists and as she rubbed them he took her face between his hands and looked into her eyes. 'I'll tell you something too, little robin. When you've grown up just a little more you will be a woman—a very lovely woman too.'

The large amber eyes opened wide as she looked at him and unable to resist her he bent and kissed her softly on the lips. Polly's heart swelled with joy. Eddie had kissed her—he had said she was lovely too. Impulsively she threw her arms around him.

'Oh Eddie!' She buried her head against his neck and pressed herself close to him. His arms closed round her as he kissed her again.

'*Polly*!' Florrie's face was crimson with fury as she stood in the doorway surveying the shocking scene before her. Polly sprang guiltily from Edwin's embrace. 'Get upstairs this minute, girl and wait there till I come up!' She held out one thin arm towards the stairs and Polly scuttled through the door. 'Where's Sid?' she heard Florrie demand. Poor Sid. He'd catch it now—she would too. But in spite of the prospect her heart sang. Eddie loved her,

12

she was sure of it and nothing else in the world mattered.

But Polly was to be sadly disillusioned. She took Florrie's nagging in her stride as she floated on the euphoric cloud of love. She hardly even listened to the words until one sentence brought her down to earth with a bump.

'Sid's told him to pack his bags, so you won't be seeing *him* again!'

She stared at Florrie disbelievingly. 'He's gone? But—where?'

'Back where he belongs, I hope.'

'But—but I love him—he loves me too!'

Florrie gave a derisive snort. 'Is that what he told you?'

'Yes!' Polly's chin came out. 'It's true. He said I was lovely too—a lovely woman—or I would be one day soon—' Her voice tailed off as she realised she was beaten. Eddie had gone—without saying goodbye—without even seeing her again. She sat on the edge of the bed dejectedly. The hard lines of Florrie's face softened a little as she sat down beside her.

'Now, listen,' she said. 'You're old enough to understand now, so listen. Your ma—who ever she was—had bad in her. Well, it stands to reason she had to do what she did—leaving you to the tender mercies of whoever might find you. Well there's some of that in you—*must* be, you bein' her daughter and you'll have to fight it all your life, my girl!'

13

Polly stared at her. How could she know so much about the woman who had given her birth when she had never set eyes on her?

'How do you know?' she asked defiantly. 'How can you tell what she was like?'

Florrie's lips resumed their thin line. 'You're telling me now, girl—by your actions! The brazen way you behaved with that young man! Don't you know why men flatter you and tell you all that rubbish?' Polly shook her head eagerly, hoping to be told but Florrie's lips shut tightly. 'Well, see that you don't find out then! Just you behave yourself!' And with this inadequate reply she left the room and a more than ever bewildered Polly.

The following day Florrie came downstairs after dinner in her best black dress with the jet trimmings. She told no one where she was going but when she came back she wore a look of triumph. The next morning she spoke to Polly:

'You're to put on your Sunday dress this afternoon, we're going out.'

Polly's eyes opened wide with surprise. It was rare for Florrie to miss her 'forty winks' on one day, but two days running! It must be important.

'Where're we going?' she asked.

But—'You'll see soon enough,' was all she could get by way of an answer.

CHAPTER TWO

It had been a long journey, first by omnibus, then on foot and now that they were entering the quiet Bayswater street Florrie squared her shoulders and ran a critical eye over Polly.

'Put your hat on straight, girl and look lively do. You look like last week's mutton!'

'Where're we going?' Polly asked for the fortieth time. 'Oh, go on, Florrie—tell me.'

Florrie stepped to one side of the pavement and took Polly's arm. 'Listen—this is Marlborough Place. We're going to number fourteen, to see two ladies. If they like you they'll give you a place.'

'A place? What kind of place?' Polly asked.

Florrie snorted impatiently and pinched her arm. 'What kind of place?' she mimicked. 'Don't show your ignorance, girl. A place in their house—in service of course!'

Polly stared at her. 'But it's too far! I couldn't come all this way every day!'

Florrie sighed. 'You won't have to—you'll live in!'

Polly couldn't believe her ears. 'You mean leave the "Bells"—and you and Sid? But why? Don't you want me any more?'

The older woman shook her head with exasperation. 'It's not that girl. You're grown now—almost a woman. You must make your own way in the world, earn your own living. Sid and me have done our best for you but you're not our own when all's said and done.'

Polly nodded and as they walked she thought about what Florrie had said. It hurt a little to be cast out but to make her own way in the world was what she wanted. A small flutter of excitement stirred within her 'Earning her own living' sounded so grand and grown-up. She looked up at the houses in the street. They were small but quite elegant with their prim railings and tall narrow windows. The front doors were solid with smooth shiny paint and there were wide, shallow steps going up to them. They weren't at all like the mean little houses at Wapping. Florrie tugged at her arm.

'Stop day-dreaming do. Here's number fourteen, come on.' She bustled down the area steps, glancing over her shoulder to make sure Polly was still with her, then gave a sharp tweak to her hat before pulling the bell.

'The ladies are sisters,' she explained in a hushed voice. 'Miss Downes and Mrs. Mears. They spend their lives doing good works and they've been once or twice to the "Bells" trying to convert sinners,' she sniffed. 'Though I'd say they were wasting their time! Well, last time they came Miss Downes asked me if I knew of a deserving girl. If I was to come across one they'd give her a place to save her from a life of sin, she said.'

Polly was silent. She supposed Florrie was

16

thinking about the afternoon with Eddie, when he had kissed her. Was *that* sin? She remembered the exciting warmth of his lips on hers and the thrilling feel of his arms about her. How could that be sinful?

Suddenly her dreams were shattered as the door opened and a large, red-faced woman confronted them.

'Yes?'

Florrie drew herself up and assumed her 'correct' voice emphasising all her aitches most carefully.

'Name of Harris. Miss Downes is h'expectin' us.'

The woman held the door wide for them to pass. 'I'll tell them you're here.' She sniffed as she looked Polly up and down. 'You're late. They likes punctuality 'ere!'

'We couldn't help it,' Florrie put in quickly. 'There was an accident at Aldgate—brewer's dray overturned—*if* it's any of your business!'

The woman gave Florrie a withering look and strutted away while Polly gazed at Florrie in amazement.

'I never saw no accident!' she hissed, but Florrie was unabashed.

'You remember, my girl—keep your eyes open—and always stay one step ahead of the likes of *her*!'

Polly looked around the kitchen. It was smaller than the one at the 'Bells' and rather dark, lit only by the one basement window but

17

there was a cheerful glow coming from the bars of the range. In the centre of the room stood a huge deal table and on the far wall shelves held an alarming array of copper pans that gleamed in the firelight. Florrie nudged her.

'Enough there to keep you out of mischief, girl,' she pointed to the pans.

Polly nodded dumbly. She thought of Kate. How was she to follow in her footsteps if all her time were taken with scouring and polishing pans? But before she had time to ponder on this thought further the red-faced woman reappeared.

'Miss Downes will receive you now,' she said grudgingly. 'If you'll come this way.'

They followed her up a flight of stone stairs to a door that gave onto the hall. Polly looked around her. The floor was tiled in black and white while the walls were hung with a richly patterned paper in dark red. The staircase curved elegantly upwards and the whole effect brought a sniff from Florrie, endorsing the remark she had made earlier about Polly being kept out of mischief. Oh yes, there was work enough here to keep the liveliest girl out of the devil's hands!

Miss Honoria Downes sat in a high-backed chair by the window, her own back as rigid as that of the chair. Polly glanced fearfully at her. It was impossible to tell her age with that thin, pinched face and those colourless eyes. She

18

wore a dress of steel grey with a high collar that emphasised her thin neck and her hair, which was screwed into a tight chignon, was of the same colour as the dress. On her board-like chest she wore a gold lorgnette on a black ribbon through which she peered at them as they entered the room.

The red-faced woman announced them briefly and without ceremony: 'The woman and girl you was expectin', Miss.'

Florrie gave Polly a push forward and launched straight into her prepared speech: 'This is the girl I was telling you about, Miss. She's a good girl and very willin' but as I told you, times is bad and much as me and Sid'd like to keep her we can't. We'd be grateful to know as she'd got a good place.' Flushed with the exertion of this monologue Florrie took a deep breath then shot a reproving look at the woman who had shown them in. Miss Downes nodded.

'You may go, Higgins, thank you.' She lifted the lorgnette and peered at Polly, scrutinising her thoroughly. 'Come over here, my girl and let me look at you.' Polly complied while the woman took in every detail of her appearance as though committing it to memory.

'What is your name?' she asked at length.

'Polly, if you please, Miss.'

'And are you really a good girl, Polly—do you read your Bible?'

'Oh, she is!' Florrie put in. 'She's been well

brought up by Sid and me—as if she was our own, as you might say.'

Miss Downes nodded. 'Can you read and write?'

Polly opened her mouth but before she could make a sound Florrie again chipped in:

'That she can, Miss. I sent her to the board school—as often as I could spare her, that is. She can reckon up too—as good as I can!'

A flicker of annoyance crossed Miss Downes' face. 'I would rather like to hear it from the girl's own mouth if you don't mind.' She looked at Polly. 'Is this true?' Polly nodded and Miss Downes leaned forward. 'I take it you *have* a tongue?'—Another nod— 'Then pray *use it*!'

Startled at the sharp tone Polly took a step backwards. 'Y-yes, Miss,' she squeaked.

At that moment the door opened and another lady entered. She was as stout as Miss Downes was thin and wore a black dress with a heavy gold chain around her neck. Her iron grey hair was dressed severely like her sister's and her small features seemed to nestle in the folds of flesh that made up her face. She obviously had no need of a lorgnette as she looked sharply at Polly with her small black, beady eyes.

'Is this the gel, Honoria?' She shot the remark at her sister without taking her eyes off the shrinking Polly.

Miss Downes nodded. 'Tell me what you

20

think, Charity.

The black eyes snapped. 'Can you scrub and polish and clean, gel?'

'Yes, Miss,' Polly muttered.

'Yes *ma'am*—and speak up! Can you sew, mend and iron?'

Polly ran her tongue over her dry lips. 'I—I think so, Miss—er ma'am.'

'Well can you, or *can't* you?'

'She can, but she's young yet,' Florrie put in. 'She's quick to learn though, aint you, Polly?'

Polly nodded miserably and Miss Downes stood up suddenly as though she had come to a decision.

'We'll give her a try,' she said to no one in particular. 'If she proves satisfactory she will receive ten pounds a year and her keep of course. One Sunday off in four, so that she can visit you, Mrs. Harris. Our cook, Mrs Higgins will instruct her as to her duties. I will get in touch with you as to her progress in—say— one month from now?' She raised an eyebrow at Florrie who nodded with satisfaction.

'Thank you, Miss. I'm sure you won't regret it.'

'That remains to be seen,' Miss Downes said stiffly, pulling a bell rope by the fireplace.

The door was opened almost immediately and Mrs. Higgins appeared as though by magic from the hall where she had been hovering, her ear never far from the key-hole.

'You rang, Miss?'

'Polly here is to be our new maid, Higgins. I want you to show her her room and instruct her in the ways of the house.' She nodded her dismissal to Florrie. 'Good day.'

Once more Polly and Florrie found themselves following Mrs. Higgins down to the kitchen by way of the stone stairs. At the bottom Florrie turned.

'Well, be a good girl and do your best.' She opened the large bag she always carried and brought forth a brown paper parcel. 'I brought a few things for you—just in case—and I'll send your box on when I can hear of someone comin' this way.'

Polly gulped. She wanted to beg Florrie to take her home again. Suddenly even the back yard at the Eight Bells, complete with rats seemed better than this unfamiliar house with its cold, unfriendly people. But knowing it would do no good to make a fuss she smiled bravely.

'Can I come and see you on my day off like she said, Florrie?'

Florrie nodded and patted her arm briefly. 'Course—Sid an' me'll miss you—but you behave now, d'you hear me? And keep away from the men,' she added in a low voice. 'They only brings you trouble, you mark my words!' She buttoned her coat, glaring disapprovingly towards the cook's back as she busied herself at the range. 'A cup of tea wouldn't have come amiss an' me with the journey back to Wapping starin' me in the face!' But the woman ignored the remark and Florrie sighed resignedly and moved towards the door. 'G'bye then, Pol—be good.'

'Give my love to Sid—' A lump filled Polly's throat. '—Tell him I'll miss him.' But the next moment Florrie had gone.

Mrs. Higgins turned to Polly. 'Well—may as well get your things off and start makin' yourself useful. I'll take you up to see your room after I've basted this meat, then you can get your uniform on.' She ran an eye over Polly's slight form. 'I'd say you'd have to take it in a bit first though.'

The climb up the back stairs seemed endless but at last they arrived at the top where Mrs Higgins paused, wheezing and gasping for breath. She clutched at her heaving bosom, rolling her eyes at Polly.

'Oh! Be the death o' me, them stairs will! I'm glad you've come, girl. I've had the cleanin' of them since Bertha went.'

'Who's Bertha?' Polly asked.

Mrs. Higgins sat down heavily. 'Bertha was the last maid. She left three weeks ago—in disgrace.'

'Why?'

The cook pulled a face. 'No better than she should be—an' it caught up with her, if you get my meanin'.' She peered at Polly. 'They don't allow followers here, you're not walkin' out, are you?'

Polly shook her head. 'Good! keep it that way and you won't go far wrong, my girl!' She opened a door. 'This 'ere's your room.'

Polly stepped inside and looked around. Tucked under the eaves the room had no straight walls at all but a series of slopes, coming almost to the floor in places. One small skylight supplied the only ventilation and light. Oilcloth covered the floor and the furniture consisted of a bed, a washstand with a bowl and a jug and a cane chair. Across one corner was a curtain which the cook drew aside.

'Here's your dresses, one for mornin's, one for afternoons and your aprons and caps—all clean, so keep 'em that way—oh and by the way, you can call me Mrs. H.' She pronounced it 'Haitch.' Polly nodded and Mrs. H. smiled. 'Make haste and get into one of them dresses then and when you come down I'll tell you what your duties are.'

Left alone in the cold little room, Polly sat down on the bed and found it as she'd expected, hard and comfortless. Her room at the Eight Bells had not been luxurious, it was true, but at least she'd had a feather bed and a rug on the floor—and a window where the sun shone in and she could glimpse the river over the rooftops. This window was too dusty to see out of and too high anyway.

Wearily she opened the brown paper parcel that Florrie had given her and set out her

24

brush and comb on the washstand, then she laid her nightdress on the pillow and began to exchange her own dress for the blue gingham one the cook had given her.

When she appeared in the kitchen doorway ten minutes later Mrs. Higgins threw up her hands in dismay.

'Oh, my dear Lord! That won't do, my girl. Indeed it won't! Come here.'

Polly went slowly towards her. The dress hung on her, the shoulder seams halfway down her arms, the neck loose and the waistline sagging while she tripped over the hem at every step.

'If Miss Downes or Mrs. Mears sees you like this they'll have a fit! Can you sew, girl?'

Polly shook her head. 'Not very well—' she sniffed back a tear, suddenly overwhelmed by the memory of Kate's beautiful wardrobe and the luxurious feel of the rich materials against her skin—that night when she had sung wearing the green dress—the night she had first met Eddie. A large drop ran down her cheek.

'Oh don't start that, girl, for Gawd's sake!' Mrs. Higgins snapped—then, more kindly: 'Better go and take it off, but first we'll pin it. I'll help you to alter them if you like—they'll have to be done—and soon!'

When she had come downstairs again Mrs. H. had taken Polly to her room which opened off the kitchen and shown her her proudest

25

possession—a sewing machine. It was the first that Polly had ever seen and she was spellbound.

'My Arthur was a great one for the horses—rest his soul,' Mrs. H. had explained. 'But say what you will he had a nose for a bargain. One day he come home with this—an investment, he said it was and he was right. Once I got the hang I made all his clothes on it—and mine, and half the street's too. It paid for itself time and again. I'd never part with it. While I've got this I can always earn myself a crust, I always say. I do all the mending jobs for Miss Downes and Mrs. Mears on it.'

'Are they rich?' Polly asked. 'They must be to have a house like this and servants.'

Mrs. H. laughed scornfully. 'Rich? Bless you no! Oh, they're comfortable enough, their Pa left them well provided for, but you'd know it if you was in a rich household, my girl. A cook and one maid! That'd be poverty to some!'

'Why—how many servants do they have then?'

Mrs. H. sat back and took a deep breath. 'Well now, there'd be a butler—housekeeper, cook and kitchen maid, a 'tweeny' and a boot boy. Then there'd be a housemaid and a parlour maid not to mention the ladies' maids and if there were children there'd be a nanny and a nursery maid—maybe a governess too!'

Polly's eyes were round. 'All those?' she breathed.

Mrs. H. shook her head. 'In the proper gentry houses there'd be footmen too and grooms for the horses and gardeners and who knows what else.' She settled back to her stitching again with satisfaction. 'Oh yes, this is a poor household compared with some where Higgins an' me've worked. Plenty of work to do though just the same.'

'Florrie told me the ladies do "good works",' Polly said. 'What sort of good works do they do?'

Mrs. H. lifted her shoulders. 'Oh— "convertin' sinners", they call it. *I* calls it a waste of time! Still I suppose they feel obliged. Their Pa was a minister, you see and they have a brother who's a missionary out in Africa,' she shuddered. 'All them savages! Let 'em stay 'eathen, I say. Better than bein' eaten alive! Still—every man to his taste, I suppose.'

While they stitched together Polly learned what her duties were to be—: To rise at five-thirty and light the range fire, first blackleading it; then, light the fire in the morning room and dust—do the hall and the front steps. Serve breakfast at eight and whilst the ladies were eating it make their beds— The list went on and on and Polly's eyes grew round. How would she ever get it all done? But Mrs. H. reassured her.

'Don't look so worried, I'll help as much as I can,' she said kindly. 'But you'll have to be thorough. If there's one thing Miss Downes can't abide it's shoddy work.'

At last the work was done and the dresses folded. Mrs. H. made a cup of cocoa and at last Polly was climbing the attic stairs to her room. As she lay in the hard, narrow little bed her last waking thought was, as always, of Eddie. Where was he now and what was he doing? Did he ever think of her? But it was not long before she was fast asleep.

She woke with a start and wondered for a second where she was, then she looked at the clock Mrs. H. had lent her. It was just five o'clock. She stretched and got out of bed, better to be early on her first day, as it was she didn't know how she was to get through all that work. As she washed in the cold water in the jug she thought briefly of the girl who until recently had occupied this room. What *had* Mrs. H. meant when she'd said—: 'No better than she should be and it caught up with her?' She'd meant to ask last night, but somehow she'd forgotten.

Down in the kitchen she struggled with the range. It was dirty, exhausting work but at last she had it clean and shining and the fire blazing merrily. What was next? Oh yes, the morning room—that was the one where she'd been interviewed yesterday. As she worked she wondered about the two ladies and hoped that she wouldn't have to come into contact with them too much. Miss Downes wasn't too bad, she decided, but there was something really

28

creepy about that Mrs. Mears. With her quick, black eyes and round body in the shiny black dress she reminded Polly of one of the black beetles she often found in the pantry at the 'Bells', the kind that *crunched* when you trod on them. Polly shuddered, yes, she'd keep well out of *her* way. Miss Downes, on the other hand was more like a fish—smooth and cold. She smiled to herself, enjoying the game of comparisons as she toiled up the area steps with her bucket. Mrs. H. was for all the world like a brown hen, clucking about, all fussy. Odd how Florrie hadn't taken to her. Polly thought she was kind and very interesting to talk to.

'Well! I must say you're an improvement on old Bertha and no mistake! What's your name then, eh?'

Roused from her thoughts Polly looked up from the steps to see a cheeky faced young man looking down at her. He wore an apron and had a thatch of straw coloured hair. By the kerb stood a trolley bearing a milk churn.

'I—I'm Polly,' she said uncertainly.

'And I'm Albert,' said the milkman with a grin. 'I hope we'll be seein' a lot of each other Polly.' He winked broadly and bending down gave Polly a resounding slap on her rear.

'You can give me two quarts and less of your sauce, Albert Potter!' Mrs. H. appeared at the top of the area steps with a milk pitcher in her hands. 'Polly here is very busy—she's got better things to do than put up with your liberties!'

Polly got to her feet and picked up the bucket. 'I've done the steps, Mrs. H. What's next?'

The cook looked at the grimy apron Polly wore. 'You'd better get that changed sharpish, girl. It'll soon be time for prayers.'

'And say one for me while you're at it!' Albert said cheekily.

In the kitchen Mrs. H. smiled at Polly. 'I've been upstairs to have a look and you've done quite well—not bad at all. Now make haste and get tidied up. We always have to go up for prayers before breakfast—oh and if I were you I wouldn't have too much truck with that Albert Potter. I shouldn't be surprised if he wasn't the cause of Bertha's trouble!'

'What *was* her trouble, Mrs. H.?' Polly asked, but the cook shook her head.

'The trouble that comes from makin' too free with a man,' she said evasively, folding her lips into a tight line. Polly shrugged. Why did nobody ever tell you *anything*?

Prayers were held in the morning room and presided over by Mrs. Mears. Polly thought they would go on for ever and her knees hurt from kneeling on the hard floor. Mrs. Mears nasal droning almost sent her to sleep twice and she was greatly relieved when the last Amen was intoned and, taking the signal from Mrs. H. she rose to leave the room. She had

30

just reached the door when Mrs. Mears spoke to her:

'Polly! Kindly do something about your hair. Tell Higgins to show you how to put it up.' The black eyes peered at her accusingly. 'Do you put rags in it?'

'No, ma'am.'

'Then why does it not lie straight like any decent gel's hair? Wet it with a comb and water. It looks a disgrace!'

As Polly closed the morning room door behind her the tears pricked her eyes. Mrs. H. took her arm.

'Come on, girl, don't dawdle, they'll be wantin' their breakfast. Makes 'em hungry, all that prayin'.' She glanced at Polly. 'Take no notice of what they say, they're only jealous 'cos you're young, dried up old pair of cats!'

Between the porridge and the bacon and eggs Mrs. H. and Polly struggled to put up Polly's unruly mop of hair, drawing it up into a knot on top of her head, but try as they might, tendrils and wisps kept escaping. At last Mrs. H. stood back and regarded her.

'Well, that's the best I can do. Where did you get a head of hair like that from—your Ma?'

'I don't know. I never had no Ma. Sid and Florrie found me down the docks when I was a baby. They never found out who my real Ma was.'

The cook's face puckered in sympathy. 'Oh!

31

Still, maybe it was just as well, eh? And you had a good home, didn't you?'

A bell jangled noisily, bobbing on its spring on the board over the door and Mrs. H. gave Polly a shove.

'Mercy me! They're ready for their bacon already! I'll swear those two eat faster every day!'

There wasn't a moment's rest for Polly all day. There were brasses and silver to clean, furniture and carpets to brush, vegetables to prepare and linen to sort and all the time she worked she learned little snippets about her employers from Mrs. H. as she bustled about at her work.

'Miss Downes is an old maid, of course but Mrs. Mears' 'usband was a curate. He ran off and left her,' Mrs. H. told her gleefully. 'I dare say she was too 'oly even for the likes of *him*!' She lowered her voice—'They do say that he ran off with a young woman from a travelling circus—dropped the church and learned to do a balancin' act!'

Polly giggled. 'Poor Mrs. Mears. It must have been an awful shock for her. Perhaps that's why she's so sharp-tongued!'

Mrs. H. snorted. 'Full of airs and graces too! Have you heard the way they call me "Higgins"? It should be "cook" by rights— either that or *Mrs.* Higgins. But put that way it sounds to visitors as though I'm the parlour maid—*sauce*!'

32

CHAPTER THREE

Time passed rapidly for Polly at fourteen Marlborough Place. There was always so much to do that the days merged one into the other and it seemed no time at all before the month had passed and her day off arrived.

'Are you going to the "Eight Bells"?' Mrs. H. asked.

Polly nodded eagerly, then she remembered something. 'Has Miss Downes said anything to you about whether I'm to stay or not?' she asked hesitantly.

'She's asked me how I thought you was shapin',' Mrs. H. replied. 'And I told her I thought you were doing well.'

'So you think I'll be staying on, then?'

The cook nodded, smiling and Polly gave a sigh of relief. It was hard work here all right, some nights she was so tired she could hardly climb the stairs to the attic room, but it was better on the whole than life at the 'Bells'. Since she'd begun to grow up Florrie had watched her like a hawk. There she would never get the chance to go on the Halls, while here she felt that anything might happen. She had no idea how it would happen but she felt sure that one day soon her chance would come, just as she felt sure that one day she'd see Eddie again. Deep in her heart there was the strongest of feelings which she hugged to her every night as she lay in her narrow bed. It was what made all the hard work bearable.

On the Sunday of her day off Polly was up bright and early and as soon as the morning chores were done she ran upstairs to change into her own clothes. Standing in front of the mirror she surveyed herself in the childish garments she had worn on the day she'd arrived at Marlborough Place and pulled a face. If only she had something smart to wear—but she hadn't, so these would just have to do.

The kitchen was empty. Mrs. H. had gone to early service at her chapel and Polly ran out eagerly with the milk pitcher when she heard Albert's cheerful cry of 'Milk-O.'

'It's my day off, Albert—I'm going to Wapping to see Florrie and Sid. Mr. Finch, the rag and bone man is taking me on his cart. He's got a married daughter that way, you see and—'

'Hey—steady on!' Albert pushed his cap onto the back of his head and surveyed her with an amused look. 'If you wear them togs folk'll think old Finch 'as gone in for baby-snatchin'!'

Polly looked down at the calf-length dress and button boots in dismay, a slow flush spreading up from her neck.

'Oh! Do I look silly, Albert?'

Albert came slowly down the area steps to

where she stood dejectedly by the kitchen
door.

'Silly?—You, Polly? You couldn't look silly
if you tried! Prettiest little girl in Bayswater,
you are.' He tipped her chin with one finger.
'Give us a kiss, eh, Pol?'

She gazed up at him, the amber-green eyes
wide with surprise. 'Ooh—Albert *Potter!*'

'Go on, Polly—just one.' He slid an arm
persuasively round her waist and drew her to
him, his lips lingering warmly on hers. It was
nice, being kissed by Albert, she reflected. But
it wasn't the same as when Eddie had done it.
It didn't make her feel all warm and sort of
soft inside—but then she *loved* Eddie and she
didn't love Albert. She pushed him away.

'You mustn't do that!'

'Why not? You liked it and so did I. Here,
Polly, don't go to Wapping today—come out
with me instead.'

'No. I've got to go—Albert, leave off and let
me go.'

But his grip around her only tightened as he
pressed her back against the wall. 'You're a
little tease, Polly, that's what you are. I'll let
you go if you give us another kiss and promise
to come out with me on your next day off.'

'No—I won't!' But in spite of her protests
Polly found herself being firmly kissed by
Albert again while his arms held her tightly
against him.

'Stop that at once—both of you!' The

flushed face of Mrs. H. peered crossly over the top of the railings. She stamped down the area steps, her feet making ominous thuds and her cheeks growing redder with every step. When she reached the bottom she raised her umbrella and brought it down heavily on Albert's shoulder.

'How dare you! You know very well that Polly 'ere's only a child! You ought to be ashamed of yourself, Albert Potter! If Mrs. Mears or Miss Downes had seen you you might have lost her her job!'

Albert looked unrepentant. 'Go on, Mrs. H. She was as bad as me—led me on something rotten, she did!'

'Get inside, girl,' Mrs H. pointed her umbrella towards the door. 'I'll deal with you in there—as for you, young man—'

But Albert didn't need telling again. He scuttled up the steps, just escaping another whack with the lethal umbrella. At the top he looked over the railings, grinning cheekily.

'See you tomorrow, Pol—be good!' And he went on his way, whistling unconcernedly.

In the kitchen Mrs. H. narrowed her eyes at Polly. 'Was it true—what he said? Come on now, I want the truth!'

'No! It wasn't true,' Polly said sullenly. 'But even if it was, we were only kissing—what's wrong with that?'

Mrs. H. stared at her and sat down heavily. 'What *are* you saying girl? Didn't your Florrie teach you any better than that? Don't you *know* that behavin' as you were out there is—is just *askin'* for it?'

There it was—that phrase again. Polly shook her head in bewilderment. 'Everyone keeps saying "don't" but nobody ever says why!' she said moodily.

Mrs. H. sniffed. 'Well then—why can't you just be obedient? You can take my word for it there's a good enough reason—but it's not my place to tell you what's what. Anyway, there's no reason why you should know. Young girls should be innocent. Just you do as you're told, do you hear? Or you'll lose your place!' Polly nodded resignedly. 'And make haste *do*! It's almost time for prayers'.

Polly stared at her in dismay. 'Prayers? But it's my day off!'

The cook laughed shortly. 'Tell that to Mrs. Mears! I daresay she forgot to let the Almighty know about your day off!'

Prayers that morning seemed longer and more tedious than ever and Polly was just escaping gratefully when Miss Downes called her back into the room.

'Are you going to visit Mrs. Harris at the "Eight Bells" today, Polly?' Polly nodded eagerly, then, remembering that Miss Downes disliked this form of answer she said:

'Yes, Miss.'

The woman rose to her feet and took an envelope from the little writing desk in the corner. 'Then perhaps you will deliver this for me. It will save me the trouble of posting it. Can you read the name on the envelope, girl?'

Polly studied it for a moment, her brow furrowed as she tried to make out the tall, spidery writing.

'Mrs—Mrs. Flor—Florence Harris!' She said at last triumphantly. It sounded so grand and formal, not at all like Florrie.

'Quite right. And you will see that she gets it?'

'Yes, Miss.'

'And do not forget that you are to be in at eight sharp this evening.'

'No, Miss.'

'That is all, Polly. You may go.'

Once outside the door, Polly ran down the stairs to the kitchen and put on her hat.

'Mrs. H. can you see Mr. Finch coming yet?' She ran to the door and the cook chuckled.

'Not from here, child—but I think I can hear his old horse coming down the road. Are you ready? Have a good time then and don't be late back.'

The ride, perched high beside old Finch on the cart was blissful to Polly. She'd hardly been out in the fresh air at all since she came to Marlborough Place, there simply hadn't been the time. Mrs. H. did all the shopping; she said that if Polly went she'd get cheated into paying more than things were worth. One day, she'd promised, she'd take Polly with her and initiate

38

her into the ways of economical marketing. It was necessary for her to bargain with the street traders and stall holders in the market, for the housekeeping money allowed to her did not stretch to 'shop' prices.

The sun shone and the air was crisp and frosty in the quiet Sunday morning streets. It would soon be Spring, Polly reminded herself. Maybe in the Spring her chance would come! Her spirits sailed high. Asked, Polly could not have said how an opportunity would arise to make a start on a stage career—or what turn of fate would turn her again in Edwin Tarrant's direction, but Polly's faith that these would happen was iron-clad.

The scent of ale and sawdust, stale air and unwashed sailors rushed out strongly when Sid opened the door at the 'Eight Bells' but to Polly it was as nostalgic and evocative as the smell of new-mown hay. Maybe one day she would regard it as Kate did, with revulsion but just at that moment it meant home to her. She threw her arms around the big man's neck, her straw 'sailor' slipping off and sliding down her back. Sid hugged her in return, then held her at arms' length.

'Well, well, Polly! Blow me if you 'aven't gone and *growed*!'

Florrie appeared in the passage behind him. 'Well bring her in and let's have a look at her then! Have you been behavin' yourself then, our Pol?'

Under Florrie's shrewd eye Polly could almost imagine she knew about the episode with Albert Potter this morning. She blushed.

''Course I have, Florrie—here—Miss. Downes asked me to give you this.' She took the crumpled envelope from her pocket and gave it to the older woman. Florrie took it from her.

'Come on then, we'd better go in the kitchen and see what she's got to say about you then, hadn't we? And I hope it's good!'

Sid continued with his morning chores in the cellar and tap-room while in the kitchen Florrie lifted the big enamel teapot from its place on the hob.

'Fancy a cup of tea, could you?' She poured Polly a cup of the strong black liquid, then turned her attention to the letter spread out on the table, but after a few minutes she pushed it across the table impatiently. 'Oh drat! It's no good, Polly. You'll have to read it for me. All them long words is Greek to me!'

Polly pored over the letter, hoping it didn't contain anything to make Florrie cross. 'Dear Mrs. Harris,' she read out slowly. 'I am pleased to say that Polly has proved sat-is-fact-ory— and that I shall be glad to make her position here as gen-er-al servant per-per-man-ent.' Polly looked up at Florrie enquiringly and Florrie nodded.

'That means they're keepin' you on—good! Well, Pol, how have you been and what's it

40

like?'

Between sipping her tea Polly recounted her impressions of the four weeks at Marlborough Place. Relaxed now that the letter was read she described Miss Downes and Mrs. Mears, imitating their voices and manners till the tears ran down Florrie's face.

'Go on with you, girl—you'll be the death of me, that you will! What about that cook? Higgins, isn't it? I bet you didn't find her so funny!'

'Oh, but she's nice, Florrie—honest! When I first went there my uniforms were ever so much too big and she helped me alter them. She's got a sewing machine! You ought to see it!'

Florrie got to her feet. 'That reminds me— our Kate was here the week before last, collecting some of her things—the last of them,' she sniffed disapprovingly. 'Too good for the likes of us, she is, now that she's got this posh gentleman friend! Anyway, I told her you'd got a place and she left you some things—dresses and that, that she'd done with.'

Polly drew in her breath. 'Oh! Where? Where are they?'

'Up in your old room—I—' But she was left in mid-sentence as Polly flew from the room, her feet clattering on the bare stairs in her haste to see what Kate had left her.

Before the spotted mirror Polly held the

dresses up in front of her. There was a soft wool plaid, another in two shades of blue and a beautiful rose coloured taffeta, trimmed with cherry red. Also in the box was a jaunty little straw boater with a blue ribbon and a little hat with feathers. Polly's eyes shone. Albert wouldn't think her such a baby in any of these. Breathlessly she struggled out of her own dress and into the plaid. The dark green and blue showed off her creamy skin and bright hair to perfection and the dimple at the corner of her mouth twinkled with pleasure.

Downstairs Sid stared at her as she walked into the taproom.

'Well! I *said* you'd growed. Quite the young lady, aren't you?'

Polly smiled and glanced round. Florrie didn't seem to be about. 'Sid—I suppose you haven't seen anything of Eddie Tarrant, have you?'

The big man looked uncomfortable. 'Well— matter 'fact, I *'ave!* He was in 'ere last week, pickin' up some bits o' gear he left behind. He asked after you.'

Polly's heart-beat quickened. 'Oh, *Sid!* Did you tell him where I was?'

He shook his shaggy head. 'No! Florrie would've killed me! I did tell him you'd gone into service though and he said to give you his regards.'

Polly could have cried with frustration. 'Oh *Sid!* Couldn't you have found a way to tell him? You will if he comes again, won't you? *Promise?*"

Sid shuffled his feet. 'Well—all right—but I don't suppose he'll be back again. Don't tell Florrie I told you though, will you?'

The day went all too quickly. Although Sunday was a busy day at the 'Eight Bells' Florrie had managed to make one of her good roast mutton dinners and had provided a high tea as well and by the time Mr. Finch called for Polly to take her back to Bayswater she was full both of good food and good spirits.

Florrie patted her shoulder briefly. 'Take care of yourself and don't forget to come and see us again,' she said gruffly.

Sid wrapped his arms around her and planted a loud kiss on her cheek. 'God bless, Pol gel. An' you look a proper treat in that frock—no mistake!'

She was silent as they drove back to Bayswater through the misty evening. Old Finch, glancing sideways at her as he sucked on his clay pipe, thought that she was homesick but inside Polly a million thoughts jostled for first place. Now she had a place—a permanent place *and* some grown-up clothes. She was independent, but above all, Eddie hadn't forgotten her. Kate always said that life was what you made it, well she was determined to make hers as exciting as she could; somehow she would have the things she wanted. If you wanted anything *hard* enough—

43

Kate said—you always got them!

Mrs. H. was glad to see her back, though Polly was a little dismayed to find the washing-up from the evening meal awaiting her.

'I never got my rest this afternoon and my leg is fair killin' me,' Mrs. H. said when she saw the direction of Polly's glance. 'You do it, Polly, then we'll have a nice cup of tea and I'll tell your fortune in the leaves.'

Polly's eyes brightened. 'Ooh—can you, Mrs. H. ?'

The cook threw up her hands as she settled herself in the chair before the fire. 'Can I? Didn't I see Higgin's death in them as plain as plain? And my cousin Emma's wedding!'

'Did you? Did you really?' Polly's eyes were round.

'That I did! But I can't read the leaves till we get the tea, can I?'

Polly set to work with a will, rolling up the sleeves of the new dress and tying on an apron. As she worked she told Mrs. H. all about her day and the dresses that Kate had left for her at the 'Bells'.

'Kate's beautiful, Mrs. H. You ought to see her. She's doing real well on the Halls and now she's got a posh gentleman friend, I hope one day I'll be just like her!'

Mrs. H. sniffed. 'You're all right as you are my girl. If I was you I'd count my blessings!'

But Polly's thoughts were very far from what Mrs. H. called 'her blessings' as she dreamed over the washing-up. 'I can sing too, Mrs. H. Real well—almost as good as Kate. Would you like to hear me? Are they out?' She raised her eyes to the ceiling and Mrs. H. nodded.

'Yes, they've gone to supper with the Reverend Chadwich and his sister. Yes, all right then Polly. Give us a bit of a song.'

The last of the dishes put away Polly rolled down her sleeves and took up her position in the middle of the kitchen floor. Then she began to sing the song she had last sung at the 'Bells' when she'd worn Kate's dress. Her strong young voice filled the room and as she grew more confident she swung her hips and raised her skirt to show her pretty ankles and calves. Mrs. H. was clearly shocked.

'Polly m'girl, you'd better not let miladies upstairs hear you sing like that! And *them words*!'

Polly pouted. 'Why—what's wrong with them? When I sang that song at the "Bells" the sailors all laughed and clapped—they joined in too!'

'Huh! They *would*!' Mrs. H. poured out two cups of tea. 'Sit down, Polly. If you take my advice you'll forget all about the stage. It's not for respectable girls and singing songs like that in public can only lead to shame!'

'But I can't see why!' Polly insisted. 'Kate's done all right for herself. Everyone treats her like a lady—she's got lovely clothes and a gentleman friend—she has a real nice time!'

45

'She'll be headin' for a fall, you mark my words,' Mrs. H. said darkly. 'Come on, drink up now if you want your fortune told.'

Polly drained her cup and handed it to the cook who ceremoniously twirled it three times and set it upside-down in the saucer. The firelight played mysteriously on her face as she peered into it.

'Go on,' Polly urged her. 'What can you see?'

'There's a great crowd of people here,' Mrs. H. said in a hushed voice. 'But one man stands apart from the rest. Then there's you—standin' alone and a fair haired woman holdin' her arms out to you.'

'Who could that be?' Polly asked. Mrs. H. nodded wisely.

'My guess is that it's your Ma. I bet she still thinks about you. I reckon she's a highly respectable woman by now—reformed like and she'll be worryin' about you—hopin' you're not treadin' the path she trod.'

But Polly was hardly listening. It was all so clear: the crowd was her audience and the man apart, Eddie. She was performing on the stage and the woman holding out her arms was her mother like Mrs. H. said. She hadn't thought a great deal about her before but now the vision in the teacup stirred her imagination. Maybe her mother was a famous actress—or a lady—someone with blue blood. She voiced these exciting thoughts to Mrs. H. and the cook laughed.

'In a minute you'll be saying your Ma was the Queen herself!'

Polly laughed with her but in her heart she had added another ambition to the growing list. Some day—somehow she would find her mother. Until now she had always thought of herself as a foundling—a nobody but now she came to think of it she might be *anybody*! The woman who had borne her *had* to have an identity—didn't she?

CHAPTER FOUR

Mrs. H's promise to take Polly to the market and instruct her in the art of buying came to fruition unexpectedly the following week. Polly thought secretly that the cook was making a great fuss about nothing. She was quite used to shopping both with and for Florrie at Wapping and the street traders here seemed models of honesty compared with those she was used to dealing with. However, she went along with Mrs. H's lectures, not knowing at the time how soon she would be called upon to put them into practice. It was two mornings later, when she took the cook her morning tea that the blow fell.

'It's my leg—it's all swollen up like a prize marrow!' Mrs. H. groaned and drew back the covers to reveal the offending limb. Polly gasped in sympathy.

'Oh, Mrs. H.! That does look bad. Can you stand on it?'

With difficulty the older woman got out of bed and put her weight on the leg. 'Aah!' she groaned, falling back heavily. 'Oh dear—look, Polly, I'm sorry but you'll have to manage without me today. When it gets like this there's only one thing for it and that's rest. You'll just have to tell Miss Downes that you'll do the best you can.'

Polly was fearful as she went upstairs to prayers that morning. It wasn't that she couldn't do all the things that Mrs. H. did. Florrie had trained her well in the kitchen—it was just a question of whether she could do them to the satisfaction of her mistresses. She dropped her usual respectful bob as she entered the room and launched straight in:

'Please Miss, Mrs. Higgins is bad this morning and can't get up. It's her leg that's giving her trouble—she can't stand on it.'

The two ladies looked at each other then at Polly. Mrs. Mears nodded to Polly.

'I shall go down to Higgins directly, gel. You may tell her I will bring her some of my herbal ointment. It is usually effective in the treatment of her leg.'

'Yes—thank you ma'am. I'll tell her.' Polly was surprised that the 'black beetle' could be so agreeable.

'Can you manage the work Mrs. Higgins usually does, Polly?' Miss Downes asked her.

Polly nodded, trying her best to look confident. 'I can cook—a little, Miss.'

'Then do your best. As it happens Mrs. Mears and I will be out to dinner this evening and I think a little fish for luncheon would suffice. Can you cook fish?'

'Oh yes, Miss,' said Polly relieved. 'Don't you worry.'

An hour later Polly pulled on her outdoor things and went into Mrs. H's room to collect

49

the housekeeping purse and her instructions.

'Now, girl—keep tight 'old of that purse or you'll have it pinched—then you'll find your wages bein' docked. You know where to buy the fish and I've made you a list of the other things we need. Can you read it?'

Polly looked down the piece of paper. 'Yes—that's all right, Mrs. H. Is there anything you want before I go?'

'No, girl, you get off.' She shifted her position in the bed. 'Phew! That ointment of Mrs. Mears don't 'alf give you gyp, but I think it's takin' the swelling down already. Make haste now—and you can do the jobs you didn't get time for this afternoon. They're goin' out so you'll have the place to yourself.'

Polly felt light hearted as she hurried along the busy streets to the market. She felt free and adventurous—as though anything might happen. The air was cool and clear and the sun shone with a promise of real warmth later. On the corner she passed an old man playing a barrel organ with a small, sad monkey in a red coat perched on top. She wished she had a penny to put into its little outstretched palm. Looking down at her dull clothing she realised that she should have worn one of her new dresses. It would have been nice to have felt like a lady for once, but there'd been no time to change.

The market was busy, teeming with noisy, bustling life. The rabbit man passed her with his long pole strung with rabbits and hares and the calls of the fruit sellers and greengrocers filled the air. A flower girl sat at the edge of the pavement, dull against the riot of colour in her basket and an oyster man lurched along, his barrel of wares perched precariously on his head. Polly breathed deeply. It was the essence of life. If only she could take her time—look at everything and enjoy it.

'Well! If it isn't young Polly! Where're you off to then?'

She turned to see Albert Potter grinning at her and blushed. Since the incident in the area on the morning of her day off she had avoided him, doing the front steps early, before his time. This morning she had left a note on the step with the milk pitcher.

'Hello,' she said briefly and hurried on, but Albert kept pace with her.

'Something up at number fourteen, is there? Mrs. H. ?'

'She's not well,' Polly explained. 'That's why I'm doing the shopping—and I'm in a hurry, if you don't mind.'

He put a hand on her arm. 'Wait a minute, Pol. Where've you been for the last few days? I've missed you.'

She stared at him coldly. 'You might well ask! I've been busy—got better things to do with my time than stand here talking to you too!'

'You're still mad about the other mornin''

aint you? I'm sorry, Pol—but can you really blame me—with you lookin' as pretty as a picture an' all?'

Polly melted a little. If only she'd been wearing one of Kate's dresses. That would have knocked his eye out! She'd meant to keep away from Albert Potter like Mrs. H. had said, but it *was* nice to be told that you were pretty.

'I've got some new dresses,' she told him shyly. 'Real *ladies'* dresses!'

He pushed his cap onto the back of his head and his blue eyes twinkled at her. 'Cor, Polly, I'd like to see you all poshed up. When're you comin' out with me, then?'

She shrugged. 'You know I don't get off again for three more weeks,' she said half regretfully.

'Come out of an evenin' then!'

She stared at him. 'What—on the sly? Miss Downs'd give me the sack. It's not allowed—evenings off.'

He nudged her playfully. 'And do you only do what's allowed? *Ain't* you a good girl! Go on, Pol—be a devil and come out with me tonight.'

She shook her head. 'You hold your tongue, Albert Potter. You know I can't do any such thing!'

He put his hands on her shoulders and swung her round. 'Oh go on, Polly—just so's I can see you in your finery. Here, look!'

Towards them shuffled an old man wearing

sandwich boards strapped to his back and front.

'See what it says?' Albert pointed. 'I'll take you there if you like!'

Polly stared at the large black printing on the board. It read: 'McKenna's Music Hall—Tonight for one night only—Patti Jordan. The Piccadilly Nightingale.' Polly felt her colour rise. Kate had told her about Patti Jordan. She turned to Albert.

'Our Kate's on the Halls. She *knows* Patti Jordan!'

'Well, there you are then—you'd like to see her, wouldn't you?'

Polly stared at Albert, then at the receding back of the sandwich man. All around her teemed the bustling life of the market, making the blood stir within her. Kate always said 'Life was what you made it' didn't she? And she had a chance to be taken to a music hall! She couldn't—*shouldn't* turn it down! Mrs. H. was laid up—Miss Downes and Mrs. Mears were going out. Surely she could sneak out and meet Albert just this once. She smiled up at him, the amber-green eyes alight with excitement that Albert fondly fancied was on his account.

'All right then—I'll come if I can.'

His grin spread from ear to ear. 'That's the ticket, Pol! See you on the corner of Marlborough Place at seven o'clock then.'

If Polly had any misgivings about the

arrangement she had made with Albert she had little time to dwell on them. As soon as she had served the luncheon and done the washing-up she began on the chores she'd neglected this morning. All afternoon she scrubbed, polished and toiled, fighting down the excitement that surged through her. At five o'clock she was finished and just filling the kettle for tea when she heard a bell ringing in the street and the familiar cry—: 'Muffins! Fresh Muffins!' Mrs. H. called from her room:

'Polly! Take some money from my purse on the dresser and get some, will you? I could just fancy a muffin for my tea.'

Polly didn't need telling twice. Muffins were a particular favourite of hers and taking Mrs. H.'s purse she ran up the area steps into the street. The sun had gone now and the gas had been lit; round each globe hung a misty aura.

'Gonna be a foggy night, missy,' observed the old Muffin man as he replaced the cloth over his wares. Polly looked up at him.

'I reckon you're right!' Somehow the prospect made her planned escapade seem even more exciting.

Mrs. H. got up for tea, announcing that her leg was a lot better.

'Say what you will about Mrs. M.' she said, 'she do know how to make ointments!' She settled herself comfortably in the chair before the fire. 'She learned it when she was in Africa with her brother, you know. They were both

54

out there, 'elpin' him before he got married. No doctors there, so you *'ave* to learn how to take care of yourself!'

She seemed in great spirits after her rest and for a while Polly was afraid she would decide to remain up, but after they had finished the last of the muffins and drained the pot of tea the cook heaved herself out of the chair.

'Well, I'm off back to bed. Now you will stay up and lock up when they get in, won't you Polly?'

Polly nodded. 'What time do you think that'll be?'

'They've gone to a meeting over at the Mission Hall in Houndsditch. That usually keeps 'em out till ten-thirty at least. But you can have a snooze in the chair by the fire, can't you? I'd stay up with you only I feel that if I get an early night I'll be all right tomorrow.'

'Oh yes, you get off to bed, Mrs. H.' Polly said quickly. 'I'll be alright. I can write a letter to Florrie and Sid while I'm waiting.'

Polly guessed that Mrs. H. was off to have a swig of her 'cough medicine'—the colourless liquid she kept in a medicine bottle in her wardrobe. She *said* it was for her 'bronical tubes' but Polly hadn't been raised in a pub without knowing the odour of gin when she smelt it! Tonight she was grateful to the 'cough medicine' though. Everyone knew there was nothing like a drop of gin for getting you off to sleep and who was she to criticise, anyway?

At five minutes to seven she came cautiously down the back stairs and listened outside Mrs. H's door. To her satisfaction loud snores vibrated the air and, heaving a sigh of relief she tiptoed to the scullery and surveyed herself in the mirror over the sink. She had chosen the blue dress. It had a high neck frilled with frothy white lace and the front drapery, which looped into a small bustle at the back was of a darker shade of blue. With it she wore the jaunty boater with the blue ribbon and a pair of kid gloves, which to her joy she had found at the bottom of the box.

As she came up the area steps she saw the muffin man's prediction had been right. A thick mist swirled in the street making Polly shiver, half with cold and half with anticipation. Albert was waiting as he'd promised at the corner and when he saw her he came towards her eagerly.

'You came then—I wondered if you would after all.'

'Yes, but I must be in before ten—that's when they get home,' Polly said breathlessly.

He laughed. 'Leave off! The evenin's only just beginning!' He took her hand and drew her under the nearest street lamp. 'Cor, Polly! You don't 'alf look a little bit of all right!'

She gave him a shove 'Go on with you—I though you were taking me to the music, hall.' But she blushed prettily at the compliment all the same.

McKenna's stood on a corner and as they came up to the entrance Polly held back, her eyes critical.

'Is this it? It looks more like a pub to me!'

'Well, so it is,' Albert admitted. 'But it's a music hall too—lots of them are. Didn't you know that?'

Polly did know, from what Kate had told her but somehow she'd imagined herself at a real theatre tonight and she was a little disappointed. She said so, pouting a little and Albert looked peeved.

'Blimey, Pol. I'm a milkman, not a ruddy belted earl! Do you want to go in then, or don't you?'

'It's not one of them "Penny Gaffs" is it?' Polly asked suspiciously.

Albert's mouth dropped open. 'What do you take me for? I wouldn't take you to one of them!' He grabbed her arm. 'Here—come on in before I loses my patience with you!'

To Polly the names: Theatre, Music Hall and Penny Gaff were just words; places that so far had only existed in her imagination. Kate had talked of them and of climbing the ladder to success in the world of the theatre and many a time Polly had dreamed of seeing the inside of one of these places. Now the time had come.

Inside McKenna's the light seemed brilliant after the gloom in the street. The place was full of people, noise and colour. At one end was a busy bar, grand with an ornate mirrored backing and aproned waiters bustling to and from it with laden trays. At the other end was a small stage, the curtain of which bore advertisements for local tradesmen. The remaining area of the room was filled with tables at which sat the evening's customers. Polly looked up at Albert with wide eyes as she clutched at his arm.

'Ooh! It's nice isn't it? When does the show start?'

Albert pulled out his pocket watch and looked at it. 'In about five minutes. Come on, Polly, let's sit down. What will you have—a drop of gin, or a nice port and lemon?'

She shook her head, overawed by her surroundings. Now that they were inside she could see how splendid Albert was. He wore a brown checked suit, the jacket of which was buttoned high and a brown, curly brimmed bowler which he now held against his chest. His unruly hair was plastered down neatly and his face shone with cleanliness.

'You do look nice, Albert,' she said shyly.

He grinned. 'Thanks! You look a fair cracker yourself! Come on, there's a table over there.'

Above them the gas chandeliers blazed and Polly's cheeks soon glowed pink with warmth and excitement. Her hair had begun to come down as it always did and hung in little curling tendrils about her neck and ears. Albert felt for her hand under the table. She would have drawn it away but at that moment something exciting began to happen—the curtain rolled itself up as though by magic revealing a small stage decorated with potted palms. The show was about to begin—and somehow Polly's hand stayed in Albert's for the rest of the evening.

There was a man with a concertina who sang and told jokes,—a lady with a little dog that did tricks—a very small boy who sang a sad song about his mother who had died—that made Polly cry a little—but at last the star of the evening appeared—Patti Jordan herself! Polly sat spellbound. She had never seen anyone so beautiful, not even Kate! Her dark hair was dressed in an elaborate style, piled high on her head and in it she wore a magnificent feather ornament. Her dress was of deep red velvet and her skin was like white satin—but her voice! The crowd, who all through the show had continued to laugh and talk, was now silent as the rich, throaty contralto filled the room. She sang ballads that brought tears to the eyes and comic songs that made the sternest of faces smile and by the time they came out of McKenna's Polly was her devoted admirer for life.

Albert tugged at her arm. 'Come on, Pol, didn't you say you wanted to be in before ten?'

Polly came out of her dream with a start.

'Why—what time is it now?'

'Quarter to,' Albert told her drawing her arm through his. 'It's all right, we'll get there —just have to step it out a bit, that's all.'

They began to walk and he looked down at her. 'Like it then, Pol?'

She nodded. 'Ooh yes, it was *lovely*. Thanks for taking me, Albert.'

The fog was thicker now and when they reached Marlborough Place Albert accompanied her down the area steps.

'It's all right, I can manage now. Goodnight, Albert—and thanks again,' she said, but he stood with her at the kitchen door.

'Don't I get a cup of cocoa to wash the fog out of my throat?'

She gasped. 'Albert! You know I daren't do that!'

He moved closer, trapping her between himself and the wall. 'Give us a kiss then.'

'No!'

'Oh, Pol—you said you'd had a nice time— go on.'

'Well—just one, mind.' She raised her face and closed her eyes. He kissed her gently once—then suddenly something seemed to happen to Albert. She heard him give a kind of gasp and his arms tightened round her while his lips crushed hers hungrily, then he was murmuring her name over and over while his fingers fumbled clumsily with the fastenings at the front of her dress. She struggled wildly.

'Albert! What are you doing? What's the matter?'

But her protests went unheeded and as his lips came down on hers again she felt his hand slide inside her dress and close round her breast. She lifted her foot and brought the heel down hard on his instep. His hold on her loosened temporarily, giving her enough time to move to the door.

'Albert Potter,' she warned. 'If you so much as touch me again—I'll scream!'

He caught her wrists, his eyes burning, 'If you do you'll lose your job. They'll know you've been out!'

'I don't care!'

'Oh yes you do!'

Suddenly Polly stiffened as the sound of horse's hooves was heard in the street above. A cab was drawing to a halt in the street directly over their heads.

'Ssh! It's *them*!' she hissed. 'Miss Downes and Mrs. Mears. Oh lor'!'

Albert drew her swiftly under the steps into the dark recess where the coal-hole was. 'Now we'll see how much you care then!' he whispered, pressing her into the corner. He kissed her greedily, once more slipping his hand inside her dress and caressing her roughly. Tears sprang to Polly's eyes, tears of frustration. She longed to hit Albert as Mrs. H. had done on that other occasion. She *hated* him for taking advantage in this mean way but

61

she was terrified of making a noise. It would be so humiliating to be found like this! There was nothing she could do but endure Albert's unwelcome attentions until her mistresses were safely indoors.

At last she heard the cab driver call to his horse and the clip-clop of hooves as it moved away—then the thud of the front door closing. The danger of discovery was past. She lifted one small foot and kicked Albert's shin as hard as she could.

'Ow!' He let her go to clutch at his leg. Polly aimed a slap at his face with her open palm but he caught her hand.

'You're a proper little spitfire and no mistake, Polly,' He grinned catching her round the waist again. 'Come on—don't say you don't like it 'cos I know different!'

'Then you know wrong, Albert Potter!' Polly's eyes blazed bright green with fury. 'How *dare* you lay your hands on me. I *hate* you!'

The cocky look vanished from Albert's face and he looked crestfallen. 'I thought you liked me, Pol. I thought you wanted me to—'

'Well I don't—and never shall!' With a final push at his chest Polly turned and let herself into the house, turning the key in the kitchen door and leaning against it in relief.

Inside all was quiet. Soft snores came from Mrs. H.'s room. Suddenly a terrifying thought came into Polly's head—suppose Miss Downes and Mrs. Mears wanted a hot drink before they went to bed? And here she was dressed up like a dog's dinner! Lighting a candle from the embers of the fire in the range she peered at herself in the scullery mirror and what she saw brought a flush of shame to her cheeks. Her hair hung in damp strands about her face and the jaunty boater sat crookedly over one eye. The front of her dress was undone and crumpled and there was a sooty mark on one sleeve. She turned away, her eyes pricking with tears. That Albert Potter!

Straightening herself as best she could she crept up the stairs to the hall door and listened—there was complete silence. Opening the door she peered through cautiously. No, it was all right, they'd obviously gone up to bed. She bolted the front door and slipped on the chain, then she made her way slowly up to her own room.

Lying in bed Polly went over the evening's adventure. She had learned a lot of things tonight. One was that you couldn't trust men! She thought she began to understand some of those phrases now, like—: 'Asking for it' and 'Making free'. She'd never *speak* to Albert Potter again as long as she lived. Funny though—her eyes gazed dreamily into the darkness. She wouldn't have minded if it had been Eddie. Was that awful? She rolled over in the narrow little bed, hugging the thought of Eddie to herself. Then she thought of the music hall and all its magical splendour. If only *she* could be on that stage, holding everyone spellbound with her voice and her beauty. She *could* do it if she got half a chance—and one day she would, or her name wasn't Polly Harris!

CHAPTER FIVE

It was one bright morning in late March when Mrs. H. came down from the morning room full of excitement.

'Here, Pol—what do you think? They're going away—indefinitely!'

'Away—who?' Polly asked.

'Who do you think, silly? Miss Downes and Mrs. Mears. Their brother's wife is ill and they're going out to Africa to nurse her and help him.'

Polly digested this information for a moment, then she looked at Mrs. H. in alarm. 'Does that mean we're to lose our places?'

The cook shook her head. 'No. The house is not to be shut up. They've lent it to Mr. William.'

'Mr. William—' Polly gaped. 'Who's he?'

'He's Mrs. Mears' son,' Mrs. H. explained. 'He's just come down from his college and he's got a position with a firm of tea importers in the city. He's looking for a place of his own but in the meantime he's to stay here.'

'What's he like?' asked Polly, intrigued.

'Well, I haven't seen him but the once and that was a long time ago,' Mrs. H. said. 'But he seemed a nice enough young gentleman. Gentlemen are much easier to look after than ladies, Polly. It'll be like a holiday!'

Polly's spirits rose. 'When're they going?'

'Two weeks from today—but there'll be a 'undred and one things to do before then. There'll be all their tropical paraphernalia to get out and go over—they'll be wantin' your help with that, I don't doubt!'

Mrs. H. was right. Polly was run off her feet during the two weeks that followed, running errands, folding, pressing and ironing clothes. The laundry woman who normally came in only twice a month was there almost constantly, filling the kitchen with steam and the smell of wet linen and Mrs. H. was kept busy hour upon hour with all the mending jobs the ladies found for her, the sewing machine whirring away in her room till Polly could almost hear it in her sleep.

At last the day came for their embarkation and when the cab had left bearing the two ladies and all their luggage Mrs. H. turned to Polly with a sigh of relief.

'Phew! Thank goodness for that! Now you and me'll 'ave a bit of a breather girl!'

'When does Mr. William arrive?' Polly asked.

'He hasn't said—any time, I suppose.'

But 'any time' proved to be sooner than they expected. The very same afternoon when Polly was dusting the drawing room the front door bell rang and she answered it to find a tall, handsome young man standing on the step with a beautiful lady on his arm. Polly dropped a respectful bob.

'Good afternoon, sir—madam.'

The young man removed his hat and Polly saw that he had a fine head of dark hair and a crisp moustache to go with it. 'Good day, my girl. I think you've been told to expect me.'

'Is it Mr. William, sir?' Polly asked shyly and the lady gave a shrill little laugh.

'Oh, Willie, how very grand! Mr. William!'

William Mears nodded and stepped inside. 'That's right—and you'd be ?'

'Polly, sir.'

'Polly, eh? Well this is Miss Fellowes and she'll be staying here too for a while. Now, can you get us some tea?'

'Oh yes, sir. Will you take it in the drawing room?'

After showing them into the room Polly ran breathlessly down the stairs, bubbling over with her news but when she heard it Mrs. H. frowned disapprovingly.

'I wasn't told to expect no Miss Fellowes! What a cheek! I don't know what his Ma'd say, I'm sure—and them not chaperoned!'

Polly stared at her. 'What do you mean, Mrs. H. ?'

The cook brushed her aside impatiently. 'Oh never you mind! Just you get that tray set. Good job I made them buns!'

But Polly thought Miss Fellowes—or Amanda as Mr. William called her was beautiful. She had such elegant clothes and she was so pretty. It was on the following morning, when Mr. William had left for the city that the guest room bell rang and when Polly answered it she found Miss Amanda standing in the middle of the room surrounded by clothes.

'Polly dear, I have no maid with me and I wondered if you would like to help me while I am here?'

Polly looked uncertain. 'I'd like to, Miss—but I don't know if I can.'

Amanda laughed her shrill little laugh, showing her exquisite white teeth. 'Of course you can—and don't look so worried. I won't *beat* you if you do something wrong!'

Polly smiled. 'Well, I'll do my best, Miss. I'm sure.'

Amanda began to pile dresses over Polly's arm. 'That's right. I'll teach you what to do, you'll soon learn.'

When Polly returned to the kitchen, her arms laden with brightly coloured dresses Mrs. H. threw up her hands in horror.

'What does she think this is—a laundry? What a nerve! Free board and lodging and now all this extra work! I'll tell you this, Polly, girl, she's no lady!'

Polly stared at her. 'Oh—I think she's ever so nice—have you seen all her lovely things?'

'Hmm—'andsome is as 'andsome does! You mark my words!' Mrs. H.'s mouth took on its buttoned look. 'Posh voice and fancy clothes she may have but clothes don't make the lady- you see if I'm not right.'

But Polly's opinion of Amanda Fellowes didn't change. During the days that followed she spent a lot of time with Amanda, she liked her way of talking, so friendly—more like a friend or a sister than a mistress. Mrs. H. disapproved more strongly every day but Polly was enjoying herself. She told Amanda all about Florrie and Sid and her life at the 'Eight Bells'; how she had been found on the step as a baby and brought up in the dockside pub. She told her about Kate and how well she had done on the Halls, also how she herself hoped one day to follow in her footsteps. Amanda seemed to find it all fascinating.

'Oh, Polly! What an exciting, romantic life you have before you! And how curious you must be about who you really are! Imagine— your mother might have been a Russian Princess who had stowed away on a ship—or perhaps a member of the Royal household in disgrace. Why, just think, Polly—you could be *anyone*!'

'I know—I'm going to find it all out one day,' Polly said dreamily. 'Mrs. H. saw it in the leaves.'

'Tea leaves? I have some Tarot cards, they could *really* tell you. I'll have to get them out one day.'

Polly clapped her hands. 'Oh, Miss—would you?'

The chores became sadly neglected and Mrs. H. grew crosser and crosser.

'It's *me* who's responsible 'ere, my girl and *I* say you're spendin' too much time with Miss Fellowes and not enough time doin' what you're paid for!'

'I can't help it,' Polly said sullenly. 'Miss Amanda says she gets lonely all day with Mr. William away and she has so many clothes that need seeing to. I like doing it and she says it's good for me to learn so's I can get a better job—as a ladies' maid. Miss Amanda says I don't want to be scrubbing floors all my life!'

'And you don't want to run before you can walk either, my girl. Them as does soon find themselves trippin' over themselves!' Mrs. H. sniffed loudly. ''Ave you seen them front steps? They're a disgrace!'

But it was when Amanda started to get interested in Polly's aspirations as a music hall artiste that the trouble really began. To begin with she insisted on Polly giving her a sample of her talents and when she had heard Polly sing she came up with a plan.

'Listen Polly, here's a lark—you must sing for Willie and I when we come home from the theatre tonight. It shall be a surprise. He'll be so amused!'

Polly shook her head. 'Oh, no, Miss. I couldn't! Not in front of Mr. William. Besides—Mrs. H.'d be so cross. When I sang for her she said it could only lead to shame.'

Amanda laughed. 'Did you ever! Sanctimonious old crow! If you listen to people like her, Polly, you'll never get your heart's desire. Now listen, William and I will be home at about eleven. I'll ring and you shall bring us some sandwiches and a hot drink— then you must put on your little performance for us. Please, Polly, don't say no!'

But still Polly hung back. 'I don't know, Miss—'

'Surely by that time cook will be asleep?'

'I suppose so—' Polly looked at Amanda's pouting, disappointed face and made up her mind—'All right then, Miss—if you really want me to—I'll do it.'

Amanda clapped her hands delightedly. 'Wonderful—I can't wait to see William's face.'

Later that night after Mrs. H. was in bed and safely asleep Polly crept up to her room to change, it would never do to sing for Mr. William in her uniform, she would wear one of her own dresses. In the little attic room she stood for a long time trying to make her choice. Which would be the most suitable? Not the blue one. Since that evening at the music hall and the subsequent struggle with the amorous Albert it reminded her too much of her humiliation. She replaced it and took down the plaid—No, too sober. It would have to be the rose taffeta with the cherry red trimming. She hadn't worn this one before.

Ten minutes later she surveyed her

reflection in the mirror over the washstand. This dress was not as demure as the others. The material was richer and the neckline was square and cut low, revealing her creamy skin and the soft curve of her bosom. She had wondered about the colour, would rose pink and cherry go well with her hair? But now she saw the combination gave her a glowing appearance which pleased her. She smiled at her reflection, her heart fluttering with excitement, one part of her wishing the whole thing were over—another hardly able to wait until it was time to begin.

She sat on the edge of a chair in the kitchen for what seemed like hours waiting for the sound of a cab in the street above. The sandwiches were cut and waiting on their covered tray and the kettle was singing on the hob. Polly's heart quickened as at last the sound of hooves was heard. She half rose as she heard the front door slam and waited with bated breath until at last the drawing room bell jangled.

When she made her appearance Amanda drew in her breath sharply. 'Why, Polly! How grand you are!' But a flicker of malice crossed her lovely face as she took in Polly's pretty face and figure and bright hair. As for William, he'd spent a boring evening and felt sleepy. When Amanda had spoken of a surprise he had been irritated, already he was beginning to tire of her constant need of entertainment and cossetting. But at the sight of Polly he pulled himself upright in his chair and the corners of his mouth curved upwards in anticipation.

'Well, *well!* What have we here? Has our little caterpillar turned into a butterfly?'

'It's Polly's ambition to be on the Halls, darling,' Amanda explained. 'And tonight, as a special treat she's going to give us a preview of her talents.' She poured the coffee and handed William a cup, then she nodded to Polly. 'Very well, Polly. You may begin.'

For a second, *just* a second, Polly wanted to run away then she took a deep breath and composed herself. The more people who heard her sing, the more chance she had of achieving her ambition. After all, this was how Kate started.

The cheeky song she sang was a different one this time, one of those she had heard Patti Jordan sing at McKenna's. She had been practising the words and movements every night in her room since and as she got into her stride she saw to her satisfaction that William Mears sat forward on his chair, watching her admiringly, a look of amusement on his handsome face. When the song came to an end he threw back his head and laughed heartily, slapping his knee.

'Well done! Well done indeed, Polly!'

Polly smiled, glowing with the pleasure of success. 'Thank you, sir. Would you like me to do another?'

73

'No—that will be all, thank you, Polly. You may leave the tray.' Miss Amanda dismissed her with a nod and although she smiled with her lips a hard brightness glittered in her eyes. Polly sensed that something was wrong and she backed out of the room, dropping a respectful bob.

'Good night then, Miss—Mr. William.'

'Good night, Polly—and thank you.'

In the hall she paused, biting her thumb nail. Miss Amanda was angry—but why? What had she done? She'd only done what was asked of her, hadn't she? Miss Amanda had liked her singing well enough this afternoon. In the kitchen she tidied up and lit her candle before damping down the fire. Carefully, she checked the bolts on the area door and was just going towards the back stairs when a sudden noise made her turn. Her heart leapt into her mouth as she saw a shadowy figure standing at the top of the stone stairs leading up to the hall.

'Oh!' her hand flew to her mouth and she almost dropped the candle till a voice said softly:

'Don't be afraid, Polly. It's only me.'

She held the candle high as he descended the stairs. 'Oh—Mr. William, it's you.'

'Were you just going to bed?'

'Yes, sir. Is there something I can get you first?'

He came closer and looked down into her eyes. 'No—I just wanted to thank you again for the entertainment you gave us, Polly. You're very talented, did you know that?'

She lowered her eyes. 'Thank you, sir.'

With one finger under her chin he raised her face again to look at him. 'And very pretty too.'

Polly blushed, not knowing what to say. She wondered what Miss Amanda would say if she could hear Mr. William speaking to her in this way and she had the uncomfortable feeling that she wouldn't like it at all. She made to move away but William laid a hand on her arm.

'Don't go yet, Polly.' His voice was soft and low. She turned and looked up at him. Very gently he took the candle from her and put it on the table.

'What would you say, Polly, if I asked you for a kiss?' She took a step backwards but he took her wrist and held her fast. 'Whilst my mother is away I am the master here—isn't that true?' She nodded, mesmerised by his dark eyes—'Well then—' he drew her slowly towards him—'If I ask you to give me a kiss, you must be a good girl and obey, mustn't you?' His lips came down on hers in a kiss unlike any she had ever known. It was deep and searching and left her breathless, half with excitement, half with a fear of something she didn't understand. At last he let her go and looked down at her, his dark eyes glowing with lazy amusement.

'Good-night, little Polly—*pretty* little Polly. I'll see you tomorrow.' He smiled. 'You know you're wasted here, terribly wasted.'

'Am I, sir?'

'Yes—oh yes, you are.' He stood looking down at her for a moment, then stooped to kiss her briefly again before he turned and ran lightly up the stairs.

Polly stood for a long moment staring after him, filled with bewilderment. He shouldn't have done it, she knew that and deep down she had an uncomfortable feeling that she should have stopped him, in spite of what he had said about being the master. Slowly she went up the stairs to check the front door bolts. It was dark in the hall with the gas extinguished and Polly started at a soft rustling sound, then she saw that someone was standing in the shadow of the drawing room door and she held up her candle.

'Oh—Miss Amanda!'

Amanda came out of the shadows and looked hard at Polly. Her face had a tight, stretched look and her eyes glittered in the candlelight.

'What are you doing, Polly?'

'I'm making the doors fast, Miss.'

Amanda drew in her breath sharply. 'Don't be impertinent—and don't try to look so innocent!'

Polly's mouth dropped open. She must have seen! Miss Amanda must have seen Mr.

William kiss her!

'It—it wasn't my fault, Miss—' she began, but she was stopped in mid-sentence as Amanda struck her a ringing blow on the cheek—then gathering up her skirts, she ran up the stairs.

Holding her stinging face, Polly watched her to the top. Just what *had* she done to bring all this about? Sometimes life could be very puzzling!'

It was after breakfast the following morning, when Mr. William had left for the city, when the guest-room bell rang. Polly stared fearfully up at the dancing bell and Mrs. H. gave her a push.

'Go on then, girl! You're not usually so slow to run to your precious *mistress!*' She said the word acidly and Polly bit her lip and started unhappily towards the stairs. Miss Amanda had been so kind to her, she didn't want to be in her bad books.

When she entered the room Amanda was seated at her dressing table a pack of strange looking cards spread out before her. She turned as the door opened and Polly was relieved to see that she was smiling and looked more like her old self.

'Oh there you are, Polly. I'm afraid I was rather horrid to you last night. It was all a misunderstanding. Am I forgiven?'

'It was nothing, Miss—thank you.'

'We were talking the other day about

fortune telling,' Amanda went on. 'And I told you I had some Tarot cards—here they are—' She pointed to the ones laid out before her. 'If you like I will tell your fortune by way of atonement. Would you like that?' Polly nodded eagerly.

'Then draw up that chair and I'll begin.'

After a great deal of curring and arranging of the cards in a ritualistic pattern Amanda began turning them over one by one.

'Ah!' She exclaimed. 'I see that you are to beware of a dark man, Polly. He can harm you and you should keep well out of his way! But there is a great future for you if you have the courage to grasp it.' She looked closely at Polly. 'Have you courage, Polly?' Polly nodded eagerly and she went on: 'You will meet someone at a gathering—soon—*very* soon and through this person you will get your heart's desire!'

Polly clapped her hands together. 'Ooh, Miss! Will it really happen soon—*really*?'

'Nothing ever happens in this life, Polly, unless we *make* it,' Amanda said. 'It's all there—the things you want. It's just knowing when to grasp the opportunity. And once you've got what you want—whatever it is—you must fight to keep it. We must all do that!'

Polly had never heard her speak so vehemently and she looked up in surprise. It was almost as though Amanda were talking to herself. Suddenly she seemed to come to and

78

her smile returned.

'Do you understand what I have been saying, Polly?'

'Oh yes, Miss.'

'And will you grasp *your* opportunity when it comes?'

'Yes—oh yes, I will!'

Suddenly Amanda relaxed. 'Do you know, Polly I think I can begin to see this fortune of yours coming true!'

'Oh can you, Miss—how?'

'I have a friend,' Amanda told her. 'She has a beautiful grand house just off the Strand and she gives a lot of parties for important people—some of them from the world of the theatre!' Polly shook her head, not understanding.

'I don't see—'

'Listen and you will. She is giving one of her parties this very evening. William and I were invited but William cannot go because he has a business dinner to attend. *Now*—if I were to take you with me—as a friend—'

'Oh, Miss!' Polly stared at her. 'Oh—I couldn't. I'm not allowed out except for one Sunday in four—and even then I have to be in by eight!'

Amanda waved an airy hand. 'Nonsense! If I wish you to accompany me, then you shall! I will tell Mrs. Higgins that I need you to help me change into a fancy dress both before and after the party.' Polly still looked uncertain and she went on: 'You could wear the pretty dress you wore last night—oh come, Polly. I thought you said you were not afraid to grasp your opportunities!'

'Well—I don't know—It's not that I wouldn't like to come, Miss—'

'Then come—please do. I want to go and I can't very well go alone. Do you want me to be disappointed?'

A tiny spiral of excitement began in the pit of Polly's stomach. Miss Amanda had been very kind, especially after last night and she seemed so anxious to make up for what she had done. Besides—the thought of going to a grand house—as a guest—just like Kate did, filled her with a sort of terrifying delight—and there was the fortune too—what the cards had said. If she didn't go she would never know whether they had been right! Suddenly she was surprised to hear her own voice saying.

'All right, Miss. I'll come—if you'll speak to Mrs. H. for me.'

Amanda clapped her hands. 'But of course I will! You leave her to me!'

For the rest of the morning Mrs. H. had not spoken to Polly. She wore a cross, closed-up expression and went about her work in an exaggerated, forceful way, banging things about. At last, unable to bear it any longer, Polly spoke to her:

'Did Miss. Amanda speak to you about me?'

Mrs. H. sniffed haughtily. 'She did!'

'Is it all right then?' Polly asked anxiously.

'Why ask me?' Mrs. H. rounded on her. 'If *Madam* says you're to go then I suppose you must—but I don't like it. I told her and I'm tellin' you! Mark my words, no good will come of it!' And with that she turned on her heel and left Polly to ponder on her words.

Polly had never driven in a hansom cab before and, dressed in the cherry dress and the smart little feathered hat she felt very grand indeed as she sat beside Miss. Amanda. Mrs. H. still hadn't spoken to her and Polly felt badly about that. The cook had been a good friend to her since she had come to Marlborough Place and she had no wish to fall out with her. But now, as they drove through the fine Spring evening Polly's heart fluttered with anticipation. Could Miss. Amanda really pass her off as a 'friend'? She'd never manage to speak with Amanda's refined accent—not that she hadn't practiced at night when she was alone in her room. What would the night before her hold? Would she really meet an important person who would bring her heart's desire? What would have happened by the morning?

But if at that very moment Polly could have known the answer to her questions she would have been surprised indeed—and not a little afraid!

CHAPTER SIX

The house 'just off the Strand' was even grander than Polly had imagined it would be. It seemed full of noise, people and colour. Although the ladies were most elegant Polly noticed that they all had rather loud voices and as she entered with Miss. Amanda they were eyed in a bold, speculative way by several of the gentlemen present. Polly hung back feeling uncomfortable. It had been foolish of her to think she could appear like these ladies here, poised and confident. But before she had time to voice these thoughts Amanda grasped her arm and drew her forward as a raven-haired woman in a dark red dress came towards them.

'Ah, Madame Hortense—this is the young lady I was telling you about. She has such a beautiful singing voice and as you can see, she is very pretty!'

Madame Hortense smiled at Polly who was at once reminded of a cat, a huge, black cat, well fed and purring. The woman held out a hand, like a paw in its black velvet glove.

'Bon soir, ma chère. Vous êtes *charmant.* I do hope that you will like my little establishment.'

She spoke with a heavy foreign accent like those Polly had often heard at the Eight Bells when a foreign ship had docked. The black eyes swept appreciatively over Polly in a way that made her squirm with discomfort, then she turned to Amanda, taking her arm.

'Most satisfactory, chère. No relatives, you say?' Amanda nodded.

'Polly is in great need of friends, aren't you, Polly? And she has a great desire to entertain.'

Madame Hortense smiled. 'Then she shall—by all means. Tonight we have a great many *good natured* gentlemen here who wish most urgently to be entertained!' She laughed and Amanda joined in, her own shrill peal contrasting with the French woman's deep chuckle.

Polly felt a little lost, although the two women were being kind to her she felt oddly uneasy. It was as though their words had a double meaning. Madame led them to a comfortable couch and a tray of drinks was brought by a maid. Amanda pressed a glass into Polly's hand.

'What is it?—I've never—' Amanda waved a hand.

'Drink it, Polly. Tonight you are doing a great many things you have never done before. This is an adventure, remember?' Polly nodded but she still looked doubtfully at the amber liquid in the glass. Although she had been brought up in a public house she had never been encouraged to take alcohol. Florrie had always been most strict in her views on that subject.

'Oh, do go *on*, you silly girl,' Amanda said impatiently. 'It's only a glass of ginger wine. Drink it down quickly, it'll buck you up—and do try to look more cheerful!'

Polly did as she was told and tossed the drink back. It burned her throat and made her gasp a little but immediately she felt its warmth spread through her in radiating waves. Amanda poured her another measure from the carafe on the tray.

'There—it's nice, isn't it?'

Polly nodded. After the second drink she felt better, more relaxed and she leant back against the soft cushions and began to take in her surroundings. The room where they sat was richly furnished in red plush and gilt. There were a great many mirrors and beautiful pictures and people seemed to be coming and going all the time. Polly had thought there might have been music and asked Amanda where the entertainment was. Amanda smiled sweetly.

'Oh, that's upstairs.'

'Would Madame Hortense let me do one of my songs upstairs, do you think?' Polly asked. She felt in exactly the right mood to sing one of her songs now and was already trying to make up her mind which one it would be.

'Presently,' Amanda told her. 'When Madame finds the right gentleman she will ask you to go upstairs and entertain him.'

Polly stared at her. 'You mean a gentleman

from the Halls? Like the one who gave Kate a start?'

Amanda giggled. 'That's right!' She poured more of the amber liquid into Polly's glass. 'Here, have some more ginger wine, it'll improve your voice.'

Polly drank the scalding ginger flavoured drink obediently and felt her spirits rise in anticipation of what the evening held in store for her. The trouble was though, that she felt rather sleepy. The room was so warm and things kept slipping away from her. She hoped she would get a chance to do her song soon.

'Polly, ma chère, will you come with me?'

Polly looked up to see Madame's sloe black eyes smiling down at her. Beside her stood a gentleman, tall and broad shouldered with grey hair and a moustache and—yes—he was smoking a cigar, just like the man who had 'discovered' Kate that night at the 'Bells'. She smiled up at them and tried to rise, but something seemed to have gone wrong with her legs, for some strange reason they wouldn't hold her up properly. She tried again with a great effort. It would never do not to be able to do her song. Madame took her arm firmly.

'This gentleman would like you to entertain him—you would like that, wouldn't you, Polly?'

Polly smiled. 'Oh yes.'

Amanda glanced at Madame. 'Do you need

my help?' she asked softly but Madame smiled wryly, shaking her head.

'I think not, chère. You have already done your job well. There will be little resistance, I think.'

In a daze Polly found herself being escorted towards the stairs, Madame on one side, the tall gentleman on the other. In a strange way she felt detached—as though she were an onlooker, witnessing something that was happening to someone else. Then something happened that brought her abruptly back to her senses. From a long way off a familiar voice spoke her name—yet not her name—'

'Robin!'

It was a voice she'd never forgotten. She'd heard it so often in her dreams, yet never thought to hear it again in reality—especially not here or now.

'Robin! Don't you remember me?'

She blinked and opened her eyes wide. It was true—she wasn't dreaming. It was Eddie. His beautiful face with the gentle brown eyes and curling hair was before her now and she put out a hand to touch his cheek as though to convince herself that he was really there.

The breath caught in her throat. 'Eddie! Oh, Eddie!' She swayed and saw the gentle expression in his eyes replaced by one of blazing anger.

He stared at Madame. 'What have you done to her? Where are you taking her?'

Madame tried to push him aside. 'Excuse me, monsieur, please stand aside and let us pass.'

But Edwin barred the way with his arm. 'I demand to be told where you are taking this girl!' His voice had taken on its deep, authoritative tone and Polly was reminded of the night Eddie had come to her rescue in the back yard at the Eight Bells. She felt his hand under her chin as he raised her face.

'She is intoxicated!' he shouted. 'Who has done this? I am acquainted with this young lady's guardians and I demand that you release her at once!'

Polly glanced at Madame and saw that her pale face now looked slightly flushed. Her eyes glowed like hot coals as she spoke, her voice sharp as a razor:

'Kindly leave my establishment at once, monsieur. I really cannot tolerate this interference!'

'Certainly!' Eddie put his hand on Polly's arm. 'I will leave gladly, as long as I take Miss Harris with me. If I am forced to leave alone it will be to return with a police officer.'

The gentleman on Polly's other arm suddenly seemed to melt into the crowd of onlookers and Madame's firm grip on Polly was released. She let out an exasperated little snort and shrugged her plump shoulders.

'Ach! As you wish monsieur. Take the wretched girl and go—and pray do not return, for you will not be welcome here!'

'Indeed I will *not* return, Madame—now that I know the practice employed here! Indeed, you will be lucky not to hear more of the matter!' And with these words Polly found herself being propelled out through the hall and into the street with a speed that made her already dizzy head reel.

A few minutes later she was in another hansom cab and Eddie was sitting next to her, demanding to know how she had come to be at Madame Hortense's. As carefully as she could she tried to tell him all that had happened since they last met at the Eight Bells and as she neared the end of her story a hard fact suddenly hit her and she stopped short.

'Oh, Eddie—I—I've got nowhere to go!'

She stared up at him, the amber eyes brimming with tears of dismay. 'Miss Amanda wouldn't have me back at Marlborough Place now and I daren't go back to the Bells and say I've lost my place!'

He put a comforting arm round her. 'I wouldn't let you go back to Marlborough Place anyway, Polly. Don't you realise what kind of place that was where your Miss Amanda took you?'

'No—I thought we were going to a party.' She glanced up at his stern face. 'What kind of place *was* it, Eddie?'

'It was a—a—bordel. A house of prostitution. You were about to be seduced and if that had happened you would have had no choice but to lead a life of sin—of prostitution.'

Polly stared up at him blankly, completely uncomprehending and after a moment his face relaxed and he gently shook his head.

'My poor Robin. You haven't the slightest idea what I'm talking about, have you?'

She shook her head. 'No, Eddie. Will you tell me?'

But he squeezed her hand. 'One day I will—for your own good, but for tonight you have had enough. Besides, I don't think you are in a fit state to take such things in.' He drew her head down onto his shoulder and the warmth and the gentle rocking motion of the cab soon sent her to sleep.

A little later she felt herself lifted from the cab and carried up a great many stairs, then she was warmly wrapped and lying on something soft. Sleepily she opened her eyes. The sight of Eddie's handsome face just above her as he tucked her up sent a glow of blissful happiness coursing through her and she reached up and put her arms round his neck.

'I always knew I'd see you again, Eddie,' she whispered. 'I've thought about you every day. Have you thought of me?'

He smiled, gently taking her arms away and tucking them under the blanket. 'Of course I've thought of you. But now you must go to sleep.'

'Eddie—don't go,' she caught at his hand. 'What will happen to me? If I go home to the Bells Florrie'll be so cross and I can't—' He put a finger against her lips.

'Hush—no more tonight. We'll talk in the morning. I won't be far away.'

'Eddie.'

'Yes?'

'Will—will you kiss me—please?'

For a moment he stood looking down at her, then he bent his head and gently brushed his lips against hers.

'Goodnight, little Robin. Sleep well.' And the next moment he was gone.

Polly gave a sigh of contentment and closed her eyes. Whatever else Miss Amanda had done she had told her fortune well. She *had* met someone important tonight and she had got her heart's desire—or part of it, anyway!

She woke to bright sunlight and the smell of coffee and bacon. Lifting her head she looked round the room. It was large and very untidy, though comfortably furnished; the window that was letting in such a blaze of light was enormous and Polly saw that it was really more like a huge skylight. They must be at the very top of the house, right under the roof. A bright fire burned on the hearth and from a half open door came the sound of a pleasant light baritone voice singing. It was Eddie—he must be cooking breakfast. She couldn't let him do that for her! She threw the rug that covered

90

her aside, then gasped as she realised that she wore only her petticoats. Where was her dress? She didn't remember taking it off last night—could Eddie have?

'Ah, you're awake then?'

She drew the rug up to her chin, her cheeks reddening as Eddie came into the room carrying a tray. At once he saw her discomfort and, putting down the tray he went into the bedroom and reappeared at once with a dressing gown.

'Here—put this on.' He threw the garment over the back of the couch and turned to the window tactfully. 'I had to take your dress off last night, Robin. It was much too tight for you to have slept in and besides, it would have been spoilt. Forgive me?'

Polly drew the gown round her and tied the cord. Forgive him? There was nothing she wouldn't forgive him.

'Thank you, Eddie,' she said quietly. 'I'm sorry to be such a nuisance.'

He turned and smiled at the little tousle-haired figure swamped in the huge gown. 'You're not a nuisance, silly girl. Come on, eat your breakfast now, it's getting cold.'

Standing on her feet Polly was aware of the throbbing in her head and the nauseous feeling in the pit of her stomach. She sat down again abruptly, shading her eyes from the bright light. Edwin laughed softly.

'Poor Robin. I'm afraid last night's drinking

91

has taken its toll. Try to eat something, you'll feel better.'

She stared at him in horror. 'Drinking! But it was only ginger wine!'

He shook his head and sat down beside her. 'I'm afraid they deceived you in that as well as in other things. It's a good thing I came along when I did. How *can* you have grown up so innocent?'

Polly blushed and hung her head, how stupid he must think her and yet she still did not know what it was he had saved her from last night, except that it was something terrible, connected in some way with men. He pushed the plate of bacon towards her.

'Come—eat. Then I want to hear all about that place where you were working. I'm afraid you were a little incoherent last night.'

Polly found that Eddie was right, the food did make her feel better and gradually, little by little she unfolded the whole story of her life at Marlborough Place right down to two evenings ago when Mr. William had shown his appreciation of her singing so affectionately. When she had finished Eddie nodded wisely.

'Ah, I think I see it all now. Your Miss Amanda was not all she appeared to be, obviously and when she saw that her well-to-do suitor was attracted to you she decided to get rid of you!'

'But how, Eddie? What *would* have happened if you hadn't taken me away?'

92

The great amber eyes looked innocently into his and Edwin, usually so eloquent was lost for words. He cleared his throat. 'I'm afraid that if I were to tell you—you would be shocked.'

'No, no, I wouldn't. Please Eddie.' She laid a hand on his arm and he looked deep into her eyes.

'You really mean, Robin, that you truly do not know what takes place—between a man and a woman?'

She considered for a moment, remembering that night when Albert Potter had taken her to the music hall.

'Well—' she said. 'Kissing—and touching—' She looked up at him. 'There's more—isn't there? Florrie and Mrs. H. wouldn't tell me, they said a young girl should be innocent.'

Edwin got up from the couch and walked about angrily. 'That's how such dreadful places are able to flourish, on that belief!' He turned and looked at her. 'Well—someone must tell you.' Seized with sudden inspiration he fetched a sketch pad from a table in the corner and a stick of charcoal, then, with a few words and some deft drawings he made clear for Polly the basic facts that had been witheld from her. In spite of his tact and sensitivity though, she turned her head in shame and embarrassment, her cheeks colouring.

'Oh, Eddie—that's horrible!'

'No!' He threw down the pad and took both

93

her hands in his. 'Never think that, Robin. The way it would have been at that place last night, maybe—but between two people who love and respect each other, it can be very beautiful. One day you'll see I'm right.'

She looked at him. His brown eyes were so sincere, so earnest and the lines of his face so sweet and dear that a great wave of love for him swept over her, yet somehow she knew now that she mustn't tell him. She swallowed hard at the lump in her throat.

'Will I, Eddie?' she whispered, wishing with all her heart that he would kiss her. He didn't, instead he stood up and went to the far side of the room where all his painting materials were. From a stack of canvasses he selected one and held it up for her.

'Look—do you remember this?'

It was the 'gutter child' painting he had done of her while he was staying at the Eight Bells. She laughed.

'Yes, I do. I look awful!'

Turning again to the pile he drew out another canvas. 'What about this one then?'

She stared at it in wonder. It was a study of her again, but this time dressed in Kate's green dress and standing on the trestle platform. Her head was thrown back, one hand rested on her hip and the other caught up the front of her skirt to reveal a frilly petticoat and one dainty foot.

'I did it from memory,' he said quietly.

'Because I couldn't forget the little girl who wanted so much to be a beautiful lady. It's yours if you want it, Robin.'

With a little cry of delight she ran to him and threw her arms round his neck. 'Oh, Eddie—it's lovely!' He *had* thought of her then—maybe he did love her—just a little. Joy filled her breast till she thought she would burst as Eddie's arms held her briefly. Then he put her gently from him.

'Now,' he said, looking at her gravely. 'What are we to do with you? I really think I must take you back to the Harris's.'

'Oh no, Eddie! I can't go back. How would I ever explain to Florrie?'

'But surely if I told her—'

'No!' She grasped his arm urgently. All the things Florrie had said about her mother and how she herself must surely take after her were suddenly crystal clear now and Polly could well imagine how Florrie would view last night's happening. 'She'd swear it was all my fault,' she said, her voice catching. 'If I go back there now, Eddie I'll never be anybody as long as I live!'

Tears began to run down her cheeks and Edwin patted her shoulder. 'Don't cry, Robin, we'll think of something but don't cry.'

'Maybe if I were to try I could get a job on the Halls,' Polly said haltingly. 'But while I'm trying couldn't I—couldn't I stay here and look after you?' She looked round the untidy room.

'This place could do with a good clean up and I'm a good cook—I wouldn't be a trouble to you, Eddie, and I wouldn't want any pay—just a home in return for my work. What do you think?'

He regarded her for a long moment, his eyes half amused, half wistful, then he said: 'And what do you think Florrie would say to that? She never trusted me and if she knew that you and I were living under the same roof alone together she would naturally imagine—' he left the sentence unfinished, spreading his hands and Polly knew what he meant. She sat down on the couch and gave it some thought.

'She won't know,' she said at last. 'And even if she did she'd be wrong so what does it matter? You and I know it's all right and that's all that counts! Anyway, Florrie's told me often enough that I'm not her flesh and blood and that I must make my own life—so—can I stay, Eddie—please?'

She stood facing him, waiting for his decision; so small and vulnerable in the huge dressing gown, yet in her he saw a kind of strength, a resolution. Something had happened to the little girl from the docks since he had painted her with dirt on her face, she knew now where she was going, she'd grown up. Maybe she was almost the woman he'd foreseen. In many ways it would not be easy, having her around all the time but with those huge luminous eyes looking so beseechingly up at him he was powerless to refuse. He smiled, inclining his head.

'Very well, Robin—welcome to my studio— for as long as you want to stay.'

A delighted smile lit her face and a sudden perverse sadness tugged at his heart. Maybe she wouldn't stay long after all. Maybe his bright little Robin would soon spread her wings.

CHAPTER SEVEN

Polly spread the white cloth over the table with a flourish, humming happily under her breath as she began to lay the supper. Today was Eddie's birthday and she had prepared a special meal for him as a surprise, he would be out till six, so she had plenty of time. Every Tuesday and Friday he taught drawing and water-colour painting in a school for young ladies in Kensington.

Today was Friday, June the fifth, 1888 and Eddie was twenty-four. Polly had been at the studio five weeks now but she had slipped so easily into his routine that she might have been here all her life. She'd cleaned Eddie's rooms till they shone like a new pin and he'd been so full of praise; even when she'd taken hours scraping the mess of paint off that board thing he called a Palette he hadn't been cross, though she realised now that the area of the room where he worked must be left strictly alone. Each day she shopped, cooked and cleaned, finding a new pleasure in the tasks that, till now she had always thought boring, she had met and made friends with the other tenants who lived in the tall house and one of them, Albert Spriggs, the elderly hump-backed printer had given her work addressing envelopes. This she did quietly in the afternoons while Eddie worked away at his easel, it was one of her favourite times, when they worked in companionable silence. But best of all to Polly were the evenings, after supper when they sat together in the firelight. Eddie would light his pipe and sometimes he would read to her from one of his books. Sometimes they'd just talk, Polly about her hopes and dreams of a life on the stage—Eddie of his aspirations as a great painter. One evening she had asked him about his family and had been thrilled to discover that Eddie and she had something in common—he had never known his true parentage either, though, unlike her, he had been brought up by a kind and loving mother.

'I grew up in the country,' he'd told her. 'In a dear little house on the very edge of a village. My mother often told me stories about my wonderful father but I never saw him—just received presents from him at Christmas and birthdays. When I was older he paid for me to go away to school and for my painting lessons and now he makes me a generous allowance, but who he is my mother never told me—and swears she never will!'

Polly stared dreamily into the fire as she sat at Eddie's feet. 'Oh, it's so romantic—just like one of those stories you read to me. It's just like me in a way.' She looked up at him. 'Do you realise, Eddie—we could be *anybody*, you and me, for all we know!'

He laughed and ruffled her hair. 'Tell you what—you can be a fairy princess, robbed of your inheritance by a wicked fairy—I am a reincarnation of Michaelangelo, sired by the Gods!'

She'd laughed with him, turning her face up to his, hoping he might kiss her but he'd got up and changed the subject abruptly as he so often did.

She put the final touch to the table, a little bunch of brown and yellow gillies she'd bought from a flower girl outside the Palace Theatre, their velvet softness and sweet perfume filled her with a strange longing, and excitement stirred within her as she thought of the news she had to tell Eddie. This afternoon she had found herself a job—a real job—in a theatre. She was still finding it difficult to believe and she could hardly contain the excitement that bubbled inside her like champagne.

It had all happened quite by accident. She'd been delivering a batch of addressed envelopes to Albert Spriggs' shop in the next street when she'd almost collided with a strange looking man who was going in at the same time. He'd seemed taken with her and asked Albert to introduce them, then he'd bowed low and asked in his deep, resonant voice:

'I'm delighted to know you, Miss Harris. I wonder—you wouldn't be looking for a refined occupation, I suppose?'

Polly stared at him. 'Lor' sir, you must be a

mind reader!'

The man threw back his head and roared with thunderous laughter while Albert joined in squeakily. Polly looked from one to the other in bewilderment. At last the tall man composed himself with some difficulty and cleared his throat.

'Forgive me, my dear. It's just that you've hit the nail on the head, so to speak—and that being the case who better to help me in my act—you see I am just what you said—a mind reader!'

Polly blinked and took a deep breath. 'You mean you do a turn—on the Halls?'

The man laughed again. 'I do indeed. I have appeared before the crowned heads of Europe. It is only my advancing age that has reduced me to these appearances before the rabble, but beggars cannot be choosers. If you were a little older my dear, I am sure that the name of the Great Maurice would be familiar to you.'

In a daze, Polly waited while the Great Maurice collected the cards he had ordered, then as he turned to leave she tapped his arm.

'Sir—Mr Maurice—what you said just now about work. I do need a job. Would I do?'

The man looked down at her thoughtfully. He had a fine, high bridged nose, domed forehead and piercing black eyes. He reminded Polly of a hawk, especially when he opened the 'wings' of his cloak to produce a play-bill from an inner pocket.

'I wonder if you would care for the work. Here, child, this is I,' he pointed to the bold black lettering on the bill: THE GREAT MAURICE. ILLUSIONIST AND MIND READER—ASSISTED BY THE CHARMING ARIADNE. Maurice shook his head. 'Alas my little Ariadne has run away to marry a fire-eater. A fire-eater! I ask you! Such a *low* class of entertainer. Still—love conquers all, they say.' He directed the piercing eyes on Polly again. 'I could try you out for a week—you may be no good at all. If you suit me I'll pay you fifteen shillings a week.' Polly nodded eagerly and he smiled, wrapping his cloak around him. 'Be at the Palace Theatre at ten sharp tomorrow morning and I'll put you through your paces—right?'

Polly swallowed hard. 'Yes, sir—I'll be there.' And without further ado the Great Maurice swept out of the little shop leaving her quite numb with shock.

She had walked past the Palace Theatre twice in order to prove to herself that it wasn't a hoax and she wasn't dreaming but sure enough there were the bills with his name posted up outside the theatre. A little thrill of excitement fluttered inside her as she read them. She was going to appear in a real theatre—*she* was! She couldn't wait to tell Eddie.

102

She stood back and surveyed the finished table with satisfaction. Although the days were warmer now she had lighted a fire and she dreamily imagined how they would sit before it when they had eaten their supper. Surely this must be the happiest day of her life.

The sound of a light step on the stairs jerked her out of her reverie. Eddie was coming! She hid behind the door ready to jump out and surprise him, excitement welling up in her like a fountain.

'Happy *happy* birthday, Eddie, dear. I've made you a special supper and I've got such news to tell you!'

He laughed gaily, disentangling her arms from his neck. 'Give me a minute to catch my breath, Robin! I'll swear you've knocked all the breath from my body!'

She drew him across to the couch and told him of the chance meeting with the Great Maurice and how she was to become the new Ariadne in his act, the whole story punctuated by impersonations of the Great Maurice's voice and dignified walk till Eddie was quite helpless with laughter.

'Oh, Robin—*Robin*, are you quite sure you didn't dream the whole thing?'

'No, honestly, Eddie it's all true,' her eyes sparkled at him. 'I'm to be at the Palace Theatre at ten tomorrow morning—Oh just think, I may even get the chance to sing!'

'Well—' Eddie looked doubtful. 'Quite

honestly, I can't see the Great Maurice letting you steal his thunder—still, you never know, I suppose.'

Polly's chin went up defiantly. 'I shall have a good try anyhow!'

'I don't doubt it!' Eddie laughed again then looked at the table. 'What's this then—a party?'

She flushed with pleasure. 'It's for your birthday, Eddie. I couldn't get you a present, I hadn't enough money—but Mr. Maurice is going to pay me fifteen shillings a week if I suit and when I get my first wages I'll—'

He put a finger against her lips. 'No, Robin, I wouldn't dream of letting you spend your money on me. You've worked so hard since you've been here, it's I who should buy you a present.'

She shook her head. 'I owe you so much— for what you did for me. If it hadn't been for you I'd—' she trailed off as her eyes fell on the box in the corner that had been delivered after he had left that morning. In all the excitment she had quite forgotten it. 'Oh—I almost forgot. That came for you this morning.'

Together they opened the box, which bore a wine merchant's label and inside found six bottles of wine, three of claret and three of hock. Eddie read the enclosed card and smiled.

'From my father. I'd guessed it was. Since my twenty-first he always sends me wine. I suppose not knowing me it's the safest thing.'

Polly laughed. 'For all he knows you might be T.T. like Miss Downes and Mrs. Mears. Going round the pubs with your little tracts, trying to convert all the wicked sinners!' She drew down the corners of her mouth and minced round the room, handing out imaginary tracts while Eddie laughed at her.

They lingered long over their meal and Polly had her first taste of good wine with the pigeon pie she had so lovingly made. Eddie smiled at her across the table, raising his glass.

'You know, this reminds me of an old rhyme I used to know—: "A boat afloat, a cloudless sky, a nook that's green and shady. A cooling drink, a pigeon pie, a lobster and a lady".'

Polly looked thoughtful. 'The only part that fits is the pie. We're not in a boat, we haven't got a lobster—and I'm not a lady.'

She looked so pensive that Eddie put down his glass and came round the table to her, taking her hands in his. 'I didn't mean it was true literally, Robin, it's more the mood we're in.' He took her chin in his hand and turned her face towards him. 'Anyway who says you're not a lady? You're the nicest little lady I know—and one day we will go in a boat *and* have lobster if that's what you'd like.' His face suddenly brightened. 'I know! I shall take you to the country—to my mother's house for a holiday. Would you like that?'

Polly stared at him. She had never seen the

country—the *real* country, much less had a holiday. Eddie had drunk a lot of wine and she wondered if he could be a little tipsy. She put out her hand and stroked the springy brown hair, tears pricking at her eyes.

'You'd better think about that again tomorrow, Eddie—when you're sober.'

He laughed and pulled her to her feet. 'Sober indeed! I should spank you for that remark! I'm as sober as any judge and I want to take you for a holiday—now, what do you say?'

'But to—to your mother's?' Polly shook her head. 'I don't think she would like me, Eddie.'

'How could she help it? She'll love you as much as I do!'

She stared at him, her eyes wide and her mouth tremulous. Did he *really* know what he was saying? Their eyes locked for one long moment then Eddie drew her to him and kissed her, softly at first, then long and deeply till her head reeled. Clasped in his arms she could feel his heart beating strongly against her own and joy overwhelmed her.

'Oh, Eddie,' her lips moved softly against his cheek. 'Eddie—I love you too—so much.'

She heard his breath suddenly catch and he put her from him abruptly. The expression on his face changed as he whirled her round.

'A party! With all this wine we must have a party. You sit there while I go and fetch the others. We'll have an evening to remember!'

He was gone and with him the moment she had so longed for and as Polly sat looking into the fire sadness turned her heart to lead. It *had* been the wine that had made Eddie say those sweet things. In his right mind he'd never allow himself to love her and she thought she knew the reason why. Eddie's father was obviously someone rich and important. He had what Mrs. H. used to call 'breeding', anyone could see that—and that being the case he'd never want to marry a nobody like her. Tears stung her eyes. If only she could trace her mother. She might even prove to Eddie that she was worthy of him after all. As it was, the lovely evening she had planned just for Eddie and herself was quite spoiled.

Besides Albert Spriggs there were two other tenants in the house, Madame Petrov, an embroideress who, Eddie had told her, was once a ballerina in far away Russia and Rose, a pretty girl who helped her brother with his fruit barrow in the market. Eddie soon had them all rounded up and they came into the studio, smiles of anticipation on their faces. Resignedly, Polly went to fetch more glasses while Eddie opened the wine. A party—when all she had wanted was to be alone with Eddie. She tried to smile, but the corners of her mouth dragged downwards.

But, being Polly she could not be glum for long. Fortified by the wine their three guests were soon laughing and calling on Polly to give them a song and she forgot her sadness as she threw herself into her robust performance. Albert clapped his hands and stamped his feet in time, Rose joined in the chorus and Eddie looked on with pride and humour in his eyes. But when she had finished her song old Madame Petrov shook her head.

'Who taught you to move like that, child?'

'No one,' Polly answered. 'I just watched Kate, my sister.'

The old woman clicked her tongue. 'You are small and dainty, your movements should be light and delicate—and you should sing songs that have feeling and pathos not those crude, bawdy ones.'

'What's wrong with them? I *like* 'em!' Rose retorted. 'You sing what you like, Pol and good luck to yer!'

But although she'd been a little hurt at first Polly now sat down thoughtfully at the old lady's side.

'Will you show me what you mean?' she asked. 'Will you teach me?'

Madame Petrov smiled and patted her head. 'Of course I will, child. Come down to my room when ever you have time and I will give you lessons.'

Polly was thinking of the evening she had seen Patti Jordan at McKenna's music hall. She had gone from comedy to tragedy at the drop of a hat and turned smiles to tears in minutes with her skill and talent. If Polly were to be a star like that she must learn as much as she could whenever she had the chance.

So the evening was not quite spoilt after all and later, as Polly lay tucked up on her couch before the dying embers of the fire she dreamed her favourite dream of the future. It would be so grand—*she* would be so grand— rich, famous and beautiful. She would make Eddie want her so much he wouldn't be able to help himself. It was like Kate had said—: 'Life was what you made it!'

At ten sharp the next morning Polly presented herself at the stage entrance of the Palace Theatre. She wore her plaid dress and looked her most demure. On the day after her arrival at Eddie's studio she had realised with some dismay that she had only the clothes she stood up in but Eddie had been undaunted. He had taken a cab and gone straight to Marlborough Place where he had demanded to speak to Miss Amanda. What he had said to her Polly had never discovered but he had returned with her box, complete with all her belongings for which Polly was grateful. She would not have liked to lose the dresses Kate had given her.

The stage door keeper eyed her with suspicion. He was an old man with a belligerant expression and put Polly strongly in mind of a water rat.

'Wotcher want?'

She lifted her chin. 'I am Mr. Maurice's new assistant. Will you please tell him I'm here—' she almost added 'my man' as Eddie would have done but couldn't quite frame the words. The old man shuffled off down a corridor and was gone for so long that Polly began to fear that he had forgotten about her, then suddenly the stage door opened and Maurice himself entered like a giant bat with a flourish of his cloak.

'Ah—my new Ariadne. Good day to you m'dear.'

'If you please, sir, my real name is Polly—Polly Harris.'

He frowned and shook his head. 'Ghastly! No, my assistants are always Ariadne. Anyway it's on all the bills. Imagine how it would look—: The Great Maurice, assisted by Polly Harris! Oh no! Oh dear me, no!'

Polly couldn't help seeing what he meant, though it would have been nice to have had her own name on the bills.

'Follow me, child.' Maurice swept down the dusty corridor with Polly running at his heels. 'I will show you the room where you are to dress and you had better try on Ariadne's costume. I fear it may be just a little too large.' He was right. Ten minutes later Polly stood regarding her reflection in the mirror. The costume that had been made for her predecessor was at least two sizes too large. It was all depressingly reminiscent of the day she had arrived at Marlborough Place and found the previous maid's frocks too large, but Polly tried her best to look on the bright side. She hoisted the dress up onto her shoulders. It was a very smart costume in black and white satin with black velvet trim. At least the colour suited her. Maybe Madame Petrov would help her to alter it. Hastily she changed back into the plaid dress and found her way down to the stage, where Maurice had said he would wait for her. Excitement stirred in her as she made her way down the stairs. She was actually in a real theatre, she could hardly believe it!

The vast, empty stage was lit by a single cold light and she peered about her. The auditorium was like a great black cave and she could only dimly make out rows of seats, circle and gallery high above. All the drapes were raised and the stage was a jumble of assorted furniture and props. It was just a little disappointing, yet there was a smell about the place—she sniffed—it was a mixture of many elusive things but there was a strange magnetic magic about it.

'I'm down here m'dear.' Maurice's booming voice came from the orchestra stalls and Polly shaded her eyes and peered out into the darkness.

'You will spend the greater part of your time down here so if you will join me I will show you what you are to do. Step down just there—' he indicated a short flight of steps leading down from the stage and Polly came down them to join him.

He explained how he required her to borrow objects from members of the audience. 'You must use your utmost charm,' he told her, 'But I have no doubt that you will do that admirably! I stand in the centre of the stage blindfolded and as you hold the objects in your hand I will tell you what they are.'

Polly gazed at him in admiration. 'Oh—can you really do that?'

He smiled ruefully. 'Not without *your* assistance m'dear—that is where you come in!' He drew a small notebook from his pocket and opened it. 'See, this is the code. If you are given a pocket watch you tell me you are holding an "object of great delight". "Delight" is the key word, you see. If you are given a hat-pin, it is a "pretty" thing, and so on. It will be necessary for you to learn the code.'

Somewhat taken aback Polly stared at the book. There were a dozen or so objects listed along with their respective key words. She looked up at Maurice apprehensively.

'What happens if I'm given something that isn't on the list?' she asked.

He waved a heavily ringed hand airily. 'You'll find that these are the things people usually give you—just disregard anything else. Now—at the end of the act comes the pièce de resistance. A man will stand up in the pit and ask me to tell him what is written on a post card. I will ask you to read it then concentrate hard. You will do so, first having passed it round for inspection. Then I will repeat what is on the card, word for word!'

'And how will you do that?' Polly asked.

Maurice placed a finger on his lips and whispered 'With the aid of an accomplice— having prepared the card myself. But that need not trouble you. Now, is all that clear?'

Polly nodded. 'I think so.'

'Be sure to learn the key words carefully and I will give you a test on Monday morning.' He wrapped his cloak round himself and strode back up onto the stage. 'Come now and I will show you the illusions.'

Polly followed him onto the stage thoughtfully.

'Mr. Maurice—' she ventured. 'Can't you do it without all that?—I mean, aren't you a real mind-reader then?'

He turned and stared at her scornfully. 'Of course I am, child! But you must understand that clairvoyance is a very delicate thing, often destroyed by the slightest wrong vibration. These people pay their money to see a show and we must make sure that they get one, therefore a little deception is necessary.'

'Oh—I see.' Polly nodded humbly.

Maurice went to the side of the stage and reappeared a moment later trundling a huge black box painted with wierd hieroglyphics. He spun it round and then opened the two doors

113

at the front to reveal the interior. 'This is how you make your entrance, child. Get in and let us see how you fit.'

Polly stepped inside and found that there was little room to spare, she wondered briefly how the previous Ariadne managed.

'What do I do now, Mr. Maurice?' she asked.

He showed her a small spring that opened a hidden compartment at the back of the box. 'When I tap thus!' he rapped on the side of the box with his cane. 'You slide into the false back. The door will slide across, then when I open the doors again—Voila! Ariadne has miraculously disappeared! Now—try it.'

Polly tried and found that it worked and though she would not have liked to remain for long in the small confined space, the idea of appearing and disappearing as though by magic appealed to her sense of the dramatic. They rehearsed the trick several times more and Maurice seemed pleased with her quickness and aptitude.

'Bravo! You are bright and intelligent. Now—over the week-end you are to alter the costume and learn the key words. Can you do that?'

'Oh yes, Mr. Maurice.'

He beamed at her. 'Good. I think we shall work excellently together!'

Encouraged by his praise she said: 'Would you like me to sing, Mr. Maurice? I sing very well.'

The smile left his face 'Sing? Why should I want you to sing?'

'I thought you might like it,' she said. 'I thought perhaps it would brighten things up a bit.'

His face turned an odd shade of purple. 'You think my act needs brightening up, do you?'

'Oh no—I just thought—'

'Then don't! I don't pay you to *think*. I pay you to do as you're told. And I haven't told you to sing!'

When Polly climbed the stairs to the studio she found Eddie preparing the lunch. He looked up expectantly as she came in.

'There—you've caught me, and it was to be a surprise. Well, how was the rehearsal?'

Polly sat down. 'It's all a cheat really. He isn't a real mind-reader, even though he says he is. I won't get a chance to sing after all and I'm to spend most of the time in the audience—not even on the stage! I don't even have my own name on the bills.' All the way home she had felt more and more depressed.

Eddie put down the saucepan he was holding and came over to her. 'Why Robin, cheer up! I thought you'd be cock-a-hoop. What are you billed as?'

'The charming Ariadne,' Polly said scathingly.

Eddie's face broke into a smile. 'But that's a

115

good omen! Don't you know who Ariadne was?' Polly shook her head glumly.

'No—who was she?'

'She was a Greek Goddess who eventually turned into a star! Surely that appeals to you. Now come and eat your lunch!'

Polly laughed as he pulled her to her feet. What would she do without Eddie?

CHAPTER EIGHT

In her tiny cubby-hole of a dressing room at the Palace Theatre Polly wriggled into the black and white dress. She and Madame Petrov had spent most of yesterday altering it to fit her and now, as Polly surveyed herself in the long mirror she was well satisfied with the result. She had spent the first twenty minutes of the evening in Maurice's room learning how to apply her make-up. She still couldn't get used to the sticky feel of the greasepaint on her face but she liked its effect. Her eyes seemed larger than ever, outlined in black liner, the lashes standing out stiffly. Her mouth was painted a clear, bright red, which gave her face an impudent look and Maurice had advised her to let her hair fall in loose curls about her shoulders.

Suddenly as she stood looking at herself her stomach contracted with a spasm of nervousness. It was amazing how different the theatre was at night with all the lights blazing and people rushing about. She and Maurice were not due to appear until the second half of the programme and now there was time to spare. Dare she go down to the stage, she wondered, and find a place where she could watch the show without being in the way?

She opened the dressing room door and

peered out into the passage, for the moment all was quiet. Somewhere in the distance she heard the audience laugh and guessed that the comedian was on. Quietly she tiptoed down the stairs, all her senses alert and sharp. The scent she had smelt on Saturday morning was stronger now and she was able to distinguish its ingredients—: coffee, beer, cigar smoke, greasepaint and dust. She stood for a moment, savouring its musty sweetness. Just at that moment it seemed to Polly the essence of all she wanted.

In the wings the Stage Manager bustled about giving orders to his stage hands. He had a sharp edge to his tongue for hands and artists alike, Polly had heard him earlier in the evening and now she kept well out of his way. The comedian on the stage was winding up his act with a song which had the audience in fits of laughter; even from where she stood Polly could feel the waves of friendly warmth coming across the footlights and her heart lifted. It must be *wonderful* to be accepted like that!

'Now then, Miss. You're not supposed to be down here!'

She spun round to see a middle-aged man in shirt sleeves addressing her.

'Oh!—I'm sorry.'

He smiled. 'All right, don't look so scared. It's Mr. Maurice's young lady, isn't it?' Polly nodded. 'New to the business, aren't you? Well if you want to watch just keep out of sight.'

'Thank you, I will, sir.'

He laughed. 'Lor' not sir. I'm Wally, I do the carpentering round here.' There was another gust of laughter and he nodded his head towards the stage. 'He's a great comedian Freddie Long, isn't he?'

'Yes,' Polly agreed. 'They seem to like him, don't they?'

'Love him's more the word,' Wally said. 'One of the most popular comedians in London. You'll have a fine job following him! Still he's done a good job—warming up a Monday house. That could help you. Maurice has got the worst spot on the bill, first on, second half!'

'Why's that?' Polly asked.

The man shrugged. 'Oh—you'll see.'

The curtain came down to loud playing from the orchestra and Wally touched her arm. 'Better get off upstairs now, love. This is the busiest time back-stage and you don't want to get in the Stage Manager's bad books your first night, do you?'

She turned away, shaking her head. Wally hurried off in answer to a shout and Polly began to make her way towards the stairs but she had only just reached the bottom step when someone cannoned into her. She staggered back against the wall.

'Oh dear, have I hurt you? I'm sorry.' She found herself looking into the brightest, bluest eyes she had ever seen. Freddie Long was of stocky build and medium height. His 'working' costume consisted of a loud check suit and bowler hat and his make-up was grotesquely florid but underneath it all there was a sparkling attractiveness about him, a magnetic warmth which captivated everyone he met. Polly was no exception.

She smiled shyly. 'No, I'm all right. I shouldn't have been here, in everyone's way.'

Freddie's blue eyes twinkled at her. 'You can get in my way any time you like! On the bill, are you?'

'Yes, I'm with Mr. Maurice,' she said proudly.

'Oh.' His eyes swept over her appreciatively. 'You surprise me. I'd have said you were a dancer—or maybe a singer if you'd asked me.'

Polly's heart quickened and she had just opened her mouth to begin telling him about her ambitions in that field when she heard her name called and looking up, saw Maurice standing at the top of the stairs, his face dark with annoyance.

'I've been looking everywhere for you, girl! Come up here at once. Don't you realise we're on in a minute?'

Freddie pulled a comic face. 'Better get your skates on, gel, or you'll be for it!' he said under his breath and as he passed her he gave her arm a friendly squeeze.

In Maurice's dressing room Polly began to

apologise but he cut her short. 'No time for that now, girl. Listen—Monday night can be tricky, especially in the spot we've got. Now, if they don't settle we'll keep it short. Take three objects from the customers unless I tell you different. When I say the words—: ' "What a wonderful audience we've got here tonight," that is the cue for the man in the pit to produce his post-card. When we've done that you return to the stage—to thunderous applause—we hope—and wind up the act as we rehearsed it. Is that clear?' Polly nodded, swallowing nervously.

'They seem a good audience—they liked Mr. Long,' she ventured.

But Maurice shrugged as he fastened on his cloak 'Not necessarily a good sign. It may just mean that they'd rather have him than us! Only time will tell. Come now, we'd better get downstairs.'

Polly's heart thudded like a drum as she waited for the 'magic-box' to open and reveal her. But when she stepped out onto the stage the audience clapped delightedly and almost from that moment her fears disappeared. Maurice introduced her and his announcement that she would be coming amongst the audience was greeted with cat-calls and ribald remarks from the gallery which Polly found disquieting. Maurice nudged her and she steeled herself and walked down the steps into the auditorium.

The first object given to her was a pocket watch by a gentleman in the front row and quickly remembering the code word she made the required remark. Maurice made a great show of concentration and came up with the correct answer. The audience was impressed and Polly heard audible gasps of surprise. Heartened, she proceeded to accept a locket from a lady in the fifth row—then a brooch from a girl further back. All went well, Polly remembered the code words and Maurice continued to amaze his audience. Then she heard him speak the cue line and immediately a voice spoke up from the pit:

'If you're so clever just you tell me what's writ on this 'ere card!'

There were gasps as heads turned to look at the unbeliever. Polly walked towards him haughtily and took the card from his hand. From the stage Maurice's voice vibrated deeply:

'I accept that challenge! Will you all remain silent please while Ariadne concentrates on the words for me?'

There was a hush as Polly stared at the four words on the card—then Maurice—his voice quivering with effort spoke them slowly, one by one: 'Wish—you—were—here.' Then he added triumphantly: 'On the reverse side there is a view of Brighton!'

Polly held the card up for all to see and the audience broke into spontaneous applause.

She returned to the stage, took a bow and stepped back into her 'magic box'. The act was over—and it had been a success. In the dressing room Maurice was delighted.

'You were excellent, m'dear! If we went down well tonight just think what we shall do to 'em on Friday!'

Polly changed out of her costume in a daze. It was like one of her dreams and she felt sure she would wake up in a minute. At the stage door the ancient keeper touched his greasy cap to her and looked over her shoulder.

'G'night Mr. Long, sir.'

Polly turned to see the comedian behind her. He smiled, looking very different from the Freddie Long she had encountered earlier. With his face cleaned of the make-up and the checked suit replaced by his own smart clothes he looked almost handsome. He smiled at her encouragingly.

'I was watching you from the side, you did well. It takes guts to go down amongst the customers. By the way, what's your real name?'

'Polly—Polly Harris—'

He pushed his hat onto the back of his head with the silvertopped cane he carried. 'Pretty Polly, eh? Just right! Well, night-night, Polly my love!' He patted her cheek and went off through the stage door, whistling cheerily.

As Polly herself came out into the street someone touched her arm, making her start, then with a cry of pleasure she saw that it was

Eddie.

'You came to meet me!' she said delightedly.

He smiled. 'I did more than that, I was in the audience!'

'You were? Oh, Eddie, why didn't you tell me you were coming?'

'I thought it might make you nervous.' He pulled her arm through his. 'You were very good, Robin. I was proud of you.'

She smiled happily. 'Oh, it was *wonderful*! I was so scared I could hardly breathe to begin with, but once we'd started I was all right. I made friends with the stage carpenter—his name's Wally and he was ever so kind—oh and guess what—I spoke to Freddie Long—*he's* top of the bill and he said—'

She stopped speaking as Eddie drew her under a street light and looked down at her in the soft gas-light.

'What is it, Eddie?'

He smiled. 'In all the time I've known you I've never seen you look as happy as you do tonight,' he said.

She laughed. 'I'd be happier if they'd let me sing!'

He slipped an arm round her, drawing her close to his side. 'That's my Robin! A true artist is never satisfied you know!'

During the weeks that followed Polly and the Great Maurice played in Music Halls and Supper Rooms all over London. Maurice made his own bookings and wouldn't agree to doing 'circuit' work where they would have to agree to giving several performances each night, travelling from theatre to theatre. 'I'm getting too old,' he told Polly 'and I don't believe in giving less than my best.'

Polly enjoyed the work and made a great many friends in the course of her travels but she still ached for a chance to sing. Whenever she got the chance she would go down to Madame Petrov for lessons in deportment and she was developing a new style, a softer, more feminine approach—but what was the use, she often asked herself, if she was destined never to get the chance to try it out?

As they went from theatre to theatre they came across the same artistes again and again and one of these was Freddie Long. He was in great demand and very popular with his fellow artistes as well as audiences. He and Polly became good friends, he could always make her laugh with his comic ways and inexhaustible fund of funny stories and she was always pleased to see his name on the same bill.

Although she still kept house for Eddie at the studio she saw little of him. Besides his teaching post he had been lucky enough to get several commissions to paint portraits and when he was at home he was always busy painting. But there were still those times when they would sit together after supper, perfectly contented in each other's company and these moments Polly cherished. Deep inside she knew she should really offer to move out now that she had a job. After all, that had been their arrangement, but Eddie never mentioned it so she held her tongue. She had no wish to leave Eddie—ever. She loved him more with every breath she took and even though he showed little more than brotherly affection in return, she was content for now to settle for that. Then, about six months later, something happened that was to alter the course of Polly's life in the strangest way.

The man who produced the post-card at the end of the act was always picked by Maurice himself, usually from among the clientele of the local tavern. Polly had always thought it an unsatisfactory arrangement but Maurice assured her that there was always someone willing to help discreetly with their little deception for a few shillings and free beer. It seemed to work surprisingly well too—until one night in early December.

When she arrived at the theatre she heard raised voices coming from Maurice's dressing room and going in, she found the man he had employed for that week trying to persuade Maurice to give him more money. He was pleading that it was nearly Christmas and that his four children hadn't enough to eat. Maurice was adamant and sent him packing. When the man had gone, uttering dark threats,

Polly turned to Maurice.

'Don't you think you should have given him a bit more? After all, it *is* nearly Christmas and if it's true what he says about his family—'

'Stuff and rubbish!' Maurice broke in. 'I thought I'd picked a wrong'un and I made a few enquiries. The man isn't even married! He's been blackmailing me all week. He's already getting twice what I usually pay. I'll have no more of it!'

But all evening Polly had a feeling of foreboding and as they neared the part of the act where the man had to play his part the feeling grew stronger. At last the cue came and the man stood up swaying slightly, his eyes glazed with drink. Polly stared at him, holding her breath.

'If the Great Maurice is so bleedin' clever let 'im tell me what's on this card!' His words were slurred though distinct enough but when he held up the card Polly saw to her horror that it was not the post-card Maurice had prepared, but a large piece of pasteboard on which was written in bold black letters an obscene word. The audience began to laugh as, one by one they turned and saw the card. On stage the blindfolded Maurice stood, anxious and bewildered.

It took Polly a moment only to make up her mind. She couldn't allow Maurice to be exposed in this undignified way. Under the circumstances there was only one thing she could do—sing! And sing she did. No time to try out her new dainty routine, this was no occasion for that! She gave it all she had, opening her throat and letting the rich sound fill the auditorium to the surprise and delight of the audience.

In a second the laughter ceased as all eyes turned to look at the diminutive figure with the rich, full voice. Encouraged, she made her way down the centre aisle and up onto the stage Maurice had now vacated. When the song was finished the applause was deafening and there were cries of 'More' and 'Give us another!' But Polly didn't hear them, she was too concerned about Maurice. She ran off the stage and would have gone straight up to the dressing room but the Stage Manager caught her arm.

'Take a bow, gel,' he urged. 'You can't ignore applause like that!'

She did as she was told and took a bow, her eyes all the time on the wings, looking for signs of Maurice. When she came off the second time Freddie Long stood smiling at her.

'Go on—give 'em more. They love you!'

'Oh—I can't Freddie.'

'Oh yes you can!' He took her arm and led her back onto the stage. 'Do you know 'The Feller With The Barrer'?' he asked in a whisper. She nodded and he bent and spoke briefly to the conductor of the orchestra then she was alone on the stage again, singing one of the songs she knew best. All the time she sang she thought of Madame Petrov. She would have hated the saucy words and bold performance—she thought of Maurice and wondered what he was thinking of it all—but when at the end of the song the audience burst into a fresh torrent of appreciation all that was forgotten, none of it seemed to matter. A miracle had happened—she was a singer at last—and her audience adored her. It was heady wine indeed.

As she came off the stage Freddie threw his arms around her and lifted her off her feet.

'Polly you're a knock out! You saved the show. I'm proud of you!'

'Where's Maurice?' she asked anxiously. 'I must explain. I'm afraid he'll be cross.'

'Cross! Why should he when you saved him all that embarrassment?' Freddie retorted, but Polly was already half way up the stairs.

Tentatively, she tapped on the dressing room door and entered. Maurice was sitting at the dressing table, his back towards her but she saw that his face, reflected in the mirror was dark with fury. He looked up at her, his piercing eyes fiery.

'You've been waiting to do that, haven't you?' His voice was controlled and ominously low. 'You've been waiting your chance. You didn't care two hoots about making me look a fool, did you?'

Polly's face fell. 'But you didn't see what

happened, Maurice. The man held up the wrong card. He was out to ruin things for you. I sang to save you—'

He swung round to face her. 'You little liar!' he thundered. 'You're all the same. Every woman I've ever known has let me down but you're the worst of all—knocking the very ground from under my feet!'

'Please, Maurice, let me explain—' she took a step forward but he got to his feet, glaring at her.

'Get out of here!' he shouted. 'And don't come back!'

As she was backing out of the room she felt a hand on her arm as Freddie Long stepped forward.

'Now listen, Maurice ' he began, but it was no use. Maurice towered above them both.

'You're in it too,' he bellowed at Freddie. 'You encouraged her. I heard you. Get out!' And with that he slammed the door in their faces.

Polly fled down the stairs, tears streaming down her cheeks. At the stage door Freddie caught up with her and held her arm tightly.

'Steady on, love. Don't go like that, he'll come round.'

'No—no, he won't. It could never be the same again. I want to go home, Freddie, please don't stop me.'

He nodded gently. 'All right. I'll take you. Wait there and I'll get a cab. You're not fit to go anywhere by yourself in that state.'

In the cab he took her hand. 'I'm sorry about all that, Pol, really sorry. Would you like me to have a word with old Maurice when he's had time to cool down?'

She shook her head. 'I'd never go back. To think he thought I'd done it on purpose. He wouldn't even *listen*!'

'He's getting old, Polly and losing his confidence. Hearing the reception you got must have shaken him.' He was silent for a moment, then he said: 'I suppose you'll be getting married soon anyway, eh?' She turned to look at him in surprise and he added: 'To that chap of yours, the one who sometimes meets you.'

Polly smiled. 'Eddie, you mean? No, I just keep house for him.'

He pressed her hand. 'You mean there's no—understanding between you?' She shook her head and he looked into her eyes for a moment, reading the wistful look he saw in them. 'Maybe you'd like there to be though, eh?' She looked away. 'Well anyway, Pol, for what it's worth, I'll always be here if you need me. I'd do anything for you, Pol, did you know that?'

She turned to look at him. His cheeky face was serious for once, the blue eyes almost sad. 'Thank you, Freddie,' she said softly. 'I'll remember that.'

He searched his pocket and found a card

131

which he pressed into her hand. 'Here—this is my permanent address. You'll always find me there. Don't forget, Pol—if that feller of yours ever treats you rough just you let me know and I'll black his eye for him!' The twinkle was back in his eye now and Polly laughed.

'I'll remember, Freddie—you bet.'

The cab came to a halt and he looked at her. 'Will you be all right, love? I'd come up with you only I have to get back to do my spot in the finale.'

She nodded. 'I'll be all right now, don't worry.' She leant across and kissed him lightly on the cheek. 'Good night, Freddie and thanks—for everything.'

' 'Night, Polly, love.' His eyes looked into hers and for a second she saw the tender look she had glimpsed before. Then she was standing watching the cab draw away, a feeling of sadness dragging at her heart. Was this to be the end of her short-lived Music Hall career— and of her friendship with Freddie?

Up in the studio she found Eddie reading one of his favourite books before the fire. He looked up in surprise as she came in.

'Why Robin, you're early!'

She threw herself down on the rug at his feet. 'Oh, Eddie—I've lost my job. It was awful!' Jerkily, she unfolded the story to him and when she had finished he drew her up gently to sit beside him on the couch.

'My poor Robin. How unfair. Still, never

mind, it will soon be Christmas, that will take your mind off it. We'll have a grand time together.'

She rested her head on his shoulder, gazing into the fire dreamily. 'I sang to a real theatre audience, Eddie and they clapped like *anything.* They liked me—they really did—but now it's all spoilt.'

Eddie slipped an arm round her. 'Mmm, I think Freddie was right when he said Maurice was getting old. You could have given that act of his some new spice. But never mind, it's not the end of the world. There'll be other jobs, you'll see. Now, I'm going to make you a cup of cocoa. You're cold and worn out.'

But although Polly was tired sleep would not come to her that night; so many thoughts were spinning round inside her head. Again and again she re-lived the scene at the theatre when she had sung for Maurice's audience. Looking back on it now she wondered how she had dared. Then there were the things that Freddie had said in the cab. He had seemed fond of her. Could he help her to find another job, she wondered. There was the question he had asked about Eddie and her too: 'Is there an understanding between you?' Polly sighed. She had been here at the studio with Eddie for eight months now. If he loved her he would have made it clear to her by now, surely. She loved him so much that sometimes it hurt her just to look at him. Maybe she should move

133

out, go right away and make a new life for herself. One of these days, she told herself, Eddie would find himself someone to marry, someone of his own sort, when that happened she wondered how she would bear it.

At last she slept restlessly, only to wake with a headache and a feeling of heaviness. She got up early and went about her every day tasks wearily. Everything seemed to go wrong. The little cooking stove in the kitchen went out and she had to re-light it before she could make Eddie's breakfast. The bacon burned, then, as she was carrying water up from the tap in the yard she spilled it all over her feet. At last she took her shawl from the door and announced that she was going out.

'Maybe some fresh air will do me good. What would you like for dinner, Eddie?'

He looked up from the table where he was setting out his painting materials. 'Oh anything, I don't mind. By the way, Polly, Rose is coming in to model for me this morning. I'd like to have a long stretch while I have her so we'll eat later, I think.'

As she went down the stairs she was puzzled. She could have modelled for him, why did he want Rose? But perhaps he was going to paint her in the coarse apron and shawl she wore when she worked with her brother on the fruit barrow. Eddie liked to paint people at their work. But in that case why didn't he go down to the market and paint her there where he could get the background in too?

It was a crisp, frosty morning and Polly's spirits lifted a little as she made her way among the familiar faces of the street traders who were now her friends. She bought what she needed and started on the journey home, her step lighter than when she had set out. It was true what Eddie had said, they would have a grand time at Christmas. Already there were oranges, nuts and holly for sale on the barrows. She would decorate the studio. Her thoughts fell to the problem of how she would cook a Christmas dinner on the tiny stove and she was so preoccupied with this that she hardly noticed as she entered the studio that Rose was there alone.

Eddie had rearranged the room and she stopped short as she looked around her.

'Is Eddie out?'

'Yes.' Rose was taking off her shawl. 'He said he wanted to borrow something to put over the couch. He won't be long.'

Polly began to put away her purchases, then suddenly she became aware that something odd was happening. Rose was unbuttoning her blouse, she turned and stared as the girl stepped out of her skirt and began to loosen her petticoats.

'W—what are you doing?'

'Undressin' o' course!'

'But why?'

Rose turned from where she stood clad in her undergarments before the fire. Hugging herself she gave a little shudder. 'Good job Eddie built the fire up. It's parky weather for this work.'

'What work?' Polly asked.

Rose stared at her. 'Modellin' o' course! What else did you think I was takin' me clothes off for?'

Polly's mouth dropped open. 'Modelling? Without your clothes?'

Rose stepped out of the last of her clothes and folded them neatly. 'Yes—why not? How else do you think Eddie can paint a nude figure? Life drawing, they calls it. Besides, he pays well.'

Polly's mouth opened and shut but no sound would come as she gazed at the naked girl. Rose laughed and reached for her shawl, wrapping it round herself.

'Here—don't look at me like that. You make me feel awful. There's nothing for you to be jealous of, it that's what's worrying you. There's never been anything wrong between Eddie and me. It started when I used to bring him the fruit and veg' we 'ad left over on the barrow. He'd paint it first, then eat it. Then one day he asked me if I'd pose for him—well, when I knew he meant like this I thought he was up to no good at first.' She shrugged. 'But the pay was good so I took a chance. Eddie's not like that though—he wouldn't take

136

advantage of a girl. Besides, I'm not his sort.'

Before Polly could answer the door opened and Eddie came in carrying a brightly coloured shawl. 'Madame Petrov lent me this,' he said, smiling. 'It's exactly what I wanted.' He spread it over the couch where it stood in its new place under the window, then he held out his hand to Rose. 'Come here and let's see how it suits you.'

Rose let her own shawl slip to the floor and spread herself full length on the couch while Polly watched with a kind of mesmerised fascination. She had to admit that Rose was beautiful; her skin was pale and fine textured, her stomach flat and her breasts full and firm. Her dark hair fell loose to her waist and she and Eddie laughed and joked together like old friends as he arranged her as he wanted her— one arm along the back of the couch, the other hanging languidly over the edge, the fingertips touching the floor.

'I want you to appear to be asleep,' he said, standing back to regard her. 'Yes, yes that's marvellous, just right.

Neither of them spoke to Polly, she might not have been there and after a little while she took her shawl up again and went out, leaving them alone. She walked for a long time, hardly knowing where she went, her mind was so full of conflicting thoughts. Why had Eddie never asked *her* to pose? Had he thought she would refuse? Or that she wasn't attractive enough?

But deep in her mind there was something else troubling her. If what Eddie had told her about human nature were true, how then could he look at Rose without her clothes—be alone with her for hours on end—without wanting to make love to her? She was seized by a jealousy so fierce that it made her feel physically sick. If Rose was good enough to pose for Eddie let her come and keep house for him too! Let *her* do the cooking and cleaning and see how they both liked that! She would leave him—she *would*. She would tell him today! Wearily she leaned against the railings. It was she who had begged Eddie to let her stay, wasn't it? No doubt he would manage very well without her. He probably wouldn't even notice that she was gone.

Heavy with misery she made her way home and climbed the stairs to the studio. Inside she found that Rose had gone. The couch was back in its usual position in front of the fireplace and Eddie was in great spirits.

'Ah there you are, Robin. You've been ages. Shall we eat now? I'm starving and I'm sure you must be. I've worked so well this morning—look!'

She glanced at the canvas on the easel. He had worked well, inspired no doubt by Rose's beauty. She nodded grudgingly and he looked at her curiously.

'What is it, Robin? Something's troubling you.'

138

She turned away. 'No, it's nothing.' She was remembering Freddie's words—'No understanding between you.' She had no right to be jealous. Eddie had never been more to her than a good friend. She had no business to reproach him either—hadn't he taken her in—given her a home when she'd nowhere to go? She turned and went into the kitchen intent on preparing the meal but after a few moments Eddie joined her, his face concerned.

'Robin—I've never seen you look like this before. Please tell me what's wrong.'

She shook her head, her throat too tight for words but he took her shoulders and turned her to face him. The brown eyes were serious as they looked into hers.

'Are you still unhappy about losing your job with Maurice? Would you like me to go and see him for you?' She shook her head, a tear spilling down her cheek. 'Then what?' Suddenly his face cleared. 'It wasn't Rose, was it? You weren't shocked?'

She bit her lip. 'No—not that, it was just that *I* would have modelled for you—if you'd asked me.'

There was a small silence and she couldn't meet his eyes. From under her lashes she looked up at him. 'You wouldn't have had to pay me,' she said, almost in a whisper. Still he didn't answer and her throat tightened again. 'Maybe you don't think I'm as beautiful as Rose though.' She began to turn away but he caught her hands in his.

'Oh Robin—don't you see? I couldn't let you do that.'

'Why not?'

'I just couldn't—not you.'

Again she bit her lip. 'You mean because I'm not good enough?'

'Of course I don't mean that!'

'Then why? I'd like to, Eddie—I would!'

He grasped her shoulders, shaking her gently. 'Don't you see, Robin, you're—different. Rose is just a girl—a model. You're—you're.'

'I'm what, Eddie?'

He lifted his shoulders. 'Oh—I can't explain.'

'You've painted me before,' she insisted. 'I wouldn't mind—not for you. I'm as pretty as Rose, aren't I?'

Her cheeks burned with colour as she looked up at him expectantly. Speechlessly, he stared back, lifting his hands, then letting them fall helplessly to his sides again.

'No, Robin—the answer's no!'

'Why? *Why?*' Her eyes blazed, green and fiery as she stamped her foot.

Suddenly he grasped her shoulders again and jerked her towards him, his voice low and husky. 'Because I couldn't look at you like that without wanting you! Because it's hard enough as it is! Because I *love* you, Robin!—Now do you understand?'

140

She let out her breath in a sigh that was almost a gasp and her lips parted as she looked up at him wonderingly. 'Oh—Eddie,' she breathed.

He drew her into his arms and kissed her hungrily. 'If only you knew,' he whispered against her hair. 'If only you knew the control it's taken not to hold you and kiss you like this before—almost every day since you've been here. I almost gave way to it once, on my birthday, do you remember?'

She nodded caressing his cheek. 'I've wished and wished that you would. Why couldn't you, Eddie?'

He smiled at her tenderly. 'You always seemed so young—so innocent. We had such a lovely relationship and I thought it would be spoilt—perhaps it will.'

'No, no,' she drew his head down to hers. 'It will be better.' His lips found hers again and as she rested her head against his chest she said softly: 'Eddie—I'd like you to paint me as you did Rose. I wouldn't mind what—what it led to—if that's what you want.'

He looked down at her tenderly. 'Darling Robin, do you know what you're saying? You know I'm not in a position to marry, don't you?'

She smiled. 'I wouldn't ask for anything—just to be with you, that's all.' Standing on tiptoe she kissed him softly, winding her arms around his neck. 'I'll never love anyone but you, Eddie,' she whispered. 'And I'd do anything to make you happy—anything.'

Eddie's bed was soft and warm and Polly lay halfway between sleep and waking, floating on a cloud of happiness. Eddie was still asleep, one arm still across her waist and she looked lovingly at his face, so young in repose. The thick, dark lashes lay fanned out on his cheeks like those of a child and his brow was smooth. Her mind lingered sleepily on what had passed since this morning and her skin tingled with reminiscence. Eddie had pronounced her a thousand times more beautiful than Rose and had told her so, not only in words but with his lips and hands as he caressed her. She had never dreamed there could be such delight in lovemaking and now, as she gently stroked back the tumbled curls from his forehead she reflected that she could give Eddie all he needed. She could cook and clean for him, she could be quiet when he wanted to work, make him laugh when he was downhearted and now—now she could give him this too. It had seemed to give him such pleasure and happiness and she felt so proud.

He stirred, opened his eyes and smiled his wonderful smile at her. 'You're so lovely, Robin,' he said drowsily. 'The loveliest thing that ever happened to me. I want to give you the moon and stars to wear.' He drew her close. 'What can I give you darling?'

She snuggled her face into his neck. 'I've got

all I want—you.'

Suddenly he sat up. 'I know! We'll go to Marvelhurst for Christmas—to my mother's. I promised you a holiday and you shall have one!' He began to get out of bed and pull on his dressing gown. 'I'll write a letter straight away!'

With a little stab of apprehension she reached out and touched his shoulder. 'Eddie—wouldn't you rather it was just the two of us?'

He picked up her hand, kissing the fingertips. 'I want to take you home and show you off. And you deserve a rest. I can't wait to show it all to you. There'll be skating on the lake if it's cold enough—and the meet! I bet you've never seen a fox hunt, have you?' She shook her head and he leant across and kissed her. 'We'll have all the time in the world to be "just the two of us",' he said. 'The rest of our lives!'

CHAPTER NINE

Polly shivered, more from apprehension than cold as she stood surrounded by the bustling life of the busy station. She had never been in a railway train before and she was more than a little afraid of the great noisy monsters and the gushing plumes of steam that hissed up into the vaulted roof to fan out against the sooty glass. There was such an air of haste and impatience about the place that she felt she might be swept helplessly away at any moment.

Eddie had left her in charge of their luggage while he went to enquire which platform their train left from. He was full of good humour this morning, but unaccountably Polly felt a heaviness dragging at her heart. For some reason she could not dispel the feeling that with this journey she was leaving something behind; something beautiful she might never again recapture.

For the past two weeks Polly had lived in a kind of dream world. She and Eddie had hardly been out of each others' sight for a moment. They had talked, eaten, slept and wakened together; walked, laughed and made love. Eddie had even begun a painting of her and now she visualised with pride the half finished picture in which she appeared kneeling nude beside a forest pool, leaves

144

entwined in her hair.

'Water Nymph' Eddie had called it. 'That's how I see you, Robin. Ethereal and wistful, yet mischievous too.'

Polly hadn't really understood what he meant, but it didn't matter. The fact that she was considered beautiful enough to be in one of his 'special' paintings was enough for her. She loved Eddie so much that she would have given him her very soul if she had been able, but at the back of her mind a memory nagged—an old saying of Florrie's: 'Enough's enough, my girl. Where there's laugher, tears aint far behind!' The happiness she had known for the past two weeks was so rare and precious. Could it be meant to last? Or would it fade like a lovely dream? The coming visit to Marvelhurst troubled her. Eddie's ma would surely not approve of her—a foundling, brought up in a dockside pub. It was true that Eddie's own father was a figure shrouded in mystery, but from the comfortable upbringing and fine education Eddie had known he must be a man of substance and Mrs. Tarrant would surely have ambitions for her son—ambitions which would not be likely to include the likes of her!

This morning when they had left the studio she had turned in the doorway, taking a last look round. Eddie had told her regretfully last night that this must be the last time they shared a bed until their return.

145

'I'm afraid my mother would not think it proper,' he said gently.

Polly had realised this. Sometimes Eddie seemed to think her even more naive than she was but she didn't mind. She snuggled against him, her arms tightly round his waist and her face buried in his neck. How would she bear the nights without having Eddie close to her? Why did they have to go to Marvelhurst anyway? But she was wise enough to keep these thoughts to herself. 'I'll miss you, Eddie,' was all she said.

He pushed her head back and kissed her. 'It will only be for a week, my love and I can't wait to show you off.'

Before the door closed on the studio she took a long look, while Eddie called from below that the cab was waiting. Then, as she started down the stairs she told herself not to be foolish. When they came back the New Year would have begun. A New Year and a new beginning. But inside the small muff she carried her fingers were tightly crossed.

In the train she sat by the window, staring out fascinated as the green fields and hedges went past—so fast that it almost took her breath away. There were cows and sheep in some of the fields and once a boy on a farm cart had waved to her. Happily she waved back and Eddie smiled.

'Enjoying it?'

'Oh yes! I never knew it would be like this,'

146

Polly said, her face alight with excitement. 'Thank you for bringing me, Eddie.' The green eyes were golden with delight as she slipped her hand into the crook of his arm.

Eddie covered the slim fingers with his own, his heart contracting a little as he looked at the soft curve of her cheek as she looked out of the carriage window. Ever since he had first set eyes on her at the quaint little dockside inn she had held an irresistible appeal for him, like a small puppy or a defenceless child she aroused all the protective instincts in him. But since they had become lovers she had shown him that she was a woman too, a real woman, capable of deep and passionate emotions. He would never have believed that another human being could have made him so exquisitely happy. Best of all, contrary to his fears, she had not been a distraction to his work. In fact he was painting better than ever. The picture of the water nymph she had posed for promised to be the best thing he had ever done. He glanced sideways at her, picturing the creaminess of her skin and the soft curves of her body and her loveliness tugged at his heart. He longed to take her in his arms there and then.

All too soon for Polly the journey was over. As the train steamed to a stop at Marvelhurst Halt Eddie began to put the cases out onto the platform, then he helped Polly down from the train, thinking again how pretty she looked with the sunlight glinting on her red hair, a vivid contrast to the dark green velvet colour of the travelling dress he had bought her. She smiled up at him apprehensively as she put on the little black hat with the bird on it, anchoring it with a long pin.

'Do I look all right, Eddie?'

He squeezed her arm. 'Fit for a Queen, my love.'

Mrs. Tarrant was waiting in the station yard with her pony and trap and as soon as Eddie introduced them she held out her hands to Polly.

'So you're the 'little Robin' Edwin has written to me of. Welcome to Marvelhurst, my dear. Hurry and put your things into the trap, Edwin. I have lunch waiting at Woodview Cottage.'

As they drove along the country lanes in the crisp, frosty air Polly looked around her in amazement. Why, there wasn't a single building in sight! And the grass was so green it almost hurt her eyes to look at it. For some distance they drove beside the river and she thought of the little rhyme Eddie had taught her—: 'A boat afloat, a cloudless sky—' One day—oh, one day, maybe it would all come true just as Eddie had said. Her spirits lifted with a sudden surge.

'Oh, it's lovely!' she said suddenly. 'Oh, I am glad I came!'

Eddie and his mother both looked at her in

148

surprise, then they looked at each other and burst out laughing.

'I'm glad you like it,' Mrs. Tarrant said. 'But I feel bound to tell you that it isn't always so nice in the country. When we have a lot of rain the river sometimes rises so high that this road we are travelling along is flooded and quite impassable. So far this winter the weather has been kind.'

'Ah, but tell her how much lovelier it can be too,' Eddie urged his mother. 'Tell her how the banks are covered with celandines in spring and cowslips in summer. Tell her about the new lambs—the dragon flies skimming the smooth water; the fields of corn, golden under the blue skies—'

Mrs. Tarrant laughed and held up her hand. 'My son is a poet, Miss Harris, but I must admit that what he says is true. I'm afraid I take it all for granted.' She smiled at Polly, who, for a second caught a glimpse of Eddie in the wide, generous mouth and observant eyes. The older woman was tall and very upright, almost aristocratic looking. She spoke well too and though her clothes were old fashioned she wore them with elegance and dignity. Her dark blue dolman mantle was of the same style as the one Mrs. Mears had worn, though her little hat sported a jaunty feather which bobbed above the thick hair, still dark brown and curling, like Eddie's.

Woodview Cottage was enchanting and like

149

no other house Polly had ever seen with its thatched roof and neat front garden. Inside, the stone floors were covered in rush matting and the ceilings were low and oak beamed. Mrs. Tarrant led them into a room furnished comfortably and invited Polly to warm herself at the blazing log fire, then she rang a little brass bell from the mantelpiece. Almost at once, as though she had been waiting on the other side of the door, a very young girl appeared.

'Show Miss Harris up to her room, Tilly,' Mrs Tarant said. 'And we will have lunch directly.'

'Yes, Ma'am.' The girl looked at Polly. 'Will you please come this way, Miss?'

The staircase was panelled in oak and covered with a rich red turkey carpet, but although Polly admired her surroundings very much she tried to look as though she were used to such things. It was a new experience for her to be shown to her room by a maidservant and though she wasn't sure that she felt quite comfortable about it she had no intention of appearing in awe.

On the landing Tilly paused and pushed open a door, standing aside for Polly to enter the room. It had a low ceiling and a tiny dormer window set into the thatched roof. The wall paper was gay with birds and flowers whilst the rest of the furnishings were of spotless white. Polly smiled, unable to hide her delight.

'Thank you—it's lovely.'

When the girl withdrew, putting Polly's portmanteau on a stool at the foot of the bed, Polly took off her hat and tidied her hair, looking thoughtfully at herself in the mirror. Well, nothing terrible had happened so far. She began to relax. Perhaps it would be all right after all. Mrs. Tarrant certainly wasn't the fearsome figure she had imagined.

Christmas day came and went in a haze of delight for Polly. At breakfast Eddie had given her a little gold locket on a broad velvet band and when she had opened it she had found a lock of his hair inside it. She had bought him a new silk necktie, which he insisted on putting on at once. Mrs. Tarrant gave her son an elegant smoking jacket in plum coloured velvet and for Polly there were lace handkerchiefs. After breakfast the three went to church and returned in high spirits to eat the Christmas dinner, expertly prepared by Tilly. It was only much later when they were seated round the fire that Polly began to talk of her career in the theatre. She told of the lessons Madame Petrov had given her and of her experience with the Great Maurice. Mrs. Tarrant made no comment and, taking the silence as encouragement, Polly asked:

'Would you like me to sing for you?'

For one fleeting moment she saw a shadow cross Eddie's face but she had drunk too well of the excellent wine Mrs. Tarrant had served with the dinner and she missed the significance of his look in her eagerness to display her talent. Getting to her feet she began with one of the sentimental ballads she knew, putting into practice the graceful movements the old ballet dancer had taught her. When the song came to an end Mrs. Tarrant smiled and nodded.

'Thank you, Polly. That was charming.'

Polly's heart lifted. 'Now I'll show you my other style,' she said. And before Eddie could stop her she had launched into 'The Feller with the Barrer' complete with its saucy words and accompanying movements.

Mrs. Tarrant looked somewhat taken-aback but she said nothing until Polly had finished when she asked politely:

'Do you come from a theatrical family, Polly?'

Polly was surprised, she thought Eddie must have told his mother all about her. 'No,' she said. 'I never had a family at all, least ways, not a proper one. Florrie and Sid Harris brought me up—at the Eight Bells at Wapping. Florrie's sister Kate sings on the Halls though and that's what set me off.'

Somehow, although Mrs. Tarrant kept her composure and continued to smile, Polly felt from that moment that all was not well and the following morning when Eddie took her to see the spectacle of the meet on the village green she felt she must speak of it to him.

The weather had held and the sun shone brightly from a pale blue sky, down through the branches of the great elms onto the scene of brilliant bustle below. The hounds whimpered and whined excitedly and the horses tossed their heads, impatient for the chase to begin. Polly looked in awe at the gentlemen in their pink coats and the ladies in their fine habits, partaking of the stirrup-cup brought out by the landlord of the 'Green Dragon.' But in spite of it all the uneasiness dragged at her mind and at last she touched Eddie's sleeve.

'Eddie—I've done something wrong, haven't I? I can feel it.'

He squeezed her arm. 'Don't worry about it, my sweet. It is just that here, in the country, people don't move with the times. Mother is rather old fashioned. I should have warned you. It was my fault.'

'But—what did I do?' she asked.

'Well—the song you sang. If you had only stopped at the first.'

She shook her head, puzzled. 'It's only a comic song. When I sang it at the Palace the audience laughed.'

He shook his head gently at her. 'Sometimes, Robin, I wonder if you know what you *are* singing. I'm afraid Mother got the wrong impression. She doesn't know how sweet and innocent you are as I do.'

153

But Polly worried all day about the slight atmosphere that had grown up between her and Eddie's mother. That night she lay awake for a long time, staring at the moonlit square of window. Suddenly she thought she heard something—a soft tap. There it was again—was it a branch tapping in the wind against the window? She sat up and as she did so the door of her room opened with a soft creak—closed again—and the next moment she felt Eddie's arms close around her.

'Oh, Robin, the nights are so cold without you.' He kissed her. 'I couldn't lie there wanting you another moment.'

His cheek was cold against hers. 'Oh, Eddie, you're freezing!' She tucked the covers round him and held him close. It was as though he had known how much she had needed him. Held fast in his arms her senses drowned in his kisses and under his caresses her body flamed with love for him.

'Oh, Eddie—you won't ever stop loving me like this, will you?' she whispered urgently.

He kissed her deeply. 'Never, my love—never. We belong to each other for ever now. Nothing could part us—*nothing*!'

Later, after he had slipped away again, back to his own room, she lay drowsy and light as a bubble; his kisses still on her lips and his words echoing in her ears. 'We belong to each other for ever. Nothing can ever part us.' She cherished each syllable, they were all the riches she would ever want or need.

But Polly's happiness was to be short-lived. It was at lunch next day that Mrs. Tarrant first mentioned Jessica Lang. She looked up brightly during the dessert course and said:

'Oh, I forgot to tell you, Edwin: Jessica is home from her travels. Her father told me so just before Christmas. She is in London and I have written giving her your address. I knew you would want her to call on you.'

Eddie looked mildly interested. 'Jessica? It must be—oh—five years since I last saw her.'

Mrs. Tarrant nodded. 'Quite. She is more beautiful than ever. Her father showed me a photograph. Widowhood seems to suit her. I always said it was a pity for such a lovely young girl to marry a man so much older than herself, but there—she is a wealthy woman now and still well on the right side of thirty.' She leaned across the table. 'She has studied art at the famous galleries in Rome and Paris and her father tells me that she wishes to become a patroness. It would do no harm to cultivate her friendship. If she liked your work, Edwin—'

He frowned. 'I hardly think so, Mother. As I remember, Jessica wasn't in the least artistic before her marriage?'

But Mrs. Tarrant shook her head. 'People develop and change, my dear. There is not a genius born that would not flourish with the benefit of money—it could be your genius!'

He laughed. 'Really, Mother! You flatter

me!'

When they were alone, Polly asked Eddie about the beautiful and mysterious Jessica Lang and he told her she was the local doctor's daughter.

'She married old Squire Lang who was old enough to be her grandfather and now she is a well-heeled widow,' he told her concisely.

'Is—is she very beautiful Eddie?' she asked, glancing up at him sideways.

He pulled a face. 'I remember her as a rather horsey young woman with big teeth and a loud voice,' he said. 'If anyone had asked me I would have said she'd look more at home between the shafts of a cart than in an art gallery!'

Polly laughed, but if the subject of Jessica Lang was not entirely glossed over, something happened later that evening to put her out of Polly's mind completely.

She was changing for dinner when she suddenly realised that she had left her gloves on the hall table. Knowing Mrs. Tarrant hated untidiness and anxious not to make any further bad impressions she crept downstairs to the hall to get them. As she passed the drawing room door she heard voices—those of Eddie and his mother; they were raised in conflict and Polly's heart gave a sharp twist as she realised that she was the subject of that conflict.

'Do you not realise that you insult me by

bringing a girl of that sort to my house?' Mrs. Tarrant's voice shook. 'A Music Hall singer—and one with the morals of the gutter, it seems!'

'Mother!' Eddie's voice was low and controlled. 'I beg you to keep your voice down and not to speak of Robin in that way.'

'Robin!' Mrs. Tarrant spat out the name scathingly. 'At least call the woman by her correct name. And pray do not stand on your dignity with me! I came to your room last night to speak to you—you were *not* in it!'

There was a slight pause before he said: 'I—couldn't sleep.'

'I do not doubt it! Please do not lie to me further, Edwin. I know all too well where you were and I must say that I never thought to see the day when you would behave in such a manner under my roof—and with a girl of that sort!'

'I see that it is no use arguing with you. We shall leave at once!' Eddie's voice was stiff with controlled anger. 'If you were not so prejudiced and if you had taken the trouble to get to know Robin you would not say such things. I do not intend to listen to any more.'

There was a rustling sound as Mrs. Tarrant crossed the room to her son.

'Edwin—Edwin, listen to me.' Her voice was softer now. 'I realise, my dear, that you are now a grown man and that as such you need your—amusements. But it will soon be time

157

for you to think of marriage.'

'I already have, Mother. I have made my choice.'

Polly held her breath in the shocked silence that followed, then she heard Mrs. Tarrant say in a whisper:

'You can't mean *her*—that girl? But that's impossible!'

'It is not impossible.' Eddie's voice was calm.

'It is—and I will tell you why—' Mrs. Tarrant's voice was low and urgent as though she spoke through clenched teeth. 'At present you receive a comfortable allowance from your father. That allowance will die with him and you cannot expect to benefit from his will.'

'Why not? *Why* can I not, Mother?' Eddie urged.

'Because it will not be possible—you must not ask me to explain, Edwin.'

Polly heard the grating of a chair as Eddie moved impatiently. 'So I am to make myself a profitable marriage without the true knowledge of my parentage? And how do you propose that I should do that, Mother?' Eddie asked, his voice rising.

'When you come to me and tell me that you have made a suitable choice—*then* I will tell you about your father, Edwin.'

'No, Mother!' There was a thud as his fist hit the table. 'I wish to know *now*! How do I know that my father is not someone of whom I would be ashamed? There must be a reason for all this secrecy and I cannot think it is to his credit to have hidden himself from his own son for all these years!'

'Your father has been generous and good to us both all these years,' Mrs. Tarrant said tightly. 'Please do not let me hear you speak so of him again. You can believe me when I tell you that he is far from being a father to be ashamed of.'

'Why then must I only be allowed to know him when I have chosen a—a—*suitable* wife?' Eddie asked.

'Because then—and *only* then shall I know that you have reached responsible maturity,' Mrs. Tarrant said evasively. 'I think you will own that you owe me a little consideration, Edwin.'

He sighed. 'Of course, Mother, of course. But as you have already said: I am a grown man. I have made my choice and I shall not be deterred, you can be assured of that.'

'Do you honestly think that your art will support a wife?' Mrs. Tarrant asked icily. 'Or perhaps you are proposing to live on that girl's *caterwauling*! Oh, do be practical, Edwin! You are used to certain standards. Do you wish to grovel in the gutter for the rest of your life?'

'You have no idea what you are speaking of, Mother!'

'Believe me, I have! Be sensible and choose a wife with the right background.'

Polly didn't wait to hear more but crept back upstairs and sat on the bed in her room. Obviously, Mrs. Tarrant set great store by money. She wanted Eddie to marry someone who had plenty of it. Her cheeks burned as she remembered the things Mrs. Tarrant had said about her. If Eddie had known his mother was so high and mighty why had he brought her here? Her small firm chin went up. She would show Eddie's ma all right! She could sing and make people laugh. Once she got on in the theatre she would make plenty of money! Eddie would be rich and famous one day too, with his painting. They just needed time, that was all. Mrs. Tarrant had forgotten what it was like to be young and in love and on fire with dreams. She and Eddie would be all right and now that she knew that he did intend to marry her she didn't care *what* his mother thought of her—at least, not very much.

Eddie didn't come to her that night. The three of them ate dinner in a difficult, strained atmosphere and Polly was glad that their visit would only last a few more hours.

They had a carriage to themselves and as soon as the train moved out of Marvelhurst Halt Polly felt the tension lift. Eddie took her hand and she smiled up at him. His fingers tightened round hers.

'I'm afraid it was not all I had hoped it would be. I'm sorry, Robin.'

She returned the pressure of his fingers. 'It

doesn't matter, Eddie. But I do think that you should have told your ma more about me. She was disappointed. She thinks I'm not good enough for you, doesn't she—common?'

'No!' He looked so upset that she couldn't help laughing.

'She does. Oh, come off it, Eddie, love. I heard her going on at you last night. I didn't mean to listen, but I couldn't help hearing.' She squeezed his fingers reassuringly. 'It doesn't matter, Eddie darling—not to me—if it doesn't to you.'

'Of course it doesn't. You know I love you, Robin and nothing can change that!' he said stoutly.

Her eyes shone as she looked at him, then, something she had heard Mrs. Tarrant say stirred in the back of her mind.

'Eddie—' she said slowly. 'When your ma said I had the "morals of the gutter" what did she mean?'

He frowned. 'Oh, Robin—don't think of it. It was nothing. I'm sure she spoke only in haste.'

'But what did she mean? I know she was talking about you being with me that night, but why am *I* the one to blame and not you?'

Eddie shook his head, at a loss for words. 'Mother has certain standards, Robin. I'm afraid that even if I explained them to you, you would not understand. Let us forget Mother for now, please.'

161

She snuggled against him. 'Eddie—'

'Yes, darling?'

'Promise me something?'

'Of course, anything.'

'If ever you get the chance—I mean if there's ever anyone who you could love more than you love me—someone who would be better for you—you will tell me, won't you?'

Eddie slid an arm round her and drew her close. 'I could never love anyone more than I love you,' he whispered. 'And no one could be better for me than you are.'

'I meant someone with money, Eddie,' she said earnestly. 'I can see what your ma means and I can see why she worries about your being poor after she's brought you up so nicely—and what with you not being left anything in your pa's will—' She broke off as she caught sight of his eyes twinkling down at her and her own eyes opened wide in protest. 'Oh! I didn't mean to listen, Eddie—really I didn't!'

He laughed and kissed the tip of her nose. 'Oh I *do* love you, Robin!' he said.

She nestled against him as the winter landscape sped past. 'When we get back to London, Eddie I'll get a job on the Halls. I'll get on, you see if I don't and so will you. We'll be rich one day!'

He rubbed his cheek against hers. 'You and I will always be rich as long as we have each other.'

She gazed out of the window and as she

watched the first snow of the winter began to fall; large flakes that softly brushed the carriage window. She gave a little shiver and pressed closer to Eddie. Once they got back to London, she told herself, everything would be all right.

CHAPTER TEN

Edwin's rooms in Islington were cold and cheerless when they returned. The snow had been falling all morning and now a thick layer lay upon the glass of the big skylight in the studio, giving the room a dim, green, under-water light. Polly shivered.

'Brrr. We'd best get a fire going or we'll freeze to death!'

Together they carried wood and coal up from the back yard and soon a cheerful fire glowed on the hearth while Polly made a meal from the food they had bought on the way from the station. After they had eaten they sat before the fire, Polly on the floor at Eddie's feet, while she told him of her plan.

'I'll get work. I'll go and see Freddie Long. He gave me a card with his address on it and he said that if I needed help I was to go to him. I'll go tomorrow!'

Eddie stroked her hair. 'You mustn't think you have to work for my sake, Robin.'

She smiled up at him, knowing he was proud. 'I don't,' she assured him. 'But I do want to show your ma that I can be someone—someone who's worthy of you, I mean.' She glanced up at him sideways. 'Eddie—*am* I common?'

He laughed, bending to kiss her. 'I think

you're the most *uncommon* person I know!'

But she frowned. 'The songs though—the words. I suppose they do seem rude to someone like your ma, who's never lived anywhere but the country where everyone is so polite and proper. But they make people laugh—and when they laugh they're happy; that can't be wrong, can it? Do you think I should only sing the other sort of songs?'

He shook his head. 'You must always do whatever is natural to you, Robin. It's when you are being natural that you're at your loveliest.'

Polly aired the bed with two large stone hot-water bottles which she borrowed from Madame Petrov and later, curled contentedly against Eddie's sleeping form she made her plans for the following day. Freddie lived at Notting Hill Gate. She would go there in the morning to be sure and catch him. He had told her she was good. Surely he would know of a manager somewhere who would give her a chance. A small spiral of excitement began in the pit of her stomach. She had been determined to make a success of herself before—now she had twice the reason! She'd show Mrs. Tarrant that she was worthy of her son—or die in the attempt!

It was a very long way from Islington to Notting Hill Gate. Polly had thought she would never get there. Several times she had lost the way. But at last she stood outside the tall house, the address of which was on the card she held in her hand. Mounting the steps she pulled the bell handle and after a few moments the door was opened by a tall woman in a black dress.

'I've called to see Mr. Long—Mr. Freddie Long,' Polly said. 'Is he in, please?'

The woman looked her over appraisingly, making her feel glad she had worn the respectable looking travelling dress. Finally the door was opened wider.

'If you'd like to step inside I'll see if he's "receiving".' The woman indicated a chair. 'Would you care to take a seat? What name shall I say?'

'Polly—Polly Harris—he knows me.' She watched the tall figure disappear round the bend in the stairs. It was a very posh house. Rooms here must cost Freddie a packet. But then he must be earning very good money. When she and the Great Maurice had appeared on the same bills Freddie was always top.

'Will you come this way, please?' The tall woman was leaning over the baluster, beckoning her. Polly got to her feet and hurried up the stairs after her.

Freddie's rooms were on the first floor and when she was shown in Polly found him wearing a blue velvet dressing gown and seated at the breakfast table in the nicest room she had ever seen. The only thing she could compare it with was the drawing room at Marlborough Place, though it wasn't really like it at all. Mrs. Mears' taste was inclined to be stiff and formal, whereas this room was the epitome of brightness and comfort, from its attractive, colourful wall paper to its comfortable armchairs and blazing fire.

'Well, well—if it isn't little Polly! Good to see you, love!' Freddie rose from the table wiping his mouth on a snowy napkin and held out his hands to her while the woman who had shown her in withdrew quietly.

'Let's have a look at you. I'll swear you're prettier than ever!' Freddie drew her towards a chair by the fire. 'I bet you could drink a cup of tea, eh? I'll pour you one, it's still nice and hot. Well now—how's the world treating you?'

'Not too badly, thank you.' Polly's mouth was suddenly dry. Now that she was here, face to face with Freddie it wasn't as easy as she had thought to frame her request. Freddie handed her a cup of steaming tea and sat down in the chair opposite.

'Well—what can I do for you?'

'I want a job.' She bit her lip. She hadn't meant to come out with it quite so bluntly. 'You—you once said that you'd help me,' she reminded him.

The corners of his mouth twitched and his eyes twinkled.

'Aha! That best boy of yours been treating you rough, has he?'

167

Polly laughed. 'Oh no. We're going to get married—only we need some money first. You see, we went to see Eddie's mother at Christmas and she didn't think much of me. I want to show her, Freddie—show her that I'm as good as anybody!'

His mouth quivered as he looked at the resolute little face turned up towards him. 'If she's a very upper-class sort of lady, Pol, do you think our sort of work would ever count for much with her?'

She shrugged. 'I don't know—but she talked an awful lot about money. She told Eddie he's got to marry someone with plenty of it—so I want to make a lot of money!'

Freddie threw back his head and roared with laughter. 'I got to give it to you, Pol—you know what you want and no mistake! First, to be a star on the Halls—then Eddie, eh?'

She blushed. 'Eddie'd marry me sooner or later anyway—and he'll make good too, with his painting. It's just—' She looked up at him, the amber-green eyes beseeching. 'Oh, Freddie—can you help me?'

He took her hand, his eyes softening. ' 'Cos you'd rather it was sooner than later, eh? No one can guarantee you immediate success, Pol, but we'll see what we can do, shall we?'

Her eyes lit up. 'Oh, Freddie, you are good!'

He excused himself and disappeared into the bedroom; reappearing a few minutes later dressed and ready to go out. He held out an

168

arm to Polly.

'Right—come on, love. We'll make a start.'

They took a cab to Waterloo Road where Freddie said his agent's office was and as they got out Polly's heart began to pound.

'What shall I have to do, Freddie?' she whispered.

He squeezed her arm. 'Just you leave it to me, love.'

Solly Cohen reminded Polly of a large frog as he squatted behing the huge desk. He operated from a poky little office on the third floor and if she had expected opulence, either from him or his surroundings she was to be disappointed. The office was shabbily furnished and grubby and there were stains on Solly's green waistcoat as well as the gold watch chain that was festooned across his rotund middle. However, she noted with some satisfaction that he was smoking a cigar. Cigars meant only one thing to Polly—success!

Solly listened wearily to Freddie's story of how Polly had saved the show at the Palace on the night that Maurice's act was sabotaged, then he turned the bulging, glassy eyes on her, taking the cigar from his lips while he moistened them with a flabby pink tongue.

'You know as well as I do, Fred boy, that singers are ten a penny,' he said without taking his eyes off Polly. 'Does the little lady have an angle?'

Nonplussed, Polly looked at Freddie but he

leaned forward across the desk.

'She doesn't *need* an angle with a voice like she's got!' he assured the agent. 'Why don't you let her sing for you, then you'll see what I mean?'

'I've got two styles,' Polly told him eagerly, her heart in her mouth. 'Just like Patti Jordan.'

'Jordan! That old hag? Phew!' Solly flapped his hands at her with an expression of disgust. 'All right, all right—give me a few bars of something and we'll see.' He folded his arms across his stomach and leaned back, looking resigned.

Encouraged, Polly launched into her favourite—: The Feller with the Barrer, making the best use she could of the small space in the office. Solly let her sing it through to the end, his face giving away nothing as he sat behind his desk puffing away at his cigar. When she had finished he leaned forward, consulting a book on the desk.

'They need an "extra turn" at the Prince's Hoxton, next Monday,' he said. 'Twenty-five bob a week. All right?' He looked up, the cigar still drooping from his lips. Freddie went a dull red.

'Extra turn? Hoxton! Oh come on, Solly— you must be joking!'

Unruffled, Solly took the cigar from his mouth and looked at Freddie. 'It's where you started. If she can keep 'em happy at Hoxton, she can keep 'em happy anywhere! Well, do

170

you want it or don't you?' He looked at Polly.

'Oh yes *please*, Mr. Cohen!' Polly's heart was beating like a drum. She had a real engagement—of her *own*! She grabbed Freddie's arm and dragged him towards the door as he was beginning to argue again. 'Come on, Freddie—Thank you, Mr. Cohen. I'll keep them happy—you see if I don't!'

Outside in the street, Freddie looked annoyed. 'He could have done better than that for you,' he muttered. 'After all the commission he's had out of me too!' He looked at her delighted face. 'Hoxton's no picnic, love,' he told her. 'There's a lot gets the "lemon" there. Why else do you think they need "extra turns"?'

"Lemon"?' Polly asked, puzzled. 'What is an "extra turn" anyway?'

He took her arm as they walked along. 'The "lemon's" what you get when they don't like you and believe me, Pol, it's not funny. As "extra turn" you have to go on and smooth them over after.'

'Then if I do that, I won't be the one getting the "lemon", will I?' Polly asked confidently.

Freddie stared at her for a moment, then burst out laughing. 'Well—put like that I suppose you won't,' he said.

They took another cab back to Freddie's rooms where he insisted that she stayed for lunch, an excellent meal provided by the tall woman Polly had met earlier, whom Freddie introduced as Mrs. Smails, his landlady. Over the pudding he looked thoughtful.

'You know, Pol,' he said. 'If you're to be a success you'll have to have some songs of your own. Those you're singing belong to somebody else.'

She stared at him. 'I didn't know songs belonged to people—I thought anyone could sing them.'

He shook his head. 'Not professionally, they can't. You'll have to have some of your own.'

'But—where do I get them?' she asked.

'We'll have to have some written for you,' he told her. 'Unless we can find an artiste with some to sell.'

Polly shook her head. 'But I haven't got any money! How much do songs cost?' Suddenly her face brightened. 'Some of the songs I know are the ones that Kate taught me. If I could find her—'

'Kate?' he looked puzzled.

'My sister,' Polly informed him proudly. 'Kate Harris—only she calls herself Kate Nightingale.'

His eyes opened wide. 'Kate Nightingale's your sister? Well, I never!'

'Do you know her?'

He nodded. 'Worked with her many a time. Haven't seen her for a long time though. I heard some wealthy feller took up with her. She seems to have retired from the business.' He looked at her curiously. 'Don't you keep in

172

touch then?'

Polly shook her head. 'Not since I left Wapping. If she's really left the Halls she won't want her songs any more, will she? I wonder where she is and if she'd let me have them?'

'Shouldn't be too difficult to find her,' Freddie said. 'Tell you what—I'll make enquiries, someone's bound to know. Come and see me again in a couple of days' time. We can't afford to waste time if you're to have an act ready for next Monday!'

When Polly returned to Freddie's room two days later he had good news for her: he had found Kate and had been to see her. She had given permission, it seemed, for Polly to sing any of her songs in public. Freddie handed her a boxful of music manuscripts.

'But—didn't she want to see me?' Polly asked, somewhat crestfallen. 'Was she pleased that I was following in her footsteps—did she wish me luck?'

Freddie shrugged. 'The circles she's moving in now, Polly girl, she doesn't want to know the likes of us! She was only too glad to give me the songs quick and see the back of me!'

Polly was disappointed. 'I'd have liked to see her.' She sighed. 'Oh, Freddie—why is it that money changes people so?'

He laughed. 'Search me, love. Never you mind Kate. You've yourself to think of now. Shall we rehearse those songs and work out a programme for you?'

Polly was grateful for Freddie's help. Without his experience she would never have known how to arrange her act to the best advantage or which of the songs would be likely to please a Hoxton audience best, also she was totally ignorant of such things as band parts. When Freddie first showed her the sheaf of music she was mystified.

'You give these to the conductor of the orchestra,' he explained. 'And make sure you get them back again afterwards—you never know what sort of musicians you'll get Hoxton way!'

They rehearsed for two days, Freddie accompanying her on the piano till she was word perfect and satisfied with her own performance. But just as she was going home on the second day Freddie startled her by asking her what she intended to wear. Her mouth dropped open as she looked at him in dismay.

'Oh Freddie—I don't know!' Her lip trembled. 'I hadn't thought of that—I haven't got anything!'

He gave her arm a squeeze. 'All right, all right. Don't look like that. We'll find you something.' He went into the bedroom and reappeared a few moments later with three dresses draped over his arm. 'Here, I think they're about your size. Anything there that appeals to you?'

Polly stared at the dresses. They were

gorgeous; gaily coloured and richly trimmed with laces and flowers. 'But—where did you get them?' she asked.

He smiled wryly. 'They were my Daisy's. I was married once. Never told you that, did I, Pol?'

She came closer, fingering the dresses, her eyes round. 'What happened, Freddie? Where is she now?' she asked gently.

'She went off with someone else,' he told her. 'Got fed up with life on the Halls, travelling from place to place. We never had much money in those days. Couldn't blame her, I suppose.' He sighed. 'She's dead now— killed in an accident.' He patted her shoulder. 'Go on, Pol—try 'em on. I'd like to see someone look pretty in 'em again, especially you.'

Polly paraded all three dresses for Freddie. he had been right—all three fitted her as though they had been made for her and to her delight he said she could take them all. Impulsively, she threw her arms round his neck.

'Oh Freddie, you are good to me! You're the best friend I've ever had.'

He kissed her cheek and held her briefly in his arms, then he put her from him with his wry, comic grin. 'Watch it, Polly girl, or that bloke of yours'll have good reason to black my eye for me! Off you go now. See you at Hoxton on Monday night, eh?'

She stared at him. 'You mean you'll be there?'

'You bet I will!' He grinned. 'Got a week out next week— wouldn't miss that for the world!'

When Polly arrived back at Islington that afternoon she was bursting to tell Eddie all about her afternoon. As she ran up the stairs, the parcel of dresses and music in her arms she was already planning to dress up and perform her act for him after the supper things had been cleared away. She would let him be the one to decide which of the dresses she would wear on Monday. He had such good taste. He should choose too, how she would wear her hair.

At the top of the stairs she paused breathlessly to tuck in an escaping strand of hair before she pushed open the studio door.

'Eddie—just wait till you see what I've got— Oh!' She stopped short. Eddie was not alone. He was entertaining a lady to tea before the studio fire and as the two heads turned in her direction Polly was suddenly shy and acutely aware of her dishevelled appearance. She flushed and put down her parcel, smoothing her skirt and brushing a hand across her burning cheeks.

Eddie stood up, smiling. 'Robin! Come and have some tea, you look exhaused. This is an old friend of mine from Marvelhurst: Mrs. Lang—Jessica, Polly Harris.'

Jessica Lang stood up and came towards

Polly. She was tall—almost as tall as Eddie and she wore her hair in a loose chignon on the nape of her neck with the front combed forward to curl over her brow. The dress she wore was like none that Polly had ever seen, loose and flowing with wide sleeves and a pattern of large flowers. She held out a slim, white hand, laden with rings.

'How delightful to meet you, my dear.' Her voice was low and husky and when she smiled Polly saw the large, white teeth Eddie had spoken of, though she failed to see the resemblance to a horse he had mentioned. To Polly she seemed more like an exotic bird of Paradise with her trailing plumes. With some difficulty she drew her thoughts together and closed her gaping mouth.

'I'm pleased to meet you, Mrs. Lang, I'm sure—' She glanced uncertainly at Eddie.

'Jessica is just back from the Continent, Robin,' he informed her. 'She has been telling me about the wonderful work she has seen there.'

Jessica nodded. 'The new Impressionists are quite remarkable,' she observed.

'Oh we have them here,' Polly put in. 'On the Halls. Very clever, they are. I like it best when they do the farmyard noises and the—' She broke off, realising that she had said the wrong thing. Eddie looked uncomfortable but Jessica Lang gave a husky little laugh.

'I'm afraid Miss Harris is teasing us, Edwin,'

she said. 'I really think I must be going. I do hope you will think over our conversation.' She paused, looking at Polly appraisingly. 'But wait—surely the little water nymph in your picture—?'

'Yes—it's me!' Polly said proudly.

'Mmm,' Jessica smiled enigmatically. 'I see. *Now*, I see.' And with an intimate, knowing little smile at Eddie she was gone, leaving behind a waft of perfume. Eddie rushed out onto the landing.

'Wait—Jessica. I'll see you to the door.'

Polly took off her outdoor things and went to the fire to warm herself. What had that woman meant—'*Now* I see'? And the way she had looked at her! As though she were some kind of insect! If she'd studied art, Polly told herself, she should know that people got painted without their clothes all the time. It was nothing to be ashamed of! Quite the opposite!

Presently there were footsteps on the stairs and Eddie came back into the room closing the door behind him with a flourish.

'Well, Robin—what did you think of her? Isn't she magnificent?'

Polly pursed her lips. 'I thought you said she looked like a horse?'

He laughed. 'She did when I last saw her. Mother was right: being a widow does suit her. People develop and change, you know, Robin and it is true that travel broadens the mind.

178

Oh, the places she's seen!' he threw himself down on the couch with a sigh. 'The mountains of Switzerland and Austria, the great cities of Paris, Rome, Venice and Naples—the beautiful island of Capri—Oh, it's no wonder those places produce such wonderful artists!'

Polly sat down beside him. 'Don't you want to know how I got on today?' she asked in a small voice.

The dreamy look left his eyes as he caught sight of her wistful face. 'Oh, my darling, of *course* I do!' He pulled her close and kissed her. 'I want to hear *all* about it—right away.'

'Then you shan't!' She pulled away from him and stood up, a mischievous twinkle in her eyes. 'Not until after supper. Fancy me coming home and finding you here alone with another woman! You—you *scoundrel* you!'

He sprang up and made a grab at her but she whirled out of his way, laughing delightedly. Round the studio she danced, dodging blithely this way and that to avoid his attempts to catch her, till at last he made a lunge for her and they fell together, laughing and breathless onto the couch. Eddie kissed her, holding her firmly.

'Now, little Miss Tease—tell me all, or I'll never let you go again!'

Her eyes sparkled up at him, green as emeralds. 'You'll get no supper if you don't!'

Slowly, he began to undo her bodice, his

eyes searching hers. 'Somehow, I don't feel very hungry at the moment—at least, not for supper.'

For a while Polly forgot all about songs and costumes, Jessica Lang was a mere passing notion and supper was forgotten completely in the ecstacy of Eddie's lovemaking. It was only later, when she unpacked the parcel in the bedroom and shook out the pretty stage dresses that she thought of Freddie's smashed marriage. Had he and his pretty Daisy been as happy as she and Eddie? Why had it gone wrong? Poor Freddie, he must have been so badly hurt, so unhappy. A little shiver went through her as she glanced up at her reflection in the mirror. 'Oh, please God, don't ever let it happen to us,' she whispered.

CHAPTER ELEVEN

On Monday night it was snowing again and Eddie insisted that Polly should take a cab out to Hoxton. He had wanted to accompany her but she wouldn't let him.

'Freddie says it's a rough place. I'd rather you waited till I was playing somewhere better. I've got to show them I can do it, you see, Eddie,' she explained gravely. 'That's why I have to go to places like this first. It's what they all do—all the big names.' She stood on tiptoe and kissed him. 'But I'll soon show them—you see if I don't! I shan't stay in the East End long!'

He laughed and gave her waist a squeeze. 'Of course you won't.' He pressed some coins into her hand. 'Here—it's the cab fare home. I'll have supper ready and I'll be waiting to hear all about it.'

When she alighted from the cab at the stage entrance to Prince's she was disappointed. It was a far cry from the places where she had appeared with the Great Maurice. But it was only a momentary disappointment. She was appearing in her own right, wasn't she? That was the main thing! She squared her shoulders and, dismissing the cab, she walked in through the grimy stage door with its peeling paint.

Inside the brick walled corridor a single gas

light burned dimly, spluttering against the broken mantle. There didn't seem to be anyone about and for a moment Polly was at a loss, then a door at the far end of the corridor opened and a young woman came out. When she saw Polly she gave a gasp, her hand flying to her throat.

'Oh Gawd! I thought you was a bloomin' ghost! What are you doing—lookin' for someone?'

'Yes—er—no,' Polly stammered. 'I'm Polly Harris and I'm booked here for "extra turn". I was wondering where to go .

The young woman laughed. 'Just wait till you've been on, love. The customers'll tell you where to go all right!' She beckoned. 'Come on, you'd better come in with me. I'm on me own and I've nabbed the best room.'

Inside the door Polly looked round. If this was the best room she wondered what the others could be like. As in the corridor the walls were of unplastered brick and the floor of rough concrete with a strip of threadbare matting in front of the dressing table. There was one small cracked and dirty window set high in the wall and a single gas jet burned over the mirror. Apart from the dressing table with its tin basin and jug of cold water for washing, the only furniture consisted of two chairs and a screen on which hung a number of male garments. Polly looked at them in surprise.

'I thought you said you were on your own?'

'So I am. Maudie Marsh is the name.' Maudie followed Polly's glance and burst into a loud laugh. 'Oh, I see—them's my costumes. I'm a male impersonator. A good 'un too, if I do say it meself!'

Polly laughed with her, turning to unpack her bag. 'Oh, I see, that's all right then.'

'You can hang your things over there.' Maudie indicated some hooks on the far wall. 'And if you take a tip from me you won't leave any greasepaint lyin' about.'

'Why not?' Polly asked.

'Rats!' Maudie said succinctly. 'We're overrun with the little bleeders and greasepaint's their favourite grub!'

Polly shuddered. It wasn't that she was unused to rats, she remembered well the huge ones in the yard at the 'Bells' but she hated them none the less for that. 'Should I change and get ready?' she asked hesitantly. 'Or should I wait to be told?'

'Gawd no! You'd better be ready.' Maudie told her. 'If you're needed it'll be quick— damn quick!'

'Do you think I will be needed?' Polly asked, watching with fascination as Maudie transformed herself from a buxom young woman into a suave young man-about-town.

'More than likely!' Maudie turned from the mirror. 'Especially tonight. Monday's the worst night of the week.'

'Oh, I know, I've been on the stage before,' Polly assured her. 'I used to work with the Great Maurice, the mind reader.'

Maudie thrust out her lower lip. 'You don't say so! You'll be used to working better dates than this then?'

'Yes,' Polly admitted. 'But now I'm working on my own so I have to start at the bottom. I don't mind,' Polly said enthusiastically.

'That's good for you. Got an agent, 'ave you?' Maudie's bright, brown eyes swept over her as she fastened up her dress.

Polly nodded. 'Solly Cohen in the Waterloo Road. He's Freddie Long's agent and he introduced me.'

Maudie's eyebrows shot up. 'My my! We do move in exalted bloody circles, don't we? He your feller then, is he—Freddie Long?'

Polly spun round. 'No! He's just a friend.'

'Well, take a tip from me, gel and don't go droppin' names like them round here. There's some as don't take kindly to them as gets into this business through the back door—if you get my meanin'.'

Polly's cheeks flamed with indignation. 'It's not like that at all! I *can* sing! And I can make people laugh too. I'll show you if I get half a chance. That's all I want—half a chance!'

Maudie laughed and shook her head. 'Keep yer wool on, gel! No offence. I only meant to warn you, that's all.' She came across to Polly and patted her shoulder. 'You'll do! I reckon you and me are gonna get on all right. When you're ready I'll take you up and introduce you to the stage manager.'

Polly gave a final pat to her hair and surveyed herself in the spotted mirror. The dress she had chosen was of pale blue taffeta trimmed with black lace and with a red rose tucked into the low neckline. She had dressed her hair high with one curl falling forward on her forehead and Maudie nodded in appreciation as she joined her at the mirror.

'I reckon we make an 'andsome couple, eh?' She winked and adjusted her monocle. 'Come on—come and meet Sid Varley, the S.M. He's not a bad sort and it aint a bad idea to make a pal out of the S.M. if you take a tip from an old trouper.'

There were more people about now and as they passed through the corridor and up the stairs to the stage they passed several people whom Polly took to be artistes. Maudie greeted them all cheerily and Polly gave them what she hoped was a modest smile. Maudie's remarks about name-dropping had unnerved her a little, she had no wish to begin on the wrong foot by making herself unpopular.

Sid Varley was a small, wiry man with a pale, dyspeptic face and a drooping moustache. He seemed extremely busy but when Maudie introduced Polly he smiled kindly and spared a moment to explain what was needed of her.

'You just stand here in the wings,' he told

185

her. 'Then if anyone gets the "lemon" on you goes before the customers starts throwin' things!' He grinned encouragingly. 'Proper little sight for sore eyes you are and no mistake. You ought to quiet 'em down all right. I 'ope you've got a good loud voice, my gel?'

Polly nodded. 'I have. What chance have I got of going on, Mr. Varley?'

Sid sucked at his teeth. 'It's the comedians wot usually cops it Monday nights. It's not easy to make a sober audience laugh, y'see. When they've 'ad a few they'll laugh at anything— then, it's the singers' turn—they can't make 'emselves heard above the din. Get the idea?' He smiled as Polly nodded doubtfully. 'Just keep yer fingers crossed, love.'

The show began and, standing in her place in the wings Polly thrilled to the atmosphere. She wished harm and misfortune on no one, but she dearly wanted to go on and be part of it all. Her bandparts had been handed over to the conductor of the small orchestra and now all that remained was to wait for the mysterious 'lemon' to manifest itself. She thought of Eddie at home, putting the finishing touches to the picture of her as the Water Nymph. And she thought of Freddie Long. Was he somewhere out there as he had promised?

Maudie's spot was last in the first half and Polly watched in admiration as she swaggered and strutted her way through her act. At the

186

end when she pulled off her wig and let the mass of dark hair tumble free the audience roared its approval and when Maudie came off, pink-cheeked and smiling, Polly felt a stab of envy.

'Come on, gel. We can 'ave a bit of a breather now.' Maudie took her arm and propelled her towards the dressing room. The corridor was full of people now, all jostling and hurrying and Polly's heart sank. The show was half over and her chance hadn't come. Surely in the second half the audience would be more relaxed and tolerant anyway?

Maudie closed the door and turned to her. 'Come on gloomy, cheer up! Worse things 'appen at sea!'

Polly's chin quivered. 'I might as well go home,' she said despondently. 'I won't go on now, will I?'

'Dunno, gel. No tellin'.' Maudie shrugged philosophically. 'All you can do is 'ope.' She opened a bag and took out a bottle. ' 'ere, 'ave a swig of this. It'll keep out the cold. It's like a bloomin' iceberg in 'ere!'

Polly took a deep draught of the colourless liquid and gasped. She had always hated the taste of gin, but Maudie was right, it was warming. She sat watching the handsome girl change her costume.

'Maudie—' she ventured at last. 'Why is it that you're appearing here at Hoxton? I mean—you're so good.'

187

Maudie grinned ruefully. 'I was doin' all right for myself a few months back, then my Billy turned up.'

'Billy—who's that?' Polly asked.

'My kid,' Maudie told her. 'I had a baby. I couldn't work for the last three months, then for another month after he was born. You soon get forgotten, you know. So that's why I'm 'ere at Hoxton—startin' from the bottom again.'

'Who looks after the baby?' Polly asked. 'Your husband?'

Maudie gave a short, bitter laugh. ''Usband! that's a laugh! As soon as 'e knew about the kid 'e was off like a shot out of a gun! Aint seen hide nor hair of 'im since! As for marryin' me—I reckon 'e never meant to anyway.'

Polly's eyes widened. 'Oh! But how do you manage?'

Maudie's chin went up proudly. 'Oh well, we've got our own house—at least, it belongs to my dad, but at least we can't get chucked out for not payin' the rent! Alice, my sister's got three kids of 'er own. She looks after Billy while I'm workin' an' I look after her three while she is.' Her mouth set in a firm line. 'I'm gonna work 'ard and make enough money to give my Billy a good education like 'is father 'ad. One of the nobs, 'e was, an' my Billy's gonna be just as good—*better*!' She glanced at Polly. 'You want to watch them y'know. They're the worst, the educated blokes. You

188

don't want to trust 'em as far as you can throw 'em!'

Polly was silent for a moment, thinking of Eddie. Maudie was wrong, they weren't all like that—still she could see why she was so bitter.

Suddenly there was a brisk tap on the door and a voice called: 'Second half, Miss Marsh!'

Maudie jumped up from her chair and grasped Polly's arm. 'Come on, kid. I'm not on till second turn but I'll come up with you. There's a comedian on first—new bloke and if you're gonna get a chance at all this'll be it!'

As they hurried up the stairs they were in time to hear the chairman making his announcement, then, as the curtains parted, a perspiring young man who was waiting in the wings bounded on. Maudie squeezed Polly's arm as they watched. The young man told two or three jokes in a confidential, chatty manner, but there was barely a titter from the audience, then a voice called out some ribald remark and a shout of laughter went up. The young man motioned to the orchestra conductor, who held up his baton and the next moment he launched into a comic song. Polly heard Maudie wince and suck in her breath.

'Phew! Worst thing he could've done!'

Polly looked at her. 'Why?'

'Just you listen.'

The words of the song were quite funny, but the young man's voice was weak and before he had come to the end of the first verse the shouts of the audience were drowning him completely. They had begun to enjoy their own form of entertainment better than what was being provided and Polly's heart went out to the young man as he leapt about the stage in a frantic effort to regain their attention, but it was in vain. One man shouted:

'Chuck 'im out!'

Another—: 'Yeah—get 'im off!'

And the next moment Polly felt a hand on her shoulder. It was Sid Varley, the Stage Manager. 'Are you ready, gel? I'm gonna ring down on the poor beggar.'

Polly nodded, her mouth dry and Maudie squeezed her arm.

'Good luck, kid. I'll be here, watchin' you.' She held up her crossed fingers and winked encouragingly.

The curtains came to with shouts of derision from the audience and the dejected young comedian hurried past them, his head down. Someone pushed Polly into the centre of the stage and she heard the chairman's gavel hammering for order. The curtains parted again and she stepped forward into the glare of the footlights, the smile on her face belying the pounding of her heart. The angry cries died down—there was a whistle or two, then the conductor nodded to her and raised his baton. Polly opened her mouth and heard her own voice, rich, strident and confident, singing the cheeky words of the song she had sung the night that seemed so long ago for the sailors at the Eight Bells. The song that had brought Eddie to her and changed her life.

As the song came to an end there was a roar of approval. Polly smiled and bowed. Her heart had stopped pounding now and a warm glow of achievement surrounded her like a halo. She went through the programme she and Freddie had rehearsed, growing more and more relaxed with each song and when she came to the end the audience cheered and clapped until the chairman had to demand that they let her go. She came off the stage walking as though on a cloud and when she felt a hand on her arm and heard voices congratulating her she had to drag her thoughts back to earth. Sid Varley and Maudie were beaming at her.

'Well done, kid!' Sid winked approvingly.

'You've certainly warmed 'em up nicely for me!' Maudie laughed.

Back in the dressing room Polly sat in front of the mirror staring at her reflection. It was as though she stood apart from herself, watching another Polly. Inside she felt the same, yet inside she was different. She no longer belonged to herself but to those people out there—her audience—her *public*! She leaned forward, pressing her hands against her burning cheeks, pinching herself to make sure she wasn't dreaming, for this was a dream she had dreamed so many times. Had she really sung alone on a stage? Had the audience's applause and laughter been real? Had it all really happened at last, just as she had willed it to?

Her thoughts were interrupted by a sharp rap on the door and she sprang up to answer it. To her surprise and delight Freddie Long stood there, wearing a smile that split his face from ear to ear.

'Oh, Freddie!' Suddenly she was overcome by her own emotions and she threw her arms round his neck, tears streaming down her cheeks.

'Hullo—what's all this then?' Freddie laughed and came inside, closing the door behind him. 'If anyone sees you they'll think I'm a bill collector, come to take your wages off you!' He tipped up her chin and dabbed at her tears with his handkerchief. 'Here—listen,' he said. 'I've been talking to the manager. He's impressed and he wants you to appear for the rest of this week and next week too! That's not all—you're to have your name on the bills tomorrow. He's asked me if you've got a stage name. How about it, Pol? What do you fancy?'

Polly sat down with a bump. Deep in her memory Maurice's words echoed—: 'Polly Harris? Ghastly! Imagine how it would look on the bills!'

'Harris isn't my real name,' she said slowly. 'I never had a name of my own—not really. So I suppose I could choose whatever I liked.'

'Polly's all right, it suits you,' Freddie said thoughtfully. 'But for the second name—is there a place you like that you could call yourself after?'

Polly pulled a face. 'I've never been anywhere—except Marvelhurst.'

Freddie jumped to his feet. 'Polly Marvel!' he shouted. 'Suits you to a T. How about it?' He half closed his eyes . . . "Polly Marvel—The warmest heart in London"—There you are. There's your billing!' Laughing, he caught her up and swung her round. 'Come on, Polly girl, get changed. I'm taking you out to supper!'

But Polly looked up at him apologetically, her green eyes wide and appealing. 'Oh, Freddie—do you mind—I'd like to—'

He smiled wryly. 'All right, don't tell me, I know: you can't wait to get home to that feller of yours—right?'

She nodded. 'I'm sorry, Freddie. You've been wonderful to me and I do appreciate all you've done—but—'

He cupped her chin with one hand. 'But you love him,' he finished for her. 'I understand, love.' He smiled wistfully. 'I just hope he knows he's the luckiest bloke in London, that's all!'

When Maudie came back to the dressing room she was surprised and pleased to see Freddie and to hear the news he had brought to Polly. Several of the other artistes looked in to give her their good wishes and by the time she got into the cab with Freddie, Polly felt slightly intoxicated by the headiness of it all. Leaning against Freddie's shoulder she sighed deeply. He smiled down at her.

'Happy?'

'Oh yes!' she nodded. There was just one more thing needed to make her happiness complete, to sit by the fire and recount the whole evening to Eddie, reliving it all herself as she did so. It meant not only the real beginning of her career as a Music Hall artiste, but the beginning of their whole future together. If she continued to be as popular as she'd been tonight—and she meant to be—she would soon make the money they needed to be married. Oh, life was *good*!

As the cab drew up Freddie kissed her cheek briefly. 'Sure you won't change your mind? A nice little champagne supper?'

She shook her head, her heart beginning to quicken at the thought of Eddie waiting for her upstairs. 'Not tonight, Freddie—but thanks all the same.' And with a light touch of her hand on his arm she was gone, leaving Freddie looking wistfully after her. He sighed and tapped on the roof of the cab for the driver to continue.

When Polly reached the top of the stairs she was completely out of breath and had to sit on the top step for a moment to recover. She was not going to rush in on him, breathless and incoherent. Those days were over. From now on she would be more composed and lady-like, as befitted Eddie's future wife. After a moment she rose, smoothing her dress and hair and taking a deep breath. How surprised he'd be. How exciting and dramatic she would make the story. Her eyes sparkled as she pushed open the door.

Standing there on the threshold, the smile faded on her lips. The fire was out and Eddie's easel stood where he had left it, the painting of the Water Nymph untouched and his smock thrown hastily over it. On the kitchen table were the remains of a half prepared meal and over the whole place lay the unmistakable atmosphere of hurried departure.

Polly went into the bedroom and took off her outdoor things, disappointment cold and heavy in her heart. All the triumph of the evening was as nothing without Eddie there to share it.

CHAPTER TWELVE

Polly sat before the mirror in the dressing room. The last curl was in place and the last dab of powder had been applied. All that remained was for her to wait for her call.

It was six weeks since that first night at Prince's Hoxton. Now she was playing three Halls a night, hurrying from one to another in a hired brougham. Solly Cohen's attitude to her had turned from indifference to attentiveness and the billing that Freddie Long had created for her—: The Warmest Heart in London was already beginning to be known and commented on.

She regarded herself in the mirror. She had never looked better—yet there was something in the amber-green eyes that only she could define—: uncertainty. She leaned forward, peering at herself, then sat back again with a small exasperated gesture. She was imagining things again. Everything was wonderful, wasn't it? Life was good. She was well on her way up the ladder of success, everyone said so, even Solly and he wasn't given to over-enthusiasm. Every night her audiences told her so too, with their warmth and appreciation. And Eddie loved her, didn't he? *Didn't* he?

On that first night, six weeks ago he had come home as excited as she was herself.

Jessica had called to take him to a party, he had told her. Such a party! He hadn't wanted to go without her, of course. He'd intended to finish the picture of the Water Nymph and have her supper ready when she came home, just as he'd promised. But Jessica had been most insistent. There would be people there whom he should meet. Other artists, writers and critics. So, against his better judgement, he had gone.

Polly had been in bed when he returned at last and before she could tell him of her triumph he was telling her all about the party, of the lavish food and wine and the exciting people he had met. Throwing himself across the bed the words had poured out of him

'I met a man there, Robin—a writer called Oscar Wilde. We talked for hours and he told me of an idea he has for a novel all about a portrait of a man—a wonderful idea—brilliant! Oh, you've no idea of the talent there was in that room tonight, Robin. If genius was an explosive material we'd all have been among the stars by now!' He turned to her, his eyes bright and his face flushed. 'Robin—what do you think—Jessica wants to finance and organise an exhibition of my work! She thinks she can get me some commissions too—really worth-while ones instead of the grocers' daughters and old ladies' pug dogs I've been doing.' She guessed, rightly that he was a little drunk as he laughed, reaching out and drawing

197

her close. 'Oh, I wish you could have been there with me, Robin!' He buried his face in her hair and she said quietly:

'And I wish that you could have been with me tonight, Eddie.'

There was a pause, then he held her away from him, looking into her eyes incredulously. 'Oh darling! I completely forgot. Tonight was your big chance and you were longing to tell me about it! What a selfish swine I am! Can you forgive me, sweetheart?'

The coldness in her heart melted as she looked into the contrite brown eyes and a smile lifted the corners of her mouth.

'They liked me, Eddie,' she told him delightedly. 'I'm to appear at Prince's all this week and next too and I'm to have my name on the bills—Polly Marvel, I'm to be billed as "The Warmest Heart in London" Freddie thought of it. Do you like it?'

He kissed her. 'I *do*! The warmest heart in London—and you're mine—my dearest little Robin.' He kissed her again, then suddenly he remembered something. 'Have you had any supper?'

She shook her head. 'No. I wanted to come home to you as soon as I could, to tell you all about it.'

'And then I wasn't here!' He frowned and shook his head. 'It's too bad. I shall make you some now and bring it to you here in bed, like a lady.'

But she smiled and held out her arms to him. 'No. I don't want anything—except you, here beside me.'

And so everything had been all right after all. But since then so much had happened. There had been fresh songs to learn and rehearse and now Solly was talking of new material, to be specially written for her by a new young song writer he had found. He seemed confident of getting better dates for her and she must be kept on her toes. Life had become hectic for her and for Eddie, and Jessica Lang had begun to feature largely in it.

Lately, almost every time Polly returned to the studio Jessica was there, talking to Eddie in her deep, persuasive voice, using long, 'educated' words that Polly didn't understand. Eddie's head was full of new ideas and often when she talked to him he seemed far away. Sometimes it seemed that it was only in bed, in the late, dark hours that she could claim him for her own. Then all was well enough. He would whisper the same endearments and make love to her as adoringly as ever. But when morning came it was as though a curtain came down on their love—as though with the daylight it was put away in a box for another time.

A tap on the door brought Polly to earth with a start as a boyish voice called out: 'Five minutes, Miss Marvel!'

She gave another dab of powder to her face

and stood up. Another evening had begun. As she turned the door burst open and Maudie rushed in breathlessly.

'Phew! Thought I'd be late. Billy's got a cold, poor little perisher. Couldn't get 'im to take 'is feed no 'ow.' She grinned. 'See you later, kid. Good luck!'

Polly smiled and nodded as she went out into the corridor. Sometimes she wondered how Maudie did it—looking after her widowed sister's children as well as Billy all day, then coming out to do her own work at night. She always seemed so fresh on the stage too—so full of high spirits and energy. Maudie had a heart of gold and above all she was determined that her fatherless baby son should have the best in life.

Polly was grateful for her work. Once she stood on the stage, the lights on her and the warm smell and feel of an audience coming to her across the footlights she forgot everything else except her act. Those people out there had paid to see *her*—Polly Harris from Wapping. They were like the family she had never had. She loved them—and they loved her in return.

Later, as they shared a brougham on their way to the next date Maudie looked at her.

'You all right? You look a bit peaky.'

Polly nodded. 'I'm all right, thanks.'

'Is it that bloke of yours?' Maudie insisted intuitively. 'Playin' up is 'e? Gettin' tired of you?'

Polly's heart gave a lurch. Maudie's brash words framed the fear that she refused to acknowledge, even to herself. 'What a thing to say! Of course he isn't!' She forced a laugh. 'I'm just a bit tired, that's all. I'm not used to this life like you are, not yet.'

Maudie shrugged. 'Aint seen Freddie Long round lately but that aint surprisin', I suppose.'

Polly looked at her sharply. 'Why do you say that?'

Maudie laughed. 'Do you really *'ave* to ask? He's potty about you, that's why. Only anyone with half an eye can see it's no use while you're besotted with that artist bloke.' She nudged Polly hard in the ribs. 'Wake up to yourself, gel. They're not worth eatin' your heart out for—*none* of them. Get out before 'e breaks your 'eart.'

But Polly only smiled softly. 'You don't understand, Maudie. We love each other and we're going to be married one day. But first we both have to make good. To do that it looks as if we'll have to go our own ways for a bit—but our love is strong enough to stand that.'

Maudie pulled a face. 'Them's not *your* words, gel! 'E's been talkin' to you, 'asn't 'e?' She smiled relenting a little as she looked at Polly's troubled face. 'Oh, I'm sorry, kid. Take no notice of me. Never could keep me nose out of other people's business.'

That night Jessica was at the studio again. Polly heard her voice as she neared the top of the stairs and her heart sank. Although she had tried hard for Eddie's sake she couldn't bring herself to like the woman. There was something about her patronising manner and the exotic, aesthete style of her dress that embarrassed and belittled Polly in spite of herself. Eddie could see nothing but good in her and it was true that she helped him a great deal. The exhibition she had arranged was to take place next week and already he had undertaken two commissions to paint portraits of quite important people. But Polly knew instinctively that she had no place in Jessica's plans for Eddie's future.

She straightened her shoulders and reached out a hand for the door handle, but before she could turn it some words of Eddie's halted her.

'I can't come without Robin, Jessica. I'm sorry.'

Jessica gave an exasperated little snort: 'Huh! Do be sensible, Edwin. You can't possibly bring a girl of that sort to Holbrook Hall for the week-end. Lady Holbrook would be—*insulted*! *I* know that in artistic circles views are more liberal, but one must know where to draw the line.'

'Very well, Jessica,' Eddie said stiffly. 'I shan't come.'

Polly bit her lip. She knew that she should go in now and make her presence known, but she couldn't resist waiting a moment longer to hear Jessica's reaction. As she had expected it was explosive, more so than she had bargained for:

'Oh! Why are you so foolish and stubborn?' The low voice rose a tone. 'This is a chance not to be missed—a week-end with one of the best connected families in the country! And with three beautiful daughters about to be presented at Court too! It could be the making of you, Edwin, yet you refuse to go because of some little mopsy who shares your bed and models for you! Do you think she won't be here when you come back?'

'Don't speak of Robin in that way!' Eddie thundered. 'I will not have my life criticized and I won't be ordered about—by you, Jessica, or anyone else!'

'Edwin—' Jessica's tone was wheedling now. 'My dear, I'm sorry if I appeared to criticize. You know how much I admire you. You have your own life to lead, I am well aware of that. You have your pride too but I want so much to help you—' there was a pause. 'I would make it my life's work if you would let me.' Her voice throbbed with feeling. 'I know much more about you, Edwin, than you imagine—because our minds are very alike. We both have ambition and we both know what we want—but you sometimes let your heart rule your head. You feel you owe that girl something don't you? You took her home at Christmas because you thought you could shock your mother into telling you your father's identity—now you feel guilty about it. Am I not right?'

Polly pushed the door, letting it swing open, and stood silently on the threshold, her cheeks flushed and her eyes blazing. Eddie was standing with his back to her, Jessica facing him, close enough to touch and as Polly's eyes met hers she lifted her fingers to his face and said, her eyes burning:

'There is no need, my dear. A girl like that would soon find someone to console her.'

But Eddie stepped back, turning as he did so and catching sight of Polly in the doorway. Just for a moment there was silence, then Polly said levelly:

'Will you be staying for supper, Mrs. Lang? I think there's enough for three.'

Jessica drew herself up and picked up her outdoor things from the couch. 'No thank you.' She turned to Eddie. 'I'll see you tomorrow—and I strongly advise you to reconsider the invitation.'

Polly heard her departure from the kitchen and a moment later as she stood slicing bread for supper she heard Eddie's light step behind her. His arms went round her and she felt his lips on the back of her neck, kissing the little spot that sent shivers up and down her spine. She closed her eyes and took a deep breath.

'Eddie—I hope you don't mind but I shall have to rehearse for most of this week-end. Solly sent word that he's got me a week's engagement at the Oxford in April and I'm to have some new songs written for me by a man he knows.' She turned within the circle of his arms. 'Mrs. Lang said something about an invitation. Why don't you go?'

He smiled and kissed her softly on the lips. 'Why is it, Robin, that you always make things seem so simple—so right for me?' he whispered, his lips close to hers.

She didn't answer, she couldn't, her throat was too tight with tears. Was she doing the right thing? Or was she throwing him into Jessica's arms? The look in her eyes when she had looked at Eddie had plainly showed that she was in love with him. How could she compete with a woman of Jessica's strength and influence. She slipped her arms round Eddie, holding him close, acutely aware of the tender thread by which she held him.

She had not lied when she had spoken of Solly getting her a week's engagement at the Oxford or about the new material that was to be written for her. Polly spent most of Sunday at Solly's house in Camden Town, working with a young man called Jimmy Golightly whom Solly had hired to write some new songs for her. They all got along well enough together, but Polly had some difficulty in persuading Solly that she wanted to include a sentimental ballad in her act.

'You've already got a name for the saucy type of song,' he protested. 'You can't be both

205

things at once!'

'I can,' Polly told him. 'My billing says: 'The Warmest Heart in London'. I can be warm-hearted with a ballad too; Patti Jordan did it—so can I!' She began to sing one of the ballads she had heard Patti Jordan sing that night at McKenna's, employing the graceful movements that old Madame Petrov had taught her. When she had finished the young song writer clapped his hands and turned to Solly.

'I think a touch of dreamy wistfulness like that'd go down well at the end of the act, Mr. Cohen. And you can't say she doesn't do it well.'

Polly gave him her warmest smile and they both looked at Solly. He took the cigar out of his mouth and tapped at the ash reflectively.

'Well—if you could come up with the right song—' He held up his hand as Polly began to twitter with excitement. 'But if it doesn't go it comes out—right?'

For half an hour Jimmy ran his hands over the keys of the piano, playing experimental little snatches of melody, while Polly hummed and added to them. Finally Jimmy looked up.

'Listen, how about this?' The wistful little melody he played struck a chord in Polly's heart and as he played it through again she began to sing:

'A boat afloat, a cloudless sky, a nook that's green and shady. A cooling drink, a pigeon pie, a lobster and a lady.'

Jimmy looked up in surprise. 'Where did you get the words? They're perfect!'

She smiled. 'They're just from an old rhyme I once heard. They need altering a bit to fit.'

Jimmy took out a pencil and after a few moments he began to play the melody again, singing the revised words of the rhyme and adjusting the melody slightly—: 'Our boat will float 'neath cloudless skies, And willows green and shady. Our loaf will taste like pigeon pie, if you make me your lady. But if you turn me from your heart, the storm clouds, they will gather. And I will drown in waters cold, And dead I would be, rather.'

Solly shook his shaggy head from side to side and thrust out his lower lip. 'It's so *gloomy*! People don't want to be sad.'

'Yes they do,' Jimmy insisted. 'There's a lot that enjoys a good cry—anyway, I can write in a happy ending to it.' He looked at Polly. 'Come on, try it out.' He played a short introduction and nodded to her.

As she sang the words, Polly swayed gracefully. The nostalgic words of the song brought out a new huskiness in her voice and when she had finished the two onlookers were silent for a moment. But Solly still was unconvinced.

'I don't know—' he frowned. 'You're a comedy artiste, Polly. When an audience have laughed at you they don't want you to make them cry. It feels like a kick in the face to them!'

'Oh, let me try it out, please, Solly just the once—at the Oxford—please?'

Solly sighed and lifted his bulky shoulders helplessly. 'All right, all right. But remember— if it doesn't go—out it comes!' He spread his hands.

Polly nodded. 'I'll remember, I promise.'

Jimmy began to pack up his manuscripts. 'I'll write some more verses and post them to you,' he told Polly. 'Do you want to take the music home so that you can rehearse it? I can jot you down a copy.'

She shook her head. 'I haven't got a piano— and anyway, I can't read music. But it doesn't matter, I can remember it all right. It's the nicest song I've ever sung.'

He looked pleased. 'Well, thanks. If I can be of any help to you in the future, Miss Marvel—'

Polly laughed. 'Polly Harris is the name— just plain Polly'll do.'

All the way home she hummed the song to herself, a feeling of excitement in the pit of her stomach. Eddie would be home later, then she could try it on him. She could hardly wait! She was convinced now that she had done the right thing by encouraging Eddie to go to Holbrook Hall for the week-end, after all, it was for the sake of his career, wasn't it? And he had always encouraged her in *her* work. Oh yes, they were doing very nicely, both of them. The time was surely drawing near when they would be in a position to marry and settle down, maybe they could buy one of the nice new houses she had seen being built at Notting Hill Gate, close to where Freddie lived. Surely then Mrs. Tarrant would approve. She would speak to Eddie about it soon. But it was very much later when Eddie returned. In fact she had given him up and gone to bed. She woke as he crept in quietly beside her.

'Eddie?' she turned sleepily. 'I thought maybe you weren't coming home tonight after all. Have you had your supper?'

He reached out and drew her close. 'Yes— Oh, I've such a lot to tell you, darling. Lady Holbrook has three daughters and I'm commissioned to paint them in a group—only not till later, ready for next year when the younger two are to be presented. In the meantime, guess what—we're going to Paris, you and I!'

The warm drowsiness fell abruptly from her and she stiffened in his arms. 'Paris—in France, do you mean?'

He laughed and drew her close again. 'I don't know of any other!'

'But when? And for how long?' she asked.

He eased the nightgown off her shoulder and began to kiss it tenderly. 'At once—and for six months—eight, maybe a year, who knows? Oh, just think Robin. What a life we'll have! I want to study the work of the Impressionists.

Jessica thinks that she knows someone who will introduce me to Renoir himself!'

She lifted her head. 'Jessica! Is she coming too?'

He nodded. 'It was her idea. She wants to help me, Robin. I'm really very lucky that she's taken such an interest in me and my work.'

'And me? I bet she didn't suggest me coming!' Polly said scathingly.

He ruffled her hair. 'That's where you're wrong, little Miss Clever! She thinks you would make the most wonderful model. She says you're just the type the Impressionists favour.'

Polly rolled away from him and slid out of bed. 'Is that all I am—a *type*? Has she made you think of me in that way too? Am I just a model now, like you once told me Rose was? Well, just let me tell you, Eddie Tarrant, I'm *more* than that! I'm an artiste. And I'm on my way up! I've got some new songs and I'm going to be a star—so *there*!' Her teeth were chattering half from cold and half from fury as she stood there in her nightgown and bare feet, glaring down at him.

He laughed lazily and caught at her hand. 'Robin! This is something new! If I could only paint you with that expression on your face. You're just like a young tigress with those green eyes flashing!'

She snatched her hand away and ran from the room, tears scalding her cheeks. Fear grasped her heart in its cold grip and she didn't know how to deal with it. If she didn't go to Paris with Eddie she would surely lose him, yet what would become of her career if she were to leave London now. Maudie had said you were soon forgotten. Oh, Jessica was clever. She had planned all this.

She stood staring out through the skylight at the rooftops and the moonlit sky. For the first time since Eddie had first brought her here she felt lonely and insecure; lonelier than she had ever felt in her whole life.

'Robin—darling, come back to bed.' Eddie's voice was soft and persuasive as he slid his arms round her waist. 'I thought you should be so pleased for me. What has made you so angry?'

She longed to turn and give herself up to his embrace but she wouldn't allow herself the luxury. Instead she stood, stiffly unyielding, not looking at him.

'I thought you'd be pleased for me too, Eddie, that I'm doing so well on the Halls. I'm doing it all for you, so that I can show your ma I can be good enough—so that I can be somebody you'll be proud of.'

He took her shoulders and turned her firmly to face him. 'But I love you, Robin—and that's all that matters—to me. I just want you near me, can't you see that?' There's no need for you to struggle like this, making yourself good enough, as you call it.'

'And what about when your pa dies and there's no more money for gadding about to Paris and places?' she said sharply. 'We couldn't *live* on love and promises!'

He dropped his hands to his sides. 'God in Heaven! Are you becoming just like all the other women I've known—obsessed with nothing but money and security and possessions? I've always thought you were different, Robin. It seems you're not after all!'

Her heart was as cold and heavy as lead as she watched him turn from her. Panic tore fiercely at her, but instead of softening, it hardened her. 'What "other women"?' She cried, her voice shrill. 'How many have there been? I suppose I was different because I let you take me to bed without expecting marriage!' She took a step towards him, a thought suddenly occuring to her. 'And while we're talking about it—what were you *doing* at that place in the Strand that night when you found me? Had you gone there to do the same as the other men—or maybe you were going to paint a portrait of Madame Hortense!' She spat out the name as though it were a bitter taste in her mouth. Her own violence shocked and sickened her and a sharp pain jabbed behind her eyes.

Eddie swung round, his eyes dark with anger. 'You've no right to question my reason for being there. It's lucky for you that I *was*! If I hadn't, you know what you'd have become by now, don't you?'

'And what else am I?' she flung back at him. 'That's how your mother and Jessica see me— maybe it's how you see me too—maybe its what you think I'm best fitted for. But I've got better ideas for myself even if you haven't!' She threw back her head. 'I've got talent and I'm going to use it—and I *won't* be coming to Paris with you and that—that stuck-up cow!'

He folded his arms, nodded his head smugly. 'Of course, we're coming to it now. Jealousy, that's what this is all about. I might have known!'

Her eyes flashed with fury. 'I'm *not* jealous! Jealous of *her*—Huh!' She threw back her head and made to sweep past him but he caught at her arm and pulled her roughly back, his face contorted with anger.

'Stop it! Do you hear me? Stop it at once!' he growled at her.

'I won't!' She struggled, lifting her other hand to strike his face but he caught her wrist, twisting it behind her and holding it so tightly that she cried out in pain. Suddenly his lips were on hers, not gently or tenderly but hard and crushing till her teeth drew blood against them.

'Robin—oh, Robin,' he whispered huskily.

Her body grew limp as his arms crushed her against him and together they sank to the floor, their anger erupting into passion like a volcanic flame, white hot and undeniable.

213

CHAPTER THIRTEEN

Polly's opening night at the Oxford was one she would never forget. She had been given the dreaded spot—: first on after the interval, but with her strong voice and personality she had overcome this disadvantage and in spite of Solly's misgivings her new ballad: 'A Lobster and a Lady', which she sang at the end of her act, brought the house down. It was true to say that she could have earned more in the East End, working three Halls a night, but here she knew she stood a better chance of being seen by the bigger and more important managers.

Since the night of her row with Eddie their life together had undergone a subtle change. Their relationship had reached a new plane. They had, for the first time, crossed swords and Polly wasn't quite sure who had won. It was true that the visit to Paris had not been spoken of since that night, but at the same time Eddie was indefinably changed. There was a new maturity about him, an assertiveness that Polly half liked, half feared. What had brought about this change in him, she wondered? Could it be the new confidence in his work, inspired by Jessica and the success of the exhibition she had arranged for him? Or had their quarrel proved to him that he could bring Polly to submission simply by making love to her? There was one other possibility, but it was one that Polly tried not to think about: Did Eddie's new maturity stem from his conquest of Jessica? She relished none of these possibilities and though she loved and needed Eddie more desperately than ever she lived in constant fear of losing him.

He had been in the audience that night and was waiting for her at the stage door when she came out.

'Robin! You were a sensation!' He kissed her cheek. 'I've a cab waiting. We're going out to supper to celebrate. I've booked a table at "Marina's".'

Polly hung back. 'Couldn't we just go home, Eddie, and celebrate by ourselves?'

But he laughed and took her arm. 'Silly girl! I want to show you off! Who will notice you if you hide yourself away?'

Reluctantly, Polly climbed into the cab but when they arrived at the restaurant she was dismayed to find Jessica waiting there with a party of her smart friends. Polly looked at Eddie, confident that he would choose to dine with her alone, but instead he sat down at Jessica's table. What she had hoped would be a quiet, intimate celebration became a noisy exchange of laughter and witicisms in which Polly had no part.

Once or twice as she sat toying with the food on her plate she felt Jessica's eyes on her and anger and resentment burned inside her.

215

She had arranged this on purpose! She must have known Polly would want to have Eddie to herself tonight, yet she had made a point of being there with all these people—people who, as far as Polly was concerned, might have been speaking a foreign language. She pushed her barely touched plate away and felt Jessica's hand on her arm.

'My dear, aren't you hungry? I expect you are too excited to eat.' She smiled and lowered her voice. 'I have been wondering if you and I might have a little talk? Will you be at home tomorrow morning?'

Polly looked at her in surprise. What could Jessica want to talk to her about? They had nothing in common, as this evening was proving.

Misinterpreting Polly's hesitation, Jessica added hurriedly: 'Oh, I won't come too early. I realise that after this evening and its excitement you will be tired.' She glanced in Eddie's direction. 'I happen to know that Edwin has an appointment at eleven o'clock. May I call soon after that?'

Polly nodded, nonplussed. 'Yes—if you like.'

Jessica had been right. On rising the next morning Eddie had announced that he had to go out. It was about a new commission, he told her and he was cheerful, whistling while he shaved. Listening to him from the bedroom, Polly recognised the tune as the new one she had sung last night and she slipped out of bed to join him in the kitchen.

'You're whistling my song.' she said, smiling over his shoulder into the mirror.

He stopped whistling and smiled back at her reflection. 'So I was—it's catchy.'

'Did you recognise the words?' she asked him. He frowned.

'No—should I have done?'

She slid her arms round his waist. 'They're the ones from that little rhyme you taught me—last year on your birthday, remember? A boat afloat, a cloudless sky—'

He laughed. 'So they are! How clever of you.' He resumed his shaving and, watching him, Polly was suddenly seized with fear and longing. Her arms tightened round him.

'Eddie—' she whispered. 'We're both making money now—we could even afford a better place than this to live. Eddie—when can we be married?' She raised her eyes to look at him in the mirror and saw that the smile had left his lips. He put down his razor and wiped the remainder of the soap from his face before he spoke.

'We still have a long way to go yet, Robin,' he said gently. 'In spite of what my mother said I still feel I must know who my father is before I marry. Can you understand that?'

She shook her head, tears filling her eyes. 'It doesn't matter to me, Eddie. I don't care who he is!'

He turned and put his hands on her

shoulders. 'But it *does* matter, darling,' he insisted. 'For all I know at the moment he might be a criminal—or a madman! Before I embark on marriage I must take the responsible view.'

She stared at him. It sounded so unlike Eddie. Could he be joking? She laughed a little uncertainly.

'Oh, Eddie! As if your ma would have married anyone like that!'

He shook his head. 'It is no laughing matter, Robin. There is also the possibility that he never actually married my mother at all. I must face that too.'

She lifted her chin. 'Well—it's no more than I've wondered—about my ma and pa. We've said so many times, Eddie—we're two of a kind.'

He opened his mouth to say something, but closed it again and kissed her instead. 'We're getting into deep water, my love and I've no time to discuss it properly with you now. We must have a long talk about it later.'

'Tonight?' Polly pressed, clinging to him.

He nodded. 'Perhaps, but I have to go now, or I'll be late for my appointment.'

'Eddie—' she wound her arms round his neck and looked up at him, her eyes wide and appealing. 'You do still love me—don't you?'

His eyes softened as he drew her close. 'You know I do.'

'Then show me.' She stood on tiptoe, raising

218

her lips to his. He kissed her, but like all his kisses lately there was a kind of desperation in it. The old tenderness had gone and it was as though she could no longer satisfy the restlessness that had grown up within him since the beginning of the year.

When he put her from him he was smiling. 'If I don't go now, I shan't want to go at all,' he said lightly and a moment later he had collected his coat and gone, whistling down the stairs as though he hadn't a care in the world. Polly stood listening till his footsteps had faded, then she went into the bedroom and finished dressing. Jessica would be here shortly. Deep inside her a foreboding was growing. Whatever it was that Jessica wanted to talk to her about it would not be to her advantage, of that she was certain.

She put on her most demure dress and tidied the studio painstakingly before Jessica arrived. She felt vulnerable. But when she opened the door to Jessica's knock she took care not to let it show.

'Will you take a glass of wine?' she asked politely. 'Or is it too early for you?'

Jessica smiled glassily. 'Nothing for me, thank you, but I would like to sit down.'

Polly blushed, annoyed with herself for forgetting this simple pleasantry. 'Please do.' She indicated the couch and seated herself on the edge of an upright chair.

Jessica looked round the room. 'You keep

219

Eddie's rooms in very good order, Polly.' It was the first time she had actually used the name and somehow she contrived to make it sound commonplace, as though she were addressing a servant.

Polly ignored the implication. 'I do my best,' she said.

Jessica smoothed the fingers of her gloves. 'He would certainly miss you if you—were not here.' She glanced up. 'Let me be frank, Polly. It is perfectly—shall we say—usual—for an artist to have a mistress, but has it occurred to you, my dear, that the time has come when you are actually holding back Edwin's career?'

Polly shook her head dumbly and Jessica went on: 'I am quite sure that you have been good for him in the past—one might almost say an inspiration of sorts, but I am sure that if you are honest with yourself, Polly, you will agree that the time has come for you to part.'

Polly's heart seemed almost to stop beating at the words, though deep inside it was what she had expected. She stared at the other woman. 'Has—has Eddie said so?' she whispered, her mouth dry.

Jessica ignored the question. 'He is a very *loyal* person. This visit to Paris, for instance. He refuses go because he says *your* career would suffer.' She laughed her husky laugh. 'Of course, I have tried to convince him that he should go alone, but he has some absurd idea that you are incapable of caring for yourself!' She paused, looking round the studio again. 'A typical male point of view when one can see that you are the one who does all the *caring*!'

Polly looked into the cool blue eyes. Jessica had made crystal clear her view that the love was all on Polly's side. She moistened her dry lips. 'Perhaps he meant that he needed me,' she ventured.

Jessica gave a dry little laugh and tossed her head. 'A man's *needs* are easily enough met in my experience,' she said. 'Frankly, Polly, what you give him he could get from a dozen others.'

The barbed words brought Polly to her feet in an instant, her cheeks blazing. 'And are they all as willing as you are?'

Jessica coloured slightly but remained outwardly unruffled. 'I see that you have taken my meaning—though somewhat crudely, as I would have expected.' She smiled calmly. 'Do give the matter some serious thought, Polly. I did not come here to make an enemy of you, but I am sure that you must see that Edwin has reached a stage in his career where he is mixing in quite high social circles. He himself has been sufficiently well brought up to do this—'

'But I haven't and you think I'll let him down,' Polly finished for her.

Jessica sighed. 'He would never allow either of you to be embarrassed in that way—and he would never speak to you as I am doing now.

221

That is why I felt it my duty to take the matter into my own hands.'

'Very good of you, I'm sure,' Polly said bitterly. Half of her was furious at Jessica's interference and wounding remarks—the other half saw painfully clearly that what she said was true. While Eddie was perfectly at home with her friends, she could not mix with his comfortably. She sat down again, her heart heavy.

'I suppose you'd better tell me what to do,' she said.

Jessica stood up, drawing on her gloves. 'I would not presume to tell you that, my dear. You are intelligent and I know that you care enough for Edwin to do what is right for him.' She looked at Polly thoughtfully. 'If I might make one suggestion, though—it might save a painful scene if you left him a note.' She smiled. 'A girl like you must have a great many admirers. One of them might help you to forget your infatuation for Edwin.'

Polly turned away so that the other woman would not see the tears in her eyes.

'I can rely on you then?' Jessica said, turning at the door. 'You do see, don't you, that if you remain here Edwin will waste his life and talent. I am quite sure you do not wish that.'

Polly swallowed hard as she turned to face Jessica. 'Don't worry,' she said. 'I won't let Eddie down.'

*   *   *

Maudie was wearing a coarse apron when she opened the street door. Her dark hair was drawn back tightly, but strands of it had escaped and hung down damply about her ears. From somewhere inside the little terraced house a baby cried.

'Oh, it's you!' She smiled. 'Come on in, love. Excuse the mess. I was just tryin' to get a bit of washing done while Billy was asleep—only as you can 'ear 'e ain't any more.'

She eyed the portmanteau and the large box which the cab driver had deposited on the pavement. 'Cor blimey! What's all that then? Chucked you out 'as 'e?'

Polly shook her head wearily. 'It's a long story, Maudie. I wondered if you had a room to spare just till I find something else, of course.' She knew that Maudie and her sister, Alice rented the little house in Hackney from their father and although with two of them and four children it would be crowded, at least they didn't have a landlord to contend with.

Maudie helped her heave the luggage into the tiny parlour that opened straight off the street. 'Phew! What's in there then—bricks?' She straightened her back and pushed a stray strand of hair out of her eyes thoughtfully. 'I suppose you could kip down on the sofa in 'ere for a night or two. I'd 'ave to ask Alice first, o'course. We've only got the two bedrooms upstairs, y'see.'

'I'd be ever so grateful, Maudie,' Polly said. 'And I'll pay, of course.'

Maudie patted her arm. 'That's all right, love. Bad job if you can't 'elp a pal, eh? 'ere— what's it like at the Oxford? Come on through to the kitchen and tell me all about it.' She looked closely at Polly's tear-stained face and her voice softened. 'Been a bust-up, 'as there, love?'

'No,' Polly told her truthfully. 'I just decided it was time for a change, that's all.'

The tiny kitchen was spotless and cosy. The bars of the range glowed warmly and a large pan bubbled gently on top of it. Maudie's eyes swept speculatively over Polly.

'By the look of you, you aint eaten lately. Like a bowl of soup, would you?'

Polly nodded, unbuttoning her coat. The aroma of the soup reminded her that she had eaten nothing at all yet today. Maudie ladled a generous portion into a bowl and cut a thick slice of bread, putting both onto a corner of the table and seating herself opposite.

'Well?' She cocked an eyebrow at Polly. 'Want to talk about it? Come on, tell Auntie Maudie.'

Polly put down her spoon, swallowing hard at the lump in her throat. 'Nothing to tell. I've left Eddie, that's all—for good.'

'Blimey, I can see that!' Maudie retorted.

'But why?'

Polly told her as briefly as she could of the change that had taken place in her relationship with Eddie since his career had improved, ending with her interview that morning with Jessica. When she had finished Maudie looked thoughtful.

'Well, you've always known what I think, gel. If you was to ask me I'd say you'd done the right thing. But by the looks o' you, you aint so sure. Look, kid, if you want to change your mind it aint too late y'know. Never mind what that old cow said to you. It's between you and Eddie when it comes down to it, after all. She just wants 'im for 'erself.'

But Polly shook her head. 'All the same, it's right, what she said. I would let Eddie down. Even last night in that posh restaurant—I was like a fish out of water. I couldn't do it to him, Maudie. I couldn't stand about and watch his love turn to hate—and it would in the end.'

Maudie snorted. 'You could always *learn* all them things—manners and such like. If you could learn the business you could learn that. We're all *born* ignorant.'

'It's breeding,' Polly told her, remembering Mrs. H. at Marlborough Place. 'You can't learn that. Either you've got it or you haven't.'

Maudie shrugged. 'Well, please yourself. As I said, I think you've done the right thing—as long as it don't play "Old 'Arry" with your work. That I couldn't abide, not with a talent like you've got!' An extra loud wail from the baby brought her to her feet with a sigh. 'All right, all right, I'm comin'.' She grinned ruefully at Polly. 'There'll be no peace till 'e's fed. Alice's lot'll be 'ome from school soon too, so I better get it over with.'

She opened the door at the foot of the stairs and went up, calling to the baby as she went. By the time she reappeared Polly had finished her soup.

'Can I do anything to help?' she asked as the other girl seated herself in the rocking chair with the baby and began to undo her bodice. Maudie looked doubtful.

'Well—there are some things in the wash-house I didn't finish. They just need putting through the mangle. Would you mind, love?'

Polly stood up, smiling. ' 'Course not. I'm used to work and I'd like to do my share while I'm here; besides, if I hadn't come you'd have been finished by now, wouldn't you?'

In spite of Maudie's fears Polly's parting with Eddie did not play 'Old 'Arry' with her work. The moment she stepped onto the stage at the Oxford that night all her misery seemed to fade and she threw herself wholeheartedly into her performance. It was only when she came to the end and sang her new song, 'A Lobster and a Lady' that thoughts of Eddie flooded in on her mind. The words evoked for her so much of their time together and as she came to the end a little sob caught at her throat, breaking the last note. The audience loved it. They brought her back again and again, till the Stage Manager grew quite impatient.

'Blimey! We won't get 'ome till midnight at this rate!' he complained.

Polly hurried past him without comment. The warmth and generosity of her audience were like kind words from a friend, as well as bringing comfort, they drew from her the tears she had, so far, shed only in private. At the back of her mind there lingered the possibility that Eddie might just might be waiting for her at the stage door—begging her to come home—that he couldn't live without her. The note she had left had been hoplessly inadequate, she knew that. But somehow she had never been any good at putting things down on paper. Her spelling was so poor that she had been forced to keep the message simple, she was ashamed for Eddie to see her ignorance. After she had written it she had stood for a long time, staring down at the paper, reading the words over and over again, but try as she would, she could think of no others to explain to him why she must go. She pictured the note now, where she had left it, pinned to Eddie's easel: 'I must go,' it read. 'If I don't we will both be hurt. Don't look for me—Polly.' She had wanted to write: 'I love you', to tell him how much he had meant to her—but it was totally beyond her. The words

227

must remain in her heart, aching and burning till she thought they would tear it in two.

Out in the street it was mild. Spring was almost here. She looked around, but among the faces she searched there was no familiar smile, no laughing brown eyes searching for her face. Was the feeling inside her relief? Lying in her narrow bed at Maudie's she stared into the darkness night after night, every fibre of her body longing for Eddie's touch—the sound of his voice and the happy times they had shared. Night after night she stuffed her fist into her mouth to stifle the sobs that shook her so violently and despairingly. She told herself over and over that Maudie was right—: she *had* done the right thing, some day she would look back and see that she had—some day she would be happy again. But always she went to sleep without believing it.

Life at Crimea Terrace went on as usual. Alice Brown, Maudie's sister was a small, wiry woman of twenty-five, though she looked at least ten years older. Her husband, George had died of pneumonia when their youngest child was a month old and since then life had been a constant struggle for her. She welcomed Polly as warmly as Maudie had, glad of the extra cash that Polly contributed to the housekeeping as well as the extra pair of hands she offered so willingly. There was little chance of their getting in each other's way. Alice worked all day at sewing buttonholes at a local shirt factory and only ever saw her children and sister for a short time each day, except on Sundays. The one big thing in their favour, as Maudie had told Polly, was the fact that the house was their own and one morning as they put their feet up for a well earned rest after finishing the housework, she told Polly how it had come about.

'Our Mum and Dad were in service when they met, but Mum, she always wanted a place of her own. It was a big house where they were and they'd both been there right from kids. They courted for six years altogether and when they got married the master and mistress gave them a nice present. With what they'd saved they 'ad enough to buy this little house so Mum got 'er wish.' She sighed. 'But poor old Dad, 'e 'ated it. 'E'd been a valet so 'e got a job in the tailorin' business but 'e never took to it like 'e 'ad to service and when Mum died 'e gave it up. That was about the same time that poor George died, so Dad let me and Alice have the house when 'e went off to 'is new job.'

'And is he happy now?' Polly asked, pouring two cups of strong tea from the pot on the hob. Maudie nodded with satisfaction.

'He went to Lord Broadfield in Buckinghamshire. The poor gentleman lost 'is wife, and 'is only son is—' She tapped her head. 'Not quite the ticket, if you get my meanin'—not mad, you understand just a bit funny. Dad was always a great one for lookin'

229

after people, so 'es in 'is element!'

It was now three weeks since Polly had come to Crimea Terrace. Her engagement at the Oxford had come to an end and she was working the East End Halls again with Maudie. Solly had told her not to worry—that he had had plenty of enquiries about her and expected offers to come in soon, but to Polly it all seemed frustratingly slow. Maudie sipped her tea, looking over the rim of the cup at Polly.

'Seen anythin' of Freddie Long lately?' she asked suddenly.

Polly looked up in surprise. 'No. Maybe he's working out of town.'

Maudie pursed her lips. 'More likely he's fed up with floggin' a dead 'orse. Now if he was to 'ear about you and Eddie—'

Polly's eyes opened wide. 'No! You're not to tell him, you won't, will you, Maudie? Freddie's been goodness itself to me and I wouldn't want him to think I was making a convenience of him.'

Maudie held up her hand. 'All right, all right. But all the same I bet if 'e knew there was a chance you wouldn't keep 'im away! Besides—' She gave Polly a shrewd look.

'You're the kind that needs a bloke. You need lookin' after.'

Polly stared at her. 'Well thanks very much but I can look after myself!' she said indignantly.

But though she sounded confident of this fact there were times when Polly would dearly have liked a little cossetting. The overwhelming nausea she had been suffering brought her downstairs again the following morning and it was here that Alice found her when she got up to go to work, leaning against the wall in the back yard, her face white and glistening with sweat.

'Oh, my Lord, Polly, you did give me a fright! What's wrong, love? You look like death!' She took Polly's arm and led her back to the kitchen. 'Want a nice cup of tea?' she asked, but Polly shook her head.

'I'll be all right in a minute,' she said faintly. 'I just felt so sick, that's all.'

Alice stirred the fire. 'I've heard you down here before. This isn't the first time, is it?'

Polly shook her head. 'It must have been something I ate.'

But Alice straightened up, regarding her shrewdly. 'You wouldn't be overdue as well, by any chance, would you?' she asked bluntly.

The amber green eyes that stared back at her out of the white face widened. 'How—how did you know that?'

Alice sniffed. 'Been there too many times meself not to know the signs,' she said dryly. 'You know what's wrong, don't you, love?'

Polly's lips moved for a moment but no sound came from them, then she asked in a whisper. 'I'm not—I couldn't be—pregnant, could I?'

Alice shook her head. 'Well, only you know that, love. But if you was to ask me, I'd say you was.'

Polly was stunned. She was going to have a baby—Eddie's baby! He had said he wouldn't let it happen till they were married. It must have been that night when they had had the awful row, he had been so angry, they both had. But afterwards he had said such beautiful things—it had been so wonderful, making up again. For a moment a warm wave of joy washed over her, then she remembered: There was no Eddie any more—and soon she would not be able to work. What would become of her and the child she carried? Her face crumpled and her head dropped low, the tears dropping onto her hands. Alice put an arm round her shoulders.

'Look, love, I've got to go to work now. I'll fetch Maudie for you.' She gave Polly's arm a squeeze. 'Cryin' won't do no good, dearie. Everything'll be all right—you'll see.'

Maudie was practical. 'You must eat!' she pronounced. 'You may not feel like it, but you can take it from me, you'll feel better if you do. I was sick in the mornin's somethin' chronic when Billy was on the way.' She patted Polly's shoulder. 'Come on, gel, dry them tears. Shall I go get that feller o'yours?'

'No!' Polly's eyes widened in alarm. 'That would be forcing him. If I did that I'd never forgive myself and he'd hate me for it in the end. It'd spoil his chances.'

'And what about *your* chances, may I ask?' Maudie faced her angrily, hands on hips and eyes blazing. 'Oh well, I suppose you know 'im better than I do.' She made Polly eat a light breakfast, then, after the children had been packed off to school and the baby settled she put on her coat, declaring that she was going shopping and that Polly had better get some rest if she were to do three shows that evening. She was gone all morning and when she came back she wore a defeated look.

'Sit down,' she instructed Polly as she unbuttoned her coat. 'I got something to tell you.'

Polly did as she was told, she was feeling better now. Maudie had been right about the breakfast, somehow after she had eaten it things had not looked so black and during the morning she had been thinking that maybe Eddie would not hate her for having his baby after all. He might even like the idea. She had even persuaded herself that it was fate working in her favour. But now, as she looked up at Maudie's face, her spirits sank again.

'What is it?' she asked. 'What's wrong?'

'I've been to see that Eddie o' yours.' Maudie told her. 'Only I couldn't 'cos 'e aint there no more!'

'Not there?' Polly echoed.

'No.' Maudie sat down heavily. 'I went up to

the top floor but I could see it was empty, so I asked the old girl on the floor below—the one with the foreign accent.'

'Madame Petrov—what did she say?' Polly asked, her heart suddenly cold.

' 'E's gone! Gone to Paris, if you please, with that fancy woman you told me about—what's 'er name?'

'Jessica Lang,' Polly said faintly. 'Did—did she say how long they'd be gone?' She was remembering Eddie's words: 'Six months—eight—maybe a year.'

Maudie shrugged. 'She didn't know. But 'e's given up 'is rooms—so that's that.'

Somehow Polly got through the rest of the day and the evening's performances, though she could only do it by closing her mind to everything but her work. She dared not think about the future or what would become of her. She knew she could not impose on Maudie and Alice for much longer, there was precious little room for her there, let alone a baby too. But for the time being she must work hard and save as much money as she could. Maybe if she asked Solly he could get her another booking each night. She felt sure she could do four if she tried.

It was when she arrived back at Crimea Terrace one night about a week later that she found a visitor waiting for her in the little parlour. He stood before the fireplace, his usually cheerful face anxious and concerned.

'Freddie!' She turned to Maudie. 'Did you—'

Maudie looked away, her face sheepish. 'I'll make some tea. You can talk in 'ere.' She hurried through to the kitchen before Polly could question her further.

They stared at each other, neither of them knowing quite what to say.

'He's let you down then?' Freddie said at last.

Polly coloured. 'No! He didn't know.' She turned away but he stepped towards her, taking her shoulders and turning her to face him.

'Oh, Pol—I'm sorry, love. What a rotten thing to happen.'

Looking into his eyes she saw that he meant it and she leaned against him gratefully, tears starting at the corners of her eyes. 'Oh, Freddie—we *were* going to be married. I didn't—I'm not—' He shook his head at her.

'I know, love. You don't have to tell me. The point is, are you going to be sensible and let me take care of you?'

She looked up at him. 'How do you mean, Freddie?'

The twinkle came back into his eyes for a moment as he put one finger under her chin and kissed her gently. 'Well, for a start, I reckon it'd be a good idea for you to marry me, don't you?'

CHAPTER FOURTEEN

It was a month later that Polly and Freddie were married. The ceremony took place on a Monday morning in June at a little church in Bethnal Green and the only guests were Solly Cohen and Maudie, who had left Billy in the care of a neighbour so that she could attend. Polly wore a pale green dress, which Alice and Maudie had helped her to make specially, though Alice was gloomily superstitious about the colour.

She had taken time over making the decision. At first it hadn't seemed fair, marrying Freddie when she was to have another man's child. But, as Maudie was quick to point out, it wasn't as if there was any deception involved. Freddie knew quite well what he was letting himself in for and anyone could see that he really wanted her. So at last Polly had said 'yes'. It was sadly clear to her that Eddie had gone out of her life never to return. He was probably married himself by now—to Jessica. Maudie said that things usually turned out for the best.

'Gawd works in a mysterious way, 'is wonders to perform,' she quoted, raising her eyes to the ceiling with unaccustomed piety. And so it was that on that bright morning in June, Polly became Mrs. Frederick Arthur

Long.

Outside the church a little knot of onlookers had gathered. Word had got round that it was two Music Hall artistes who were getting married and as they came out of the church, Polly on Freddie's arm, blinking a little in the sunlight, a small cheer went up. A passing chimney sweep paused to give her a lucky, sooty peck on the cheek and Maudie laughed.

'That ought to see you all right!' She took out her handkerchief and wiped a smear from Polly's cheek, her eyes suspiciously bright. 'That's you two spliced then, eh? Well—Gawd bless the pair o' you!'

Freddie wanted her to join them for lunch at his rooms in Notting Hill Gate but she refused, saying that she must get back to Billy.

'Don't forget to keep in touch now, will you? Cheerio.' And she was gone, walking briskly down the street towards Crimea Terrace and her beloved Billy.

Over lunch Solly announced that he had a wedding present for Polly—two weeks' booking at the Alhambra and a week to follow at Gatti's Royal Music Hall.

'Once you've done this you'll be in the West End to stay,' he said, beaming. 'There'll be plenty of work for you from now on, my girl!'

Polly and Freddie exchanged glances. Solly didn't know yet about the baby. When he did he might not be too pleased, even though Polly intended to keep on working for as long as possible. When Solly had left Freddie held out his hands to her, smiling.

'Well—Mrs. Long?'

Suddenly she was shy and tongue-tied. He laughed and drew her towards him. 'What's this—blushes?'

She shook her head. 'It's the wine. I'm not used to it.'

He drew her close and kissed her. 'Oh, Pol. I feel like the luckiest bloke in England today!' He looked down at her. 'There's just something I want to say, love, then I won't speak of it again. It'll be understood between us—right?' Polly nodded and he went on: 'I know that you don't love me—I've always known that and I won't expect anything of you that you don't feel free to give. But I intend to make you love me, Polly. With everything that's in me, I intend to make you love me—or die in the attempt. So now don't ever say I didn't warn you!'

Tears filled Polly's eyes as she stood on tiptoe to kiss him. 'It's not you who's lucky, Freddie,' she said huskily. 'It's me."

As the months went by she did grow to love him too. Not in the way she had loved Eddie; that love, she knew all too well, could never come more than once in a lifetime. But for Freddie she developed a deep, warm affection that enriched her life. Her appearances at the Alhambra and at Gatti's Royal were a great success and as Solly had predicted, more engagements followed. Jimmy Golightly was a frequent visitor at the flat in Notting Hill Gate as more and more material was needed for Polly's new dates.

The Longs also became well known for their Sunday evening parties at which Maudie was an ever welcome and frequent guest. She too was under Solly's management now and doing very well. As Billy grew into a strong, healthy child she was no longer so tied to him. One Sunday evening she announced triumphantly to Polly that she had engaged a girl to help Alice, whom she had now persuaded to give up her job at the shirt factory.

'Nearly 'ad a fit, she did!' she laughed. 'You'd a'thought I'd suggested to 'er that she went on the streets or something! 'Ere—' She looked Polly up and down critically. 'Where're you keepin' that baby, then? Must be all of six months now and it don't show at all!'

Polly smiled. She was lucky. Since the early nausea had abated she had felt remarkably well and though, as Maudie remarked there were only three months to go before the baby's birth, her waistline had increased very little. The small bulge she had developed, she disguised by wearing dresses she had had made in the floating 'Aesthete' style so much favoured by Jessica Lang. The wearing of these did not necessitate the tight lacing of the more conventional dresses and the result was flattering and attractive.

239

'You know, you look 'appy,' Maudie remarked. ''Appier than I've ever seen you look. I'm glad!' She hugged Polly warmly.

One crisp Sunday morning in September Freddie suddenly turned to her at the breakfast table and said:

'How long is it since you went back to the Eight Bells?'

She looked up at him in surprise. 'It must be a year and a half, I suppose.'

He put his head on one side. 'Don't you ever feel you'd like to go and see them?'

Polly sighed. 'To tell the truth, Florrie wouldn't have understood about Eddie, that's why I never went. She never liked him anyway. Then—somehow, it seemed too late.'

He leaned across the table and grasped her hands. 'It's never too late. You're a respectable married lady now, a rising Music Hall star— *and* about to give them their first grandchild. I'm sure they'd be pleased to see you.'

Polly looked doubtful. 'It won't really be their grandchild, Freddie. Florrie always left me in no doubt that I wasn't their flesh and blood. I don't know after all this time—'

Freddie came round the table and sat beside her. 'Look, I've been thinking: now that you're going to have a baby of your own it'd be nice to know who your real mother and father were. It's my guess that Sid and Florrie Harris know more about that than they've let on.'

She stared at him. 'Do you really think so?'

He nodded. 'It's just a guess, but I do. We might persuade them to tell us the truth. Besides, it's a shame to lose touch with people you've known all your life.'

She smiled. 'All right. When shall we go?'

'What's wrong with now? There's no time like the present.' He stood up, smiling at her sudden apprehensiveness. 'Come on, love. They can't eat you. And if they chuck us out—well no one can say we didn't try, can they?'

Neither Wapping or the Eight Bells had changed at all. As they stood at the door Polly's heart began to quicken. She put a hand on Freddie's arm but he winked encouragingly and thumped on the door with his silver-topped cane. It was Sid who opened the door and stood blinking at them incredulously.

'Why—Polly!' he said at last. 'If it ain't our Polly! Come on in. 'Ere—just you wait till I tells Florrie'. He turned and bellowed down the passageway—: ' 'ere—Florrie! Come and see what the wind's blown in!'

She came out of the kitchen wiping her hands on a cloth and stared at them.

'Oh—so you've decided to come and see us at last, 'ave you?' She sniffed disapprovingly and looked Freddie up and down. 'And who might this be, if I might make so bold?'

'This is my husband, Freddie. I'm Mrs. Long now,' Polly said.

Freddie stepped forward and grasped Florrie's damp hand. 'Well, well! So this is the

Mrs. Harris I've heard so much about—or may I call you Florrie? You know, your Polly's making quite a name for herself on the Halls these days. Quite the little celebrity. You should be very proud of her.' He looked round. 'And this is where it all started, eh? Well, I am pleased to meet you both.'

Sid stepped forward. 'Come through to the tap-room, Mr. Long and I'll draw you a pint of me best. I expect Polly and the missus'd like to talk.'

Freddie followed Sid into the tap-room and Florrie nodded unsmilingly to Polly. 'You'd best come into the kitchen. I aint got time to stand idle!' Her eyes swept over Polly as she closed the door. 'How long've you been married, then?'

Polly coloured slightly. 'Early in the year, it was,' she said evasively.

'And when's it due?' Florrie nodded unceremoniously towards her middle.

'After Christmas.'

Florrie sniffed. 'Ain't wasted no time, 'ave you? So you got on the 'Alls then, just like you wanted?'

'Yes,' Polly told her eagerly. 'Polly Marvel is my stage name and I'm billed as "The Warmest Heart In London". I'm earning good money and doing really well.'

'Warmest heart in London, eh? Huh!' Florrie threw back her head. 'Well, I s'pose you knows what you're doin' girl.' She peered at Polly. 'You 'appy then, are you?'

Polly smiled. 'Oh yes. I'm happy, thank you, Florrie.'

The ghost of a smile played about Florrie's thin lips 'Well—*that's* all right then, though mind you, I still think you're a bad girl for stayin' away so long. And while I think of it, what 'appened to the good place I got you with Mrs. Mears and Miss Downes?'

But before Polly could fabricate a story Sid burst into the kitchen. 'Come on the two o'you. We must all 'ave a drink! It's not every day we get famous people visitin' us. 'Ow about a nice drop o' port, Florrie?'

But Florrie threw up her hands. 'You take Polly—if I've got two more to cook for I'll 'ave to do some more veg. Anyway, Sid 'Arris, you know I don't 'old with strong drink!'

Polly stood in the tap-room doorway and breathed in the atmosphere. It would always hold a special nostalgia for her, the scent of the place. Sid slipped a brawny arm round her shoulders.

'So my little Polly's goin' to be a mother, eh? It don't seem possible. It only seems like yesterday she was a young 'un 'erself!'

Freddie nodded to her meaningly from where he stood by the bar and she cleared her throat. 'Yes—that reminds me, Sid. That story about finding me on the doorstep—it isn't really true, is it?'

The big man stared at her, his jaw dropping.

' 'Ow did you know that?'

Polly shrugged. 'Just a guess. Only now that I'm expecting a baby of my own I'd like to know about my real mother. Is there anything you can tell me, Sid?'

Slowly, he walked round the bar and began to polish a glass reflectively. 'Well—I dunno,' he muttered, chewing his lower lip.

Freddie touched Polly's arm. 'I think I'll take a walk round the docks—get up an appetite for my dinner.' He winked as he kissed Polly' cheek, then went out, tactfully leaving them alone. Sid looked up and nodded approvingly.

'Fine chap you've got there, Pol. He'll look after you all right. I s'pose it's for him you want to know about your ma?' Polly nodded and he moistened his lips before continuing. 'You won't tell Florrie if I tell you, will you? We never meant you to know y'see, though I must say, it never seemed right to me.'

Polly leaned forward on the bar. 'Please Sid. I just want to *know,* that's all. I won't tell anyone—except Freddie.'

He put the glass he was polishing down on the counter and leaned towards her confidentially. 'All right then. It—she—your ma was—Kate.'

She stared at him. 'Kate? You mean—*our* Kate?'

He nodded. 'It must've been one of the sailors. She wasn't much more'n a kid at the

244

time.' He sighed. 'So you see Polly, that was why Florrie was so feared for you when you started growin' up—it was why she sent you away. When you was born we took you on to give Kate a chance in life and Florrie couldn't stand the thought of 'istory repeatin' itself.'

Polly was stunned. Kate! Whom she'd always thought of as her sister! She swallowed hard. 'May I tell *her* that I know?' she asked. 'I'd like to go and see her.'

Sid shook his shaggy head. 'Please yourself, love. Though I daresay it won't please 'er after all these years. Just s'long as you don't tell Florrie. She'd flay me alive if she knew I'd let the cat out o' the bag!'

Polly smiled and patted his arm reassuringly. 'Don't worry, Sid. I won't tell.' She turned. 'I think I'll go and find Freddie now.' She was almost at the door when he spoke and his words stopped her in her tracks.

'Ever seen any more of that artist chap, 'ave you?'

'No.' She put her hand on the door handle.

'Only 'e was in 'ere askin' for you a while back.'

Her heart seemed to stop beating as she turned slowly to face him. 'Asking for me—when was that?'

His brow furrowed with concentration. 'Must've been about April—or May.' He shook his head. 'The weeks go past so quick, it's hard to say, he asked if I'd seen you, but o'course, I 'adn't. I told 'im that as far as I knew you were still at Marlborough Place.'

'What did he say?' Polly asked, her mouth dry.

He shrugged. 'Nuthin'—he just went away. Just thought I'd tell you while I remembered, that's all.'

Outside, Polly leaned against the wall, gulping in the fresh air, her world spinning. So he had tried to find her after all. Though maybe it was just to say goodbye before he went away. The thought of Eddie overshadowed everything else. Even the revelation that Kate was her mother seemed of little importance for the moment.

It was against Freddie's better judgement that he gave her Kate's address, but she had been so insistent about wishing to visit her that in the end he hadn't liked to thwart her in her present condition. But when she had announced her intention of going alone he had been adamant. At last they had compromised: he would accompany her to Kate's small house in St. John's Wood but he would wait for her outside.

The maid who answered the door was pretty and immaculately turned out. She asked Polly to wait in a sunny little morning room and after a few minutes, reappeared in the doorway.

'Madam will see you now if you would care to step this way, please.'

Polly followed her down a thickly carpeted corridor and into an elegant drawing room. Kate rose from a small writing desk. She wore a beautifully cut dress of rose coloured silk and her hair was fashionably coiffeured. To Polly's delight she came towards her, hands outstretched.

'Polly! What a surprise. How delightful to see you after all this time!'

But it was obvious that this show of hospitality was purely for the benefit of the maidservant for as soon as she had withdrawn Kate's smile vanished along with her pleasant manner.

'What ever possessed you to come here?' she asked abruptly. 'And how did you find out where I lived?'

'Freddie gave me your address,' Polly told her. 'Freddie Long. I'm married to him now.'

'Really?' Kate said disinterestedly. 'Have you come here expecting a wedding present or something then?'

Quick tears of hurt sprang to Polly's eyes. 'May I sit down?' she asked quietly.

Kate looked at her properly for the first time since she had entered the room and her expression softened a little. 'Of course. I'm sorry Polly. I hadn't noticed.'

Polly sat down gratefully and looked at Kate. She still had difficulty in seeing her as anything but a sister. She took a deep breath.

'Last Sunday I went to see Florrie and Sid at

the Bells,' she began. 'Because of the baby I'm expecting I wanted to know more about my own birth and I managed to persuade Sid to tell me the truth.'

Kate's colour drained and her hand went involuntarily to her throat. 'He—he—told you?' she whispered.

Polly nodded. 'Yes. I know now that you are my true mother, Kate. Though it still seems very strange to me.'

Kate stood up, her hand on the mantelpiece as she turned her face away from Polly. 'What do you want? Why have you come here,' she asked, her voice shaking.

Polly frowned, puzzled by her attitude. 'I don't want anything—except to see you and talk to you,' she said.

Kate sank into her chair again and Polly saw with surprise that there were tears in her eyes. 'Please—forgive me for being so sharp with you,' she said. 'Ever since I've known Reggie I've dreaded something like this happening. If he knew—' She broke off and gave an apologetic smile. 'We're not married, you see. Reggie already has a wife so we can't be. She's an incurable invalid, so I live here and he visits me when he can. Sometimes I'm very lonely, Polly, but that is the price I knew I'd have to pay. I believe that if anything happened to—set him free he would marry me and I live only for that thought. But if he knew that I had a grown-up daughter—' she broke off and stood up again, walking to the window to hide the fear in her eyes. 'I've seen you perform, Polly,' she said presently, turning. 'Reggie loves the Halls, that was how we first met. Sometimes he takes me and I've seen you at the Alhambra and at Gatti's. You're good—better than I ever was or could be. You have a career, a husband—soon, a child. You have so much. Please—will you let me keep this one thing?'

Polly stared at her. From an arrogant, aloof woman she had become vulnerable, pathetic and pleading. She made Polly feel somehow ashamed. Her heart contracted. She knew only too well the feeling of insecurity Kate must be suffering. She nodded.

'Of course I wouldn't dream of telling anyone, Kate. No one shall know but us. There's no need anyway.' She paused. 'There is just one thing I'd like to know though—'

'You want to know who your father was,' Kate anticipated. 'Well, it's natural, I suppose, but there's nothing much I can tell you. He was a foreigner—from Denmark, I think. We didn't even speak the same language and I can't remember much about what he looked like—except his red hair.' She smiled. 'You've got that.' She touched Polly's hand. 'I'm sorry I can't tell you more, love.'

Polly shook her head. 'It's all right. And I'm sorry if I upset you, coming here, Kate. I just wanted to know, that was all.'

Kate put her arms round Polly, holding her

close for a moment. 'Don't be hurt, Polly—but I'm going to ask you not to come here again.' She looked at Polly, her eyes brimming with tears. 'I wish we could have got to know each other better—as mother and daughter, I mean. I think we could have been good friends. But I gave you up a long time ago and now it's too late. Reggie is my whole life now—all I have. I couldn't live without him.' Her voice broke a little and she clung to Polly. 'Go home now, love,' she whispered. 'Go back to your Freddie and be happy. Good luck.'

In the cab Freddie wiped the tears from her cheeks with his handkerchief, his face concerned.

'Do try to stop now, Polly, there's a good girl, or you'll make yourself ill.' He shook his head. 'I knew it was a mistake to come. The woman must be heartless, turning her own daughter away like that!'

But Polly was not weeping from Kate's rejection but from the knowledge of what it had cost her. She understood so well the longing and fear that tormented Kate and the newly discovered fact that she was her daughter made her feel it all the more keenly.

It was by the following morning's post that the letter came asking Freddie to appear in Manchester at a benefit concert for his old friend Cyril Capper, the comedian.

'It's an honour to be asked to appear, love,'

he told her. 'And I'd like to do it. Old Cyril's almost eighty now and he's a grand old boy. He helped me so much when I was on the way up. I'll only be away a couple of nights and the baby's not due for a few weeks yet, is it?'

Polly looked doubtful. 'I don't mind you going, but do you feel up to it? You've had that sore throat and I've heard you coughing at night.'

He laughed. 'It's nothing. A relaxed throat through over-working the voice. I often get it. I'm as fit as a fiddle. I can't let old Cyril down, Polly.'

She smiled. 'No, of course you can't. I'll be all right. Don't worry about me. You'll be home before I've had time to turn round!'

She was appearing that week at the Tivoli and it was to be her last week of work before the baby's birth. Though she knew she would miss her work and her beloved audiences she was looking forward to getting everything ready for the baby and having more time to look after Freddie for a while.

Freddie left for Manchester on the Sunday afternoon and Polly saw him off at Euston station, although she was still concerned about his health.

'You really don't look very well,' she fussed. 'You should have seen a doctor with that throat. I'd have been happier. What will you do if you've lost your voice by the time you get there?

Freddie laughed huskily. 'Oh, you are cheerful!' He put an arm round her waist and gave her a squeeze. 'I've told you, love. I often get these throats. They vanish as quick as they come. What it is to have a wife to worry about you, eh?' He kissed her. 'You just be sure and look after yourself, do you hear?'

He was to be away for three nights. There was a rehearsal on Monday and the benefit concert was on Tuesday. He had promised her that he would be home in time for her performance on Wednesday evening. Polly hoped he was right about the throat. She felt sure it was worse than he said—yet he was a good deal older than she was and he had looked after himself for a long time without coming to any harm.

Freddie had not returned by Wednesday evening's performance, but Maudie, who was on the same bill as Polly that week was not surprised.

'They'll 'ave 'ad a rare old knees-up last night after the show,' she said. 'I doubt if they'll 'ave recovered yet. Give 'im a chance, Polly, love!' She laughed. 'I know you're married but you'll 'ave to let 'im off the 'ook sometimes, you know!'

And Polly laughed with her, though she wasn't reassured. Usually Maudie's down to earth common sense put things into perspective for her but this time she couldn't help the disturbing feeling that something was

252

wrong. She wouldn't rest till Freddie was safely home again.

It was as she came off the stage the following night that Maudie met her in the wings. And this time her face wore an expression that Polly had never seen on it before. The orchestra was still playing the chorus of A Lobster and a Lady with which she had finished her act and the audience was applauding riotously.

'What is it?' Polly asked, grasping Maudie's arm. But the other girl pushed her back towards the stage.

'They want you back again—go on—take your bow.'

But Polly's audience would not let her go without another chorus of the sad, beautiful little song, in which they all joined. All the time she sang for them, Polly could see Maudie out of the corner of her eye. She still stood in the wings and now she had been joined by a police officer and Mr. Crouch, the house manager. A feeling of dread crept over her and when the audience finally let her go she ran to Maudie, her eyes wide with anxiety.

'What is it? Tell me, Maudie—please!'

'Polly —Freddie's been taken ill—very ill—' Maudie broke off, her eyes swimming with tears as she turned to Mr. Crouch. 'Oh God! I can't—I can't tell her!'

The manager's face was grave as he took her arm and led her to one side to allow the next act onto the stage. 'My dear—Freddie was taken ill on his arrival at the theatre two nights ago. He was taken to hospital and—died of diphtheria early this morning. He wouldn't have you sent for because of the infection. Now if I can do anything—' But he broke off as Polly slid to the floor in a dead faint.

Maudie sent word to Alice that she would not be home that night and took Polly home in a cab. She threw a shawl round the shocked girl's shoulders and held her close in her arms all the way home but it seemed that nothing could stop the shudders which seemed to shake Polly to the very soul. Once inside the house she summoned the help of a shocked Mrs. Smailes and together they put Polly to bed, where Maudie sat, trying vainly to comfort her into the small hours of the morning.

It was at five-thirty that the pains began and Maudie woke Mrs. Smailes in a panic.

'We'll 'ave to get a doctor quick! I think she's goin' to 'ave the baby and it aint 'er time yet! Nothin' *like* 'er time!'

The doctor came and did all that he could but at nine o'clock on that bleak, foggy November morning Polly's baby son came into the world—never to breathe its air or see the light of day.

'You have so much' Kate had said such a short time ago. Now, once more, Polly had nothing and no one.

CHAPTER FIFTEEN

For several days Maudie and Mrs. Smailes feared for Polly's life. Day after day she lay motionless, her face to the wall in the double bed she had so briefly shared with Freddie. Maudie was terribly afraid that she might be sickening for the same disease that had struck Freddie down but the doctor shook his head. It was not her physical condition that gave rise for concern, he told her, but her mental one. Although Polly was young and strong she seemed to lack the will to get well.

'If she'd only *cry*!' Maudie said despairingly to Mrs. Smailes. 'She never 'as, you know. Not even when we told 'er about poor Freddie. It don't seem natural some 'ow.'

Freddie Long being such a popular figure, the news of his tragic death appeared in some of the daily papers and a flood of callers and letters began to arrive at Notting Hill Gate. At first Maudie was pleased, thinking they might help Polly, especially when Sid and Florrie arrived all the way from Wapping. But she remained unchanged, numb, expressionless and uncommunicative; turning deeper and deeper within herself, till at last the doctor forbade any further visitors. So it was that the tall, fair woman who arrived one afternoon was turned away at the door by Mrs. Smailes.

'I'm very sorry, madam. Mrs. Long is not allowed visitors. She's lost her baby as well as her husband, you see and she has been very ill.'

The woman turned away, her face sad. 'I see—I'm so sorry. Will you give her my love, please?'

Mrs. Smailes nodded. 'Who shall I say called, madam?'

The woman turned. 'I am her—' She bit her lip. 'Just tell her that Kate called and was asking after her.'

As for Polly, her mind was like a dense fog. The only clear thought that formed itself out of the morass was—: Why didn't I die too? What is the point of living now? But even the effort of dying seemed hardly worth while.

Maudie never left her except to go to the theatre and make brief excursions to Hackney, but she knew she could not stay for ever. A messenger from Freddie's solicitor had called twice to see Polly and had stressed that she must call on the firm as soon as she could. There were so many things that needed attention. Maudie was at her wits' end when Jimmy Golightly arrived one afternoon, his cheerful young face grave behind the bunch of flowers he carried.

'I've heard she can't have visitors,' he said. 'But I thought these might help to cheer her up.'

He handed Maudie the shaggy bronze and

yellow chrysanthemums and she buried her face in their spicy fragrance. 'Oh, Jim! That was thoughtful of you. Come on in for a minute.' As she held the door open for him a sudden inspiration struck her. ''ere, Jim—do you feel like playin' the piano for a bit?'

He looked shocked. 'What—here? Freddie's piano? When she's—'

She took his arm and drew him into the sitting room, closing the door behind them. 'Just some of 'er songs,' she whispered. 'The ones you wrote for 'er. The ones she always loved so much. Go on, *please!*'

'Well—' He shook his head. 'If you really think she'd like it—but it hardly seems right at a time like this.' Doubtfully, he sat down at the piano and began to play. Maudie opened the bedroom door a little, standing where she could see the bed reflected in the dressing table mirror. A little hesitantly, Jimmy began to play the familiar melodies and Maudie watched as the white face on the pillow turned, listening as she had listened to nothing for days. Slowly, she raised herself up and Maudie nodded to Jimmy.

'That's it—go on. Don't stop now!'

His hands moved over the keys and the bitter-sweet tune of A Lobster and a Lady filled the room. There was a small sound from the bedroom and Maudie went in to see Polly sitting up in bed, her eyes swimming with tears.

'Maudie,' she whispered. 'Why did it happen? What can I have done to be punished like this? They're all gone now. Eddie—the baby—and Freddie—poor, poor Freddie!' The tears overflowed and slid down her cheeks while silent sobs racked her frail body. Maudie sat on the bed and gathered her close. The piano stopped playing and Jimmy's distressed face appeared round the door.

'Just go now, Jim,' she said quietly. 'You've done 'er a big favour. You'll never know 'ow big. Come and see 'er tomorrow. She'll be all right then.'

He withdrew, looking slightly reassured and Maudie rocked Polly to and fro in her arms. 'That's right, love. Cry it all out. You take as long as you like. Maudie's 'ere—Maudie's got you.'

*   *   *

The offices of Longstaff and Braithwaite were on the top floor of a tall building in Long Acre and though Polly had been breathless after climbing the four flights of stairs, she was even more so when she joined Maudie in the waiting room after her interview with Mr. Longstaff, the senior partner. Maudie got quickly to her feet, concerned at the sight of her friend's white face.

'Lord love us! What's up? You look as if you've seen a ghost!'

Polly smiled uncertainly. 'It's all been a bit of a shock. I'll tell you about it on the way home.'

Freddie, it appeared had been prudent with his earnings, saving the bulk of his money and investing it wisely so that Polly was now left with a steady income from the interest. His one extravagance was a recent acquisition—a small theatre in the Midlands which he had bought shortly before their marriage.

'I feel he saw it as an interest, perhaps to resort to after his retirement from the stage,' Mr. Longstaff had told her. Poor Freddie. Little did he know then what was to come.

'Whereabouts in the Midlands?' Maudie asked.

Polly took a slip of paper from her pocket and looked at it. 'Halesbury in Buckinghamshire,' she said.

Maudie beamed. 'That's where Dad is! Broadfield Hall is about three miles out of Halesbury. I suppose you'll sell it though?'

But Polly looked thoughtful. 'Maybe I'll keep it for *my* retirement. I like the idea of owning a theatre.'

Maudie laughed. 'Retirement! Gawd, gel, you're not twenty yet and 'ere you are talkin' about retirement!'

'Age has nothing to do with it. I could retire now if I liked!' Polly said, a slight edge to her voice. 'I don't have to work any more if I don't want to. What's the use anyway?'

Although Solly had been pressing her to accept engagements again, she had so far refused to commit herself.

Maudie shook her arm. 'Oh, Polly, do stop talkin' like that. You've got talent—*real* talent, and you were doin' so well—really makin' a name for yourself. If you don't soon get back folks'll begin to forget you. Oh *do* listen to me, love. I know what I'm talkin' about!'

Polly shrugged. 'What's it all for though, Maudie? Somehow there doesn't seem any point any more. Everything I have I lose sooner or later anyway. I can't seem to help it! But a theatre—a Music Hall of my own— that'd be different. I'd have more control over that.'

'But you don't know the first thing about how to run a theatre!' Maudie argued.

'I could learn,' Polly insisted. 'It'd be something new—a challenge.'

'What about your friends—what about me?' Maudie asked. 'I'd never see you all that way off.'

But Polly smiled wryly. Solly had already told her of the American tour that looked likely in the near future. Maudie was a certainty for it. Polly herself could have gone if she'd chosen but the idea, which once would have excited her beyond bounds now left her cold. She looked at Maudie, her head on one side. 'And if you go to America?'

Maudie blushed hotly. 'Who told you about

that? Anyway—I aint made up me mind yet. I'm not sure that I want to go.'

Polly laughed. 'Of course you want to go. You mustn't mind about me—except of course that I shall miss you. You deserve it, Maudie-no one deserves it more. And you know, Solly tells me that you'll even be able to afford to take Billy with you—and a nurse to look after him too!'

Maudie looked at her doubtfully. 'But—what will you do?'

'It's time I picked up the broken threads of my life and tried to weave them together again,' Polly said. 'And I must do it alone, Maudie. It's the only way.'

Although she protested to the end, Maudie sailed for America four weeks later with a star-studded company of Music Hall talent, taking Billy and his nurse with her. At the end she could no longer conceal her excitement.

'We're to sail on the same ship as Ellen Terry and Sir Henry Irving went on when *they* toured America!' she told Polly excitedly. 'I reckon that's a good omen, don't you?'

Although she had urged her to go, Polly was lonely and desolate after Maudie's departure. She had come to depend so much on the generous, big-hearted girl who had become such a close friend to her and suddenly, with her absence, life seemed bleak and empty. Polly put off all decisions about the future, sitting quietly in the flat day after day.

261

Christmas came and went almost unnoticed to her. Sid and Florrie had invited her to spend it with them at Wapping but she had refused. Again and again her mind went back to last Christmas. She wondered if Eddie had returned from Paris and if he was at Marvelhurst again—maybe with Jessica. Sitting alone in the firelight her mind dwelt on the warmth of his arms, his lips on hers and the words he had spoken that she would never forget-: 'We belong to each other for ever now—nothing can ever part us.' For her at least, those words would always be true and though she was tortured with guilt about poor Freddie nothing could ever change the way she felt.

It was New Year's Eve when Jimmy arrived, bringing with him a copy of the popular stage paper, the *'Era'* in which she was mentioned.

'You see, they want you back,' he said after reading the piece aloud to her. 'It says here that they have had scores of letters asking about you.'

She shrugged and turned away, but he caught at her sleeve. 'Polly—listen. It used to mean so much to you. I can't believe you've really lost all interest. Solly's talking about giving you up and you can't blame him. After all, he's in it for business like the rest of us. If you don't get a move on, love, it'll be too late.'

Polly lifted her eyebrows. 'Let it be, Jimmy. What does it matter? Freddie left me well provided for. Why should I bother?'

He leaned back in his chair, folding his arms and regarding her. 'I see. So you're perfectly happy, are you?' He spread his arms. 'This is all you ask of life, is it? These four walls? Oh, come *on*, Polly! You're not the same girl! It's— it's as if the light has gone out in you. You can't go on like this.' He got up suddenly and went to the piano. 'I want to hear you sing! *Now*—this afternoon—and I shan't leave here until you do!' He began to play a medley of her songs but she turned away angrily.

'It's over, Jimmy—all that. It belongs to the time before Freddie died!'

'My God!' he said exasperatedly. 'If he could see you now! After all the work he put in on you—throwing it all in!'

She rounded on him. 'Stop it! You don't understand about me and Freddie. He was too good for me. I didn't love him as he deserved to be loved. I wasn't there when he was ill and needed me—I couldn't even go to his *funeral*!' Her voice broke and painful sobs tore at her throat, shaking her whole body. Jimmy let her cry for a while, watching her uncomfortably. At last, when the sobs had quietened into helpless tears he went to her.

'I think I understand, Polly,' he said gently. 'But don't you see—you could make it up in this way. He wouldn't want you to throw your talent away. If you came back it would be a— well, a sort of tribute to him in a way.'

Slowly she lifted her swollen face to look at him. 'Do you think so? I never thought of it that way. It seemed so wrong to go on singing—heartless, somehow.'

'Brave, I'd call it,' Jimmy said. 'Brave as I know you are at heart.' He turned back to the piano. 'Come on, give it a try eh? Just for me.'

And ten minutes later Polly's voice was filling the room; rich, sweet and strident as ever. The words and melodies seemed to lift her, bearing her up and carrying her along on their cheerfulness till at last she threw herself, exhausted, into a chair.

'Oh! That's enough, Jimmy! I couldn't sing another note! Not today, anyway.'

He raised an eyebrow at her quizzically. 'But in the future? The *near* future? Can I give Solly a message from you?'

She nodded, ,laughing breathlessly. 'Yes—all right. Tell him Polly Marvel is ready to work again!'

He hugged her. 'That's the ticket! That sounds more like our Polly.' He picked up the copy of the *Era* that had slipped onto the floor. 'The bloke who wrote this piece about you,' he said thoughtfully. 'I know him slightly—met him in the 'York' a couple of months ago. He's interested in the publicity angle—got a flare for it. He might do you a bit of good.'

Polly frowned. 'How?'

'Oh, all sorts of ways. Song sheets and albums with your picture on the covers;

Personal posters. Look, he's always in the 'York' at lunch times. Can I ask him to come and see you?'

'Well—'

'Come on, Polly. In for a penny, eh?'

She smiled. 'Oh, all right then—if you come too. He sounds frightening!'

Jimmy laughed. 'Not a bit of it! You'll like him. I'll bring him tomorrow if I can.'

He was as good as his word. The following afternoon at three o'clock Mrs. Smailes knocked on Polly's door to tell her that Mr. Golightly and another gentleman had called to see her. She told the landlady to ask them to come up and rose to look at herself in the mirror. The face that looked back at her was pale and though still small and pointed it had lost the pinched look it had had since her illness. About the amber-green eyes there was a new depth and maturity, a new resolute firmness about the mouth. In the black dress and with her bright hair dressed severely she looked much older than her nineteen years. She smoothed her hair and turned as Mrs. Smailes opened the door and Jimmy walked in, followed by a tall, good looking man.

'Polly—' he said stepping forward. 'This is the clever fellow I was telling you about— William Mears.'

They stared at each other incredulously. Polly was the first to recover. 'Last time we met I seem to remember that you were in the tea business,' she said levelly.

He took her hand and raised it to his lips, smiling down at her in the lazy, amused way she remembered from their brief encounter at Marlborough Place. 'And you were out to enchant the world even then,' he said.

Jimmy stared from one to the other. 'You—you know each other then?'

This time it was William who spoke: 'I think I can safely say that I have the honour of being one of Miss Marvel's very first admirers.' He looked again at Polly. 'And if I can be of service to you now I shall be more than happy.'

The three of them sat down and as Mrs. Smailes brought in the tea, William began to outline a publicity programme that took Polly's breath away. There were to be personalised posters, song sheets and albums with her photograph and signature; press campaigns and personal appearances at social gatherings. At last she held up her hand, laughing.

'Wait! Please. It seems to me that all this will cost a lot of money—and there is my agent to be considered. As for appearing at social gatherings, surely I would have to have an escort?'

William smiled. 'As to the cost—naturally there would be a small outlay, which would also be a good investment and I would, of course do nothing without the permission of Mr. Cohen. Escorts, I cannot believe to be a problem to you, Miss Marvel.'

'Please—call me Polly. Marvel is only my stage name,' Polly said, choosing to ignore his last remark. 'I shall have to think it over carefully. May I write and let you know, Mr. Mears?'

He rose. 'If I am to call you Polly, surely you can call me William? I think, after all that we could be described as old friends?' He took a card from his pocket and handed it to her. 'I can always be reached through the *Era* offices but you will find my home address on the back.'

She took it, glancing at the address. 'I see that you are not at Marlborough Place now,' she said.

He laughed. 'Like you, I found the atmosphere there a little too rarified for my taste and escaped as soon as I could.'

'Your mother and aunt—are they well?' she asked. 'And Miss Fellowes?'

'Mother and Aunt Honoria are as ever—holier than holy,' he said gravely. 'As for Amanda—she was one of my more unfortunate mistakes—the less said, the better.'

When they had gone Polly propped the card up on the mantelpiece and sat down to think. William Mears—of all people! Her last encounter with him had brought her trouble—near disaster in fact. If it hadn't been for Eddie's providential appearance that night—she tried to push the memory out of her mind but it refused to go. If it hadn't been for William Mears she might never have met Eddie again and her whole life would have been different. Probably she would still have been at Marlborough Place—never have met Freddie or Maudie—never have realised her ambition to be a Music Hall artiste even! When she thought about it in that way it quite took her breath away. Why, if it hadn't been for William she might never have known what it was to *live* at all! She might still have been wearing her knees out scrubbing floors and praying in the cold house in Bayswater. Maybe she should give some consideration to his proposals after all!

*   *   *

Polly's reappearance on the Halls brought her a rapturous reception. Her first date was at the 'Oxford' and for Polly it was like waking up after a long sleep. She had walked the length of Tottenham Court Road that night before going into the theatre. Partly from nervousness and partly from the sheer joy of mingling with people again. She badly missed her friends— Maudie with her breezy, good-natured kindness and Freddie—for she still thought of him more as a friend than a husband.

The gas lights in the shops, the naptha flares on the costermonger's barrows, the smells and the bustle of the street warmed Polly's heart.

The stage doorman's cheery welcome, and the familiar atmosphere of backstage—: expectant, exuberant, yet at the same time, routine and business-like, almost made her feel she had never been away—until she stepped out into the glare of the footlights. It was then that she realised how much she had been missed. The audience clapped, roared and stamped its approval. They brought her back again and again to sing to them until she had to beg them, laughing and with tears in her eyes, to let her go.

'God bless you, Polly!' A man shouted from the gallery. And others took it up from all parts of the house.

In the dressing room Polly stared at herself in the mirror. It was as if she had been frozen all these weeks and the generosity of those dear people out there had thawed her with their warmth. It was then that she made her decision: from now on she would live her life for them. They should be her reason for living. She had been denied her lover, her husband her child and her mother. Those people should fill the void in her heart, they should be her family. Elated by the thought she jumped up and began to change her costume, her heart light.

A brief knock on the door preceded Solly's presence as his bulky form bounced into the room. 'Polly, my dear!' He was beaming so broadly that the cigar had great difficulty in hanging onto his lips. 'Polly my dear, you were wonderful! Better than ever.' He addressed the top of Polly's head over the top of the screen. 'Why haven't you got a dresser? I must see the management about it. An artiste of your calibre!'

Polly laughed, stepping out from behind the screen. 'I don't need one, Solly! If I can't dress myself at my age it's a poor look-out!'

But he shook his head. 'It's a matter of status, my dear. It don't look right, you dressing yourself.' He sat down throughtfully. 'You know, you stayed away for just the right amount of time.' His eyes gleamed. 'Though of course, the publicity helped.'

Polly stared at him in dismay. 'You mean— they're being good to me because of what happened? Because of Freddie?'

'Oh, no, *no*!' he said hastily. 'Let's just say that because of it they didn't forget you though, which reminds me, Polly—I've had this chap Mears up to see me. He wants to handle some publicity for you. I think you should let him.'

She frowned. 'I'm still not sure about it.'

'Well, I am,' he said decisively. 'Besides, there's money to be made—extra perks to be had.'

She flapped a hand at him. 'Oh *money*! Extra perks! Do you ever think of anything else, Solly? There's more to life than money, you know!'

270

'When you've *got* it, there is!' he rejoindered. 'Don't forget, Polly, that you'd be doing other people a good turn as well as yourself—creating employment.' He stood up 'Look—he was in front tonight. I said I'd ask if you'd see him. Will you?'

She sighed. 'Oh—all right, if you think so, Solly.'

After congratulating her on her performance William insisted on taking her out to supper, using all the persuasive charm that was so much a part of his character. Polly had refused at first, saying that it wouldn't look right, her dining with a man so soon after Freddie's death, but William swept her objection away:

'Then we shall go somewhere quiet, I know just the place. Just as well too, if we're to talk business—though why any man should waste time talking business to a woman as beautiful as you I can't think.'

Polly picked up her hat and put in on at the mirror. 'Perhaps, because, as Solly says, there's money to be made out of it,' she said caustically. She wasn't going to have him thinking she was the same naive little skivvy he had surreptitiously kissed in the kitchen at Marlborough Place. She would start as she meant to carry on!

But in spite of herself she soon found herself warming to William's attentive charm. They dined at a little restaurant in St. Martin's

Lane where William knew the proprietor and soon she was fascinated at the plans he laid before her. All he needed, he told her, was her permission and they could go ahead with their plans to make her the toast of London. She must be photographed first, of course and maybe painted by a good artist.

'It will be an experience!' He said heartily. 'I don't suppose you've ever had your portrait painted before?'

Her eyes rose sharply to meet his across the table. There it was again. Whenever she thought she was happy there was always something to remind her. 'No,' she said quietly 'No, never.' And she lowered her eyes again before he could see the pain in them.

'There—you see?' He made some notes in a little book. 'And as soon as your period of mourning is over I will see that you get some invitations to fashionable occasions.'

'What sort of fashionable occasions?' Polly asked apprehensively. 'And how will you get invitations for me?'

He tapped the side of his nose. 'You forget—I know a lot of what are known as "the best people". There are the races, charity balls, previews of exhibitions—oh, all sorts of things.'

'But—would someone like me ever be accepted at those places?' She stared at him, wide-eyed and he laughed.

'Just you leave it to me. If we cause a stir—

well, what better publicity?' He reached out his hand to cover hers as it lay on the table. 'I am assuming that you will let me be your escort, of course. It would be the easiest way—not to say the most pleasant task I have ever had the good luck to perform.'

She drew her hand away firmly. 'I'll let you know about it all, William,' she said. But she knew that he would not take no for an answer.

The speed with which William went into action took Polly's breath away. He brought a photographer to her rooms the very next day and personally supervised the taking of the photographs, even choosing what Polly should wear. He became a regular visitor, both to her rooms and to her dressing room at the theatre and he never came empty handed. There were the proofs of the song sheets and albums he had organised, then the final product for her approval. Soon every theatre she appeared at had her personal poster ouside and in the foyer. The song books sold like hot cakes and her bookings increased. She had as much work as she could cope with—and she revelled in it all, enjoying a love affair with an adoring public.

Letters came from time to time from Maudie. She was also enjoying a great popularity in America, which she loved, but, she said, she was homesick for her beloved London, her family and, of course, Polly. So that she could report back, Polly made frequent visits to Hackney to see Alice and the children and it was on one of these visits that she heard of the death of Lord Broadfield's son.

'Dad came to see us last week,' Alice told her. 'He was up in London with his gentleman, Lord Broadfield—for him to see his doctor in Harley Street. Dad says he's gone right down-hill since his son was killed.'

'Is that the one who was—not quite—?' Polly asked.

Alice nodded. 'They found him in the lake one morning. An accident, they said it was. Dad says it's fair bowled his poor Lordship. That poor lad was the heir to the estate, you see.'

'Was that his only child?' Polly asked.

Alice leaned forward. 'Well, no. Some years ago there was a scandal—young Mr. George— the one who was drowned—had a governess and his Lordship is supposed to have fallen in love with her. She left the place suddenly and Mum and Dad heard afterwards that she'd had a baby boy. It was terrible because her Ladyship was still alive at the time—not that she knew much about anything, poor soul. It was her the son took after, you see, though she wasn't struck down with the illness till she was older.'

'Do you think it was true, or was it just talk?' Polly asked.

'Oh, it was true all right,' Alice assured her.

274

'And there are those who say that he married her in secret after he was free, to give the child a name.'

'How thrilling!' Polly exclaimed. 'It's just like something out of a novel.' She looked thoughtful. 'And if it is true it means that there will be an heir after all—and a healthy one.'

'I suppose so,' Alice agreed. 'Though I hope his Lordship gets better and lives on for many a year yet, God bless him.'

The bleak days of winter melted into spring, then into early summer. Polly's popularity knew no bounds. Everyone seemed enchanted by her. Jimmy worked hard and produced his best songs yet and her picture was seen all around London, thanks to William. Solly was talking of a new American tour later in the year. Polly was now a familiar figure at many of the important social gatherings, just as William had promised and, with him at her side she soon lost her diffidence. His energy and enthusiasm were like a tide, carrying her along and she let him take charge, depending on him more and more as the weeks went by.

As she grew to know him better her opinion of him changed. Although he was shrewd, glib and clever; well educated and socially acceptable—the complete man-about-town, in fact, this was only a facade he showed to the world. Beneath it all she sensed a vulnerability which, though she found him attractive, warned her instinctively at first to keep him at arms' length. They became good friends, however. With Maudie away she was glad of his companionship and it was easy to let him slip into the role of escort.

One night, after supper at a fashionable restaurant William had come back to Polly's rooms for what he called a 'nightcap'. Polly kept a bottle of brandy there specially for him, she still had no taste for alcohol herself. It was a chilly evening and Mrs. Smailes had lit a fire in the sitting room. Polly poured William a generous measure of brandy and then sat, as she loved to do, on the floor in front of the fire, taking the pins out of her hair and letting it fall to her waist in a glorious red-gold curtain. William smiled.

'You look exactly like a Botticelli madonna,' he said. 'You know, you really should have your portrait painted, Polly.' He reached out, putting his finger under her chin and raising her face towards him. 'What is it about you, Polly? Sometimes you're a child, eager and without a care, then at others there's a sadness in those bewitching eyes of yours. A sadness that has nothing to do with losing your husband.' He looked into her eyes. 'You weren't in love with him, were you?'

She pulled her head away from his hand, frowning. 'You mustn't say things like that. Freddie was a good man. He was so good and kind to me. I don't know where I'd be today if it hadn't been for him.'

'That's no answer to the question, Polly,' he said. 'Not loving him doesn't make you into some kind of monster, there's no need to feel guilty about it.'

'I don't!' Her chin went up.

Gently, he slid to the floor beside her so that his face was on a level with hers. 'When you're working—when you give yourself to an audience there's a kind of incandescence about you. I've a feeling that the man who could make you look like that would have to be someone very special.' He looked into her eyes. 'I think there was once someone like that, Polly—someone you still think of—and miss.'

His eyes were almost hypnotic as she looked into them and after a moment's hesitation she nodded. Suddenly she wanted to talk about Eddie. It was months since she had spoken his name aloud, although he was never far from her thoughts. Almost without her realising it the words came pouring from her, spilling over like fermented wine. She told him everything, from their first unromantic meeting in the yard at the Eight Bells to the still-birth of his child last November. When she had finished she looked at him.

'It doesn't sound very pretty, does it? Put into words I must sound like the kind of girl your mother and aunt go around 'saving'. But I only know one thing—I'll love Eddie till the day I die. I've tried to put him out of my mind

277

and heart, but I can't. I did wrong in marrying Freddie and I'll never marry again. When I wrote that note and walked out of Eddie's life that day a part of me died.'

He smiled, his eyes shining softly in the light of the dying fire. 'Poor little Polly. Is that why you throw yourself so wholeheartedly into your work? It's not so hard for me to understand, my dear. We're very much alike, you and I. There was once someone in my life too. I treated her very badly—let her down and I've hated myself for it ever since.' He touched her cheek. 'We could comfort each other, Polly. We both have so much to give—why not to each other? There need be no illusions between us—no pretence.' His lips were gentle on hers and she felt excitement stir in her veins. It was so long—oh, so long since she had been kissed like this. He drew her close, stroking her hair.

'My lovely Polly.' His voice was husky as his lips found hers again, passionate this time— demanding. Her body responded with its own demand. 'No illusions,' he had said. 'No pretence.' Why not give each other the comfort they craved for?

It was two weeks later that Maudie arrived back from America. She had written to tell Polly of her arrival and Polly had written back at once asking her to come to the theatre. 'There is someone I want you to meet,' she had written. 'Maybe we can get him to take us

278

both out to supper.'

When she came down to her dressing room after her act Maudie was waiting for her there, looking so smart and sophisticated that Polly exclaimed aloud.

'Well! Don't you look a swell? Oh, Maudie it's so good to see you!'

They hugged each other, both of them laughing with delight and both talking at once:

'How's Billy? How was America? Where *did* you get that dress?'

'How well you look! Where's this feller, then? 'ere—let me get me breath back for Gawd's sake!'

They fell into chairs, laughing breathlessly and Maudie held up a hand. 'I know all about you so don't start boastin'. Alice has been sendin' me the *Era* regular. But who's this clever bloke who's been handlin' your publicity? Take me on too, will he, do you think?'

'I'm sure he would. It's him I want you to meet, Maudie. He'll be here in a minute. His name is William Mears.'

The smile faded from Maudie's face as though it had been wiped off with a sponge, taking the colour with it.

'William Mears?' she said in a whisper. 'Tall 'andsome feller with a moustache?'

Polly nodded. 'Do you know him?'

Maudie gave a wry little smile. 'I should do, love—he's Billy's father!'

CHAPTER SIXTEEN

It was the letter that decided her. It had been forwarded from Longstaff and Braithwaite's and was from Gilbert Seymore, the House Manager of the Gaiety Theatre, Halesbury. It told a dire story of the financial difficulties the theatre was experiencing. It took her a moment only to make up her mind. It was her theatre now, it was up to her to see what she could do. She owed it to Freddie to see that his little theatre did not go down. She had no bookings for the next month. She had persuaded Solly that she needed time to rehearse some new material before signing up for a tour of the provinces and then the American tour he had in mind. The cry for help couldn't have come at a better time.

But there was another reason for her wanting to get away from London for a while: the look on Maudie's face last night in the dressing room when she had mentioned William's name—and, a moment later when he had entered the room, the look on William's. The two of them had stood staring speechlessly at each other, Maudie's face devoid of all colour. Polly had made an excuse and left the room, returning later to find it empty—a note from William on the dressing table—: 'Forgive me. I will explain tomorrow—W.'

But there had really been no need to explain. Maudie was obviously the girl he had spoken to her of, the one he'd let down and hated himself over. Well, now he had a chance to put it right and Polly hoped that the outcome—whatever it turned out to be— would make Maudie as happy as she deserved to be.

She dressed quickly and went first to Solly's office to tell him what she intended. As she had envisaged, he pronounced her mad.

'A fine way of rehearsing new material, I must say!' he said, shifting his cigar from one side of his mouth to the other and waving his hands at her. 'How do you think *you're* going to put the place on its feet again?'

Her chin went up determinedly. 'Well, I'll get *you* to send me up some good acts for a start!' She said.

He laughed shortly. 'Huh! And who do you think is going to waste their time appearing at the back of beyond?'

'Well, *I* will for one!' she retorted.

He stared at her. 'For *no money?* Now I know you're mad!'

'Well, I'm going anyway,' she told him defiantly. 'And if I haven't got things right by the date the tour starts—you can get someone else to fill my place.'

This brought him to his feet. 'Polly! Now you listen to me, my girl—' He came round the desk. 'What you're talking about is breach of contract and don't you forget it!'

She rounded on him, a small bundle of red-haired fury.

'Contract! There's nothing in my contract that says I can't look after my own interests, so don't tell me there is! In fact there are things in that contract that want looking into! You never played quite straight by Freddie either, only he was too soft to tackle you about it. If you want to keep me as a client, Solly Cohen, you'd better co-operate. You help me and I'll help you—right?'

He stepped back as though he could actually feel the heat of her anger. 'All right, Polly, my dear—all right,' he said placatingly. 'No need to get upset about it. You know, you're tired. You need a rest.'

'No I'm not!' she shouted. 'I've never had more energy in my life and I'm going to put it to good use—and you can do what you like about it!'

Wound up like a spring she went straight to the post office and sent a telegram to the Gaiety. She had never done such a thing before and it made her feel quite adventurous. Finally, she went to enquire the times of the trains. When she got back to Notting Hill Gate her cheeks were bright with colour and the blood was singing in her veins. William was waiting for her.

'Polly—I hardly know where to begin—'

She smiled. 'Then don't try. Maudie said something that made me guess. She was your girl, wasn't she, William? The one you told me about.'

He nodded. 'I have a son, Polly. Such a beautiful child.'

'I know. I even helped Maudie to look after him for a while, when I lived with her at Hackney.' She frowned. 'What I can't understand, William, is why you never said anything before. I talked about Maudie often enough.'

He bit his lip. 'When I knew her she called herself Molly Neame. After I left her she decided to go back to her own name and make a fresh start.'

Polly took both his hands. 'Are you going to marry her now?' she asked quietly.

He lifted his shoulders. 'If she'll have me, I'd like to. But she's not sure she'd ever be able to trust me. You can't blame her for that, I suppose. For that reason I want to ask you a favour, Polly: You won't mention to her that you and I—' He broke off, turning away 'Oh God! I sound like the worst kind of rotter, don't I?'

Polly smiled gently. 'Don't worry about it, William. I never did see myself in the part of mistress, anyway. It doesn't suit me. But I do think we were good for each other, don't you?'

He grasped her hands again, relief smoothing his brow.

'Bless you, Polly.' He bent and kissed her cheek.

'There's only one thing I couldn't forgive you for,' she said, shaking her head at him.

'And what's that?'

'If Maudie, you and I ever stopped being friends. I couldn't bear that.'

'That will never happen. I promise you solemnly.'

She laughed. 'Then I'll put in a good word for you, though I'll have to do it quickly. I'm going up to Halesbury tomorrow morning.'

She waved to him from the window, watching as he ran down the steps, his step light with happiness. He looked so handsome and debonair that her heart gave a little twist. She could never have loved him but what they had shared had been very agreeable. She sighed. It seemed she was never to keep the sweet things of life in her grasp for very long. Sooner or later she always had to let them go.

Maudie came to see her off at the station the following day and fussed around her like a mother hen.

'Now are you sure you'll be all right on your own?' she asked anxiously for the fourth time. 'Have you got enough clothes with you? Where will you stay?'

Polly laughed. 'Oh, Maudie! If you could go all the way to America by yourself I should think I'll get myself to Halesbury safely!'

But Maudie shook her head. 'It's like I've

284

always said: You need lookin' after.' She grinned wryly. 'Though I'll say this for you— you can speak up for yourself all right when you 'ave to. You gave old Solly a proper wiggin' by all accounts!'

The train steamed in and they found an empty compartment where Maudie helped Polly to settle.

'Tell you what!' She said with sudden inspiration. 'I'll come up to Halesbury and give you a week! 'Ow about that? I've got some free dates. 'ere—you could bill me as—: "Fresh from 'er triumph in the United States of America!" What a lark!'

Polly gasped with delight. 'Oh, Maudie! Would you really do that for me?'

Maudie smiled. 'It's the least I can do when you've gone and found my feller for me again, aint it?'

'Are you going to marry him?' Polly asked. 'I know it's what he wants.'

'I dunno. I'll have to see 'ow 'e be'aves 'imself, won't I? Her voice was brusque but nothing could disguise the look of happiness in her eyes.

'You could visit your father too, couldn't you?' Polly reminded her.

Maudie nodded. 'Yes, that would be nice. He's had a rough time lately, poor Dad. His gentleman, Lord Broadfield died, you know and for a time Dad didn't know whether 'e'd 'ave to look for another job. But the new Lord

B. didn't 'ave a valet of 'is own, so it's all right after all.'

The guard blew his whistle and Polly jumped to her feet in alarm. 'Maudie! You must get out. You'll be carried away!'

Maudie giggled. 'Wouldn't be the first time, would it, love?' Still laughing she scrambled out onto the platform and Polly leaned out of the window as the train started to move.

'See you soon, then. Be kind to William!' she called.

When she alighted at Halesbury station Polly took a cab and went straight to the Gaiety. The theatre was in a narrow street leading off the market square; an unimposing edifice of crumbling stucco work and peeling paint. For several minutes she stood on the pavement surveying it.

In the foyer an air of mustiness hung heavily over everything. On the floor was a fraying red carpet and the only adornment was a collection of drooping ferns in pots. Polly sniffed. Well, the place needed a good clean for a start!

Behind the glass of the box office a short, fat man was busily writing something in a book. He didn't look up when Polly tapped on the widow.

'Booking office is shut,' he said gruffly.

Polly cleared her throat. 'Er—can I speak to Mr. Seymore, please? I'm Mrs. Long.'

The man looked up in surprise. 'Oh!—Oh, I

see. I'm Gilbert Seymore. How do you do.' He came out of the box office and stood looking incredulously at her, his feet scuffing the frayed carpet. 'I'm sorry—I didn't expect anyone so—so—' He peered at her lifting his steelrimmed spectacles onto his forehead. 'I've seen you before—at least, your picture—on the song sheets. Aren't you Polly Marvel?'

She nodded. 'Yes, but I'm Mrs. Long too and the owner of this theatre. You wrote a letter to my solicitors, Mr. Seymore and I'm here to see what I can do to put the Gaiety back on its feet again.'

His round face broke into a smile and the spectacles dropped back onto his nose with a small plop. Reaching into the box office he found a jacket and thrust his arms into it, muttering excuses all the time:

'You really must forgive me, Miss Marvel,' he twittered. 'We're short staffed. I've had to let a lot of our employees go—a case of economics, you understand. I—er—expect you'd like to inspect the theatre and the—er—books?'

Polly frowned. 'The sooner the better, don't you think?'

It was the strangest theatre Polly had ever seen. To her surprise she found that the doors opening off the foyer led into the circle. They walked down a narrow flight of stairs to the stalls and pit. Gilbert Seymore told her it had once been an opera house and the gilded cupids and swags of laurel decorating the proscenium arch told of past splendours. Now it was sad, grimy and neglected.

'I'd like to see backstage,' Polly said and Gilbert Seymore nodded.

'If you'll just come this way.'

Back up the narrow staircase and along a corridor to a heavy pass-door which Gilbert opened for her. Down a short flight of stone steps and they were standing in the wings with its tangle of ropes and tackle. Polly walked onto the stage and looked around her. Gilbert cleared his throat, hovering anxiously.

'Ahem—the dressing rooms are on the floor below if you'd like to see them.'

Down more stairs to where a large rectangle opened out. Numbered doors led off it and the centre space was stacked with a jumble of scenery and stage props. Polly guessed by the dankness of the air and the number of steps they had descended that they were deep underground. She opened the door of one of the dressing rooms and found it as ill-equipped as the one she had encountered at Hoxton on her first booking. She wrinkled her nose and shut it again.

'Who's on the bill next week?' She asked.

Gilbert Seymore shuffled his feet. 'We're—er closed at the moment—till further notice.'

Polly ran a finger along a ledge and held it up in front of his face. 'While the place is closed it would have been a good idea to have it cleaned,' she said accusingly. 'What self-respecting artiste do you think would pig it in a place as filthy as this?' His eyes slid guiltily away from hers and she began to walk back up the stairs. 'I think I'd better see the books next,' she said with a confidence she didn't feel.

He ran after her. 'Of course—if you'd care to come to my office.'

Polly had very little knowledge of business or economics but it didn't take a financial genius to see that the Gaiety was in a bad way and had made no money for the past twelve months. She closed the ledger with a bang and a flurry of dust.

'I don't understand!' she said. 'How did things get into this state? What have you been doing as manager to allow it.

He sighed. 'I'd better come clean, Mrs. Long. I'm not really manager—not official like. Tommy Seaton—him that was, ran off—did a bunk and took most of the money with him. He couldn't be found and that's when the place was put on the market. I was chairman and bar manager and I've been trying to keep things going till the new owner arrived. I heard that Mr. Long had bought it but he never came up to see us. I don't suppose he had time.' He hung his head. 'Well, that's about the size of it, Mrs. Long. What are you doing to do?'

Polly drew herself up to her full height. 'We'll get going again, Mr. Seymore. That's what we'll do—and we'll start by giving the place a good clean!'

The staff at the Gaiety was skeletal, consisting of a resident stage manager, a few part-time stage hands, three or four usherettes and a motley handful of musicians, known as 'the orchestra'. Polly sent Gilbert Seymore to find them all and at three o'clock that afternoon she held a meeting in the foyer.

'I don't think I need to tell you that we have an emergency on our hands,' she told them. 'Either we make a special effort to get the Gaiety back on its feet or I shall be forced to sell up. If you all want to keep your jobs here I ask that you help me.' There was a murmur of assent and she continued, encouraged. 'First the place must be thoroughly cleaned. I shall not ask you to do anything I am not prepared to do myself and if we work on it together I think I can promise you a better place to work in and a rise in your wages when we are successful again.' She looked around at their faces. 'It will be hard work, so anyone who is not willing to put their back into it with me had better leave now. I only want workers!'

No one moved or spoke for several seconds, then one of the musicians, an elderly man with greying hair, stood up.

'I'm with you, Mrs. Long.' He looked round. 'Anyone know where the buckets and brooms are kept? I'll make a start on the band room. It's a bloody disgrace in there!'

They worked with a will, inspired by Polly's determination and enthusiasm. Dressed in an old overall she found she scrubbed and cleaned alongside them till her hands and knees were raw and, gradually she earned, first their respect, then their undying loyalty. Under the grime, the giltwork was in surprisingly good condition and even the peeling paintwork benefited from soap and water. The dressing rooms were aired, cleaned and made as comfortable as possible and gradually, the Gaiety began to shine again.

Polly hadn't spent the last few months under William's guidance without learning the value of publicity and as soon as she could she paid a visit to the local newspaper offices giving him an exciting story for his front page. 'Revival of the Gaiety'. The headline was to read—'New Owner Makes Clean Sweep! Grand Reopening With A Glittering Array of London Stars!' Back in her room at the Greyhound Inn, overlooking the market square, Polly wrote letters till the small hours of the morning; letters to Maudie and Solly which she hoped would make the newspaper headline reality.

She persuaded a local carpet firm to re-carpet the foyer 'on tick' in return for a free advertisement in the programme and in their turn, the printers promised to do an extra fine job for complimentary tickets all round.

Much to her relief Solly came up with some

artistes. They hardly lived up the newspaper's description of 'A Glittering Array' but Polly was satisfied. With Maudie on the bill and a personal appearance herself she felt confident of a good show.

A fortnight later they were ready to open. The bills were posted all over the town as well as outside the theatre, together with personal posters of herself and Maudie. The local paper carried a special feature about Polly's career and already the box office was taking money for advance bookings. Even the Mayor of Halesbury had been persuaded to attend the opening night—on Polly's personal reassurance that the entertainment was to be perfectly respectable, and the whole town was buzzing with curiosity to see the dynamic lady who had brought it all about.

Maudie arrived on Sunday afternoon, a little ahead of the rest of the company. She was to share Polly's rooms at the Greyhound but lodgings had been found for each one of the other artistes; Polly inspecting them herself to see that they were clean and comfortable. She wanted everyone to be happy. That way they would have the successful show they badly needed.

Maudie hugged her warmly, then looked her over critically. 'You look done in!' she announced. 'Done in, but 'appy. This place 'as got into your blood, 'asn't it? But won't you 'ave to think about gettin' ready for that tour soon?'

Polly sighed and sat down on the bed. 'To tell you the truth, Maudie, I'd rather stay here. I like the place and I like the challenge. I think I'll put the tour off for a while. After all, nothing was finalised.'

Maudie pulled a face. 'Solly won't like it. But I think 'e's 'alf expectin' it.'

They rehearsed on Monday morning. The orchestra had been augmented by some talented amateurs that Polly had found. Band parts were distributed and each act went through its paces. The stage manager bustled around, ordering everyone about and bossily organising; glad to take up his position of authority again after the period of enforced equality. After lunch Maudie announced that she was off to Broadfield.

'Why don't you come too, Pol?' she asked. 'It's a lovely day and you're lookin' pale. You could do with some fresh air.'

But Polly shook her head. 'No. You go, Maudie. You and your father will have a lot to talk about. I'll have a rest. I'd like to be by myself for a while.'

Maudie opened her mouth to insist, then thought better of it. 'All right, love. I expect you're right. Don't go worryin' yourself silly about tonight though, will you. It's in the laps of the Gods now.' She pulled on her gloves. 'See you later then.'

Alone in the room, Polly went to the

window. Below her the little market square was quiet and sleepy. She opened the window and closed the curtains so that the light filtered through, making dim, moving patterns on the wall. She lay down on the bed and drew a deep breath. So much had happened to her in the past year. She felt the time had come to stand back and take a look at herself. Fifteen months had passed since she had written the note and walked out of Eddie's life—a year and a quarter—yet in some ways it seemed much longer. She had experienced so much in those months, had become a different person—she had grown from a young girl into a woman. She gazed up at the ceiling. Who would have thought that in such a short space of time she could have been married and widowed—lost a child and made a name for herself on the Halls? Not to mention becoming the owner of a theatre! She smiled a little, wistful smile. Deep down inside, she knew she would turn the clock back if she could. Her heart yearned to be back in the little studio in Islington with Eddie. In her mind, behind her closed eyelids she saw his face, the laughing brown eyes and curly hair, felt the touch of his hand and heard his voice as he used to call to her, taking the stairs two at a time—: 'Robin! Where are you, Robin?' Tears squeezed out from under her eyelids and ran slowly down her cheeks. She would *always* love him—all her life, whatever happened—however old she grew. Silently her lips framed his name—: Eddie—oh, Eddie— my Eddie.

The foyer of the Gaiety was transformed. The new red carpet was thick and plushy and there were fresh flowers everywhere. Among the front-of-the-house staff there was an excitement and anticipation that grew as the audience began to arrive. They had all helped with the transformation of the theatre and they felt that a share of the triumph they all hoped for so eagerly was theirs.

In the best dressing room, the one nearest the stage, Polly and Maudie dressed together; Maudie chatting companionably while Polly fidgeted nervously. She felt more excited and keyed up than she ever remembered and for once Maudie's chatter made her feel worse.

' 'Ere—you know that the Mayor and some councillors are to be in one of the boxes? Well who do you think is to be in the other one?'

'I can't guess—tell me.'

'Lord Broadfield 'imself and my *Dad*!' Maudie told her triumphantly. 'I met 'im this afternoon—'is Lordship, I mean. 'E's ever so nice, quite young for a Lord and not a bit toffee-nosed. I bet you'd like him.'

But Polly was hardly listening, only irritated, her nerves stretched like violin strings. 'Oh, Maudie, do stop chattering for a while, you'll give me a headache!' She got up from the dressing table. 'I think I'll go and see what's going on.'

But Maudie took her arm and pulled her firmly down onto her chair again. 'Now you know the stage manager won't thank you for interferin'. Bossy little devil, 'e may be, but 'e's doin' 'is job—an' doin' it well. You stop 'ere and calm down a bit!'

Polly smiled. 'You're right. I'm like a cat on hot bricks. Oh, Maudie—it *will* be all right, won't it?'

Maudie hugged her. 'You bet it'll be all right. We're gonna give this town the best show it's ever seen. By the time William gets down 'ere on Saturday we'll 'ave turned the place on its ear!'

A sudden call in the corridor made Polly catch her breath.

'Overture and beginners, please!'

She grasped Maudie's arm. 'Thank you, Maudie—and good luck!' she whispered.

'And to you too, love,' Maudie replied. 'As much as you deserve and more besides.'

The house was full to bursting, everywhere the atmosphere of anticipation crackled in the air. The conductor of the orchestra raised his baton and Gilbert Seymore took the chairman's seat at the side of the stage, resplendant in evening dress, a diamond winking ostentatiously on his little finger. The first turn was announced with a flourish—the curtain rose. The show had begun.

For Polly the evening was a kaleidoscope of

colour, noise, laughter and applause. She went on herself right at the end and gave the performance of her life. The audience brought her back again and again and she felt she could have gone on all night, intoxicated with the delight of her new achievement.

The following morning she slept late, waking only when Maudie shook her.

'Wake up, dozy! Look what's come for you!'

She blinked. Maudie was holding a huge basket of red roses, the scent of which filled the room.

'Who—who are they from?' she asked sleepily.

Maudie took an envelope from the basket. 'I expect it says in 'ere.'

Polly opened it and read the enclosed note—: 'Congratulations on a wonderful opening night! I enjoyed it very much. You and the company and staff are cordially invited to a picnic in the grounds of Broadfield Hall next Saturday afternoon at three o'clock. I will send transport to the threatre at two-thirty.' And it was signed: Lord Broadfield.

Polly passed the note to Maudie. 'How kind of him. Will you get someone to pin that on the notice board so that everyone sees it?'

By the end of the week Polly was quite exhausted. They had played to capacity audiences every night and at each performance Polly had given every ounce of her strength and vitality. By Saturday morning

Maudie was quite concerned about her and insisted that she should stay in bed.

'You'll never be fit for no picnic if you don't get some rest,' she said. 'Let alone tonight's show!'

Polly lay back against the pillows with a sigh. 'The picnic! I'd forgotten. Oh, I don't think I'll go, Maudie.'

Maudie looked shocked. 'Not go?' But the whole thing's in your honour. You must go! I've been up at the Hall every afternoon this week and believe me it's going to be quite an occasion.'

'But I've nothing to wear,' Polly protested.

'Rubbish!' Maudie opened the wardrobe and produced a frothy summer dress in white voile with a tucked bodice and hundreds of tiny frills decorating the skirt. 'This and the pretty straw hat with the yellow roses,' she suggested. 'You'll look as pretty as a picture in those!'

Polly shook her head. 'It's really a stage costume, Maudie. Oh, must I come?'

'Don't talk daft. It's perfect for a picnic—and yes, you *must* come! 'Ave some sleep now and I'll wake you up when it's time to get ready.' She held up her hand as Polly opened her mouth again. 'Don't argue! I won't listen. You know what I'm like when I've made me mind up!'

So Polly slept—and dreamed. She was at the Eight Bells again, standing on the trestles and

298

singing for the sailors. One of them stepped forward and smiled. He had red hair and blue eyes and she knew in that moment that he was her father. She reached out her hands to him but when she looked again Eddie stood in his place. 'Oh—I've found you!' she cried. 'I've been looking for you for such a long time. Please—don't go away again.' He lifted her down from the trestle and his arms closed around her——she raised her lips to his—

'Come on, love. Time to get dressed now.' Maudie was shaking her.

Wearily, she dragged herself out of bed. The dream had been so vivid and so sweet, she wished she could have gone back to sleep and dreamed it all over again.

Dressed in their prettiest clothes, Polly in the white voile with her straw hat and a frilly parasol; Maudie in gay yellow and white striped cotton, they walked to the theatre together. Lord Broadfield was sending wagonettes for the other artistes and staff but when they arrived they found that he had sent his own carriage for them. It was a beautiful afternoon and as they drove Polly thought wistfully of the pony and trap ride at Marvelhurst and the way Eddie had described the summer countryside. 'My son is a poet' Mrs. Tarrant had remarked. Polly sighed, the dream still warm and vivid in her heart.

'You're quiet. Feelin' all right?' Maudie asked.

Polly nodded. 'I'm perfectly all right, thank you.'

Maudie shook her head. 'I don't like the look of you at all! You've been overdoin' it. Melancholia—that's what you've got. You'll 'ave to 'ave a good rest or you'll crack up!'

'Oh, Maudie!' Polly forced a laugh. 'Who could have melancholia with you anywhere near them?' But the feeling she had was certainly melancholy. Suddenly she saw the life that lay ahead of her—devoted only to people at a distance, people who only saw her from the outside. Maudie had always said she needed someone and suddenly she knew it was true. She gave herself a little shake. It would never do to let Maudie see that she was right.

They drove in through tall iron gates and up a long, straight drive lined with trees. Broadfield Hall stood before them, square and magnificent, the sunlight gleaming on its many windows. As the carriage drew up to the door a liveried footman came forward to help them down.

The rest of the company had already arrived and were sitting or strolling about on the smooth pasture that sloped down to a lake at the back of the house. Food was laid out on long trestle tables and maids moved about busily serving. Maudie and Polly made to join them but the footman spoke:

'Will Miss Marvel please come with me?'

Polly looked at him in surprise. 'Me? Yes,

but why?'

Maudie gave her a little push. 'Go on—you didn't expect to eat with the rabble, did you? You're a big-wig theatre owner now, you know!' She winked but Polly shook her head crossly.

'I don't want special treatment. Everyone here is responsible for the success of the Gaiety. Not just me!'

'Oh, don't be so awkward!' Maudie said impatiently and, turned on her heel she walked towards where the others were enjoying themselves. The footman looked at her uncertainly.

'If you please, miss—'

She followed him across the grass, down a path that sloped gently towards a clump of willows that trailed their fronds in the water.

'If you will go through the trees and wait there—' the footman told her.

She turned to him. 'But what for?' She felt annoyed. Was this Maudie's idea of a joke? But the footman, his face expressionless had already turned and was walking back towards the house.

She looked around her. Through the trees, he had said. She walked through the curtain of willow fronds and found herself in a world of green, dappled with sunlight. It was quiet and peaceful, just the singing of the birds and the gentle lapping of the water against the bank. It was a beautiful place, but why had she been asked to come here? Then she heard it—someone calling her name—yet not her name—:

'Robin—Robin, are you there?'

She put up her hands to her ears. Was she still dreaming? Following the sound she pushed through more of the thickly hanging fronds till she came to the water's edge and saw a boat moored to the bank. In it were cushions and a picnic basket. Then she felt rather than saw a movement among the green shadows.

'Robin!'

She stared at him, her heart beating wildly against her ribs till she thought she would stop breathing. She must still be dreaming. But he stepped towards her, his hands outstretched and the next moment their fingers touched.

She shook her head. 'I—I don't understand—why are you here?' she whispered.

He smiled gently, his eyes lighting up in the dear way she remembered so well. 'I sent you roses. I invited you here. It would have been very rude of me not to have been here to meet you.'

She swallowed, her mouth dry. 'You're—Lord Broadfield?

He laughed. 'It was a surprise to me too! I wasn't sure I liked the idea at first but it led me back to you so now I know there was sense in it.' His eyes looked into hers. 'I'm still Eddie

Tarrant, the foolish young artist who lost his dearest love.' His eyes were tender as he drew her into his arms. As they kissed Polly closed her eyes, hardly daring to believe that it was really happening. Surely she would wake soon and find it was all a dream. But when she opened them again his face was still there above hers, the eyes smiling tenderly down at her, his arms holding her tightly as though he would never let her go. She shook her head.

'There is so much to tell you, Eddie. I don't know where to begin.' But he put a finger against her lips.

'Your friend Maudie has told me all of it. All you have to do is to listen to me. I have so much to make up to you, Robin and I have wasted so much precious time. Will you marry me?'

Her eyes widened. 'Marry you—*me*? But—now that you have all this you must marry someone—someone *worthier*.'

His eyes were tender as they looked into hers. 'You don't understand, Robin. There can be no one else. I am not a free man. Ever since the first time I took you in my arms I have been married to you in my heart. When you left me that note and went away I thought you had grown tired of waiting and at that time—when I was so unsure of my parentage I thought it kinder to set you free.' He drew her close, his lips against her cheek as he spoke. 'But I have never known a moment's freedom,

Robin. The bond that is between us can never be severed till the day my heart stops beating.'

Her heart was full as he kissed her. 'I will have a lot to learn, Eddie,' she whispered. 'But I will do my best, I promise.'

He smiled. 'Just love me, that's all I ask. Oh, Robin, I need you so much.' He pointed to the gently rocking boat. 'Do you remember a promise I once made to you? I intend to begin by fulfilling that promise.'

He helped her in, then settled himself at the oars. 'A boat afloat—' he quoted, smiling. 'A cloudless sky. Do you remember the rest?'

She nodded. 'A nook that's green and shady. A cooling drink, A pigeon pie, A lobster and a lady.'

Their laughter rang out across the water as the boat emerged from the leafy shade into the bright sunlight. Far away a crowd of small figures waved and cheered them—they waved back. The first of the promises was being fulfilled. The first of many dreams coming true.